HER FORGOTTEN GRAVE

DI RITA GUPTA MURDER MYSTERY

BOOK 1

SAM CARTER

CHAPTER 1

Thirty years ago

Wind whipped at Clara's body, dragging hair across her face. Fear thudded in her heart, knocking against her ribs. The howling wind was like a dragon's mouth, drowning her in its frigid wake. She wrapped the coat tightly around her, wondering why she'd come here. It was too risky, but she had no choice. Well, the choice offered to her wasn't really one that bore thinking about.

She stepped backward into the rocky surface of the hillside, sheltering herself from the wind's brutal onslaught. Her eyes remained on the pitch black road below. It was barely visible, curling like a serpent around the corner of the hill, then vanishing from view. She had parked her car at the base of the hill, then climbed up slowly.

There was no rain, she was lucky. A little further up, and the cliff opened up, facing the sea. In the cold darkness, it was a nightmarish landscape. The wind died, then picked up again, knocking against the rocks and peaks like a tortured soul looking for some respite. It whined against her ears, and made the sea far below dash against the rocks in restless fury.

Clara checked her watch. The green dials showed it was close to midnight. He was late. How long would she wait for? She didn't feel safe here. Her jaws hardened as she thought of what she had sacrificed for him. How low she had to slip – in her own esteem. Ultimately, nothing mattered but what she saw in the mirror. She could live to everyone, but not herself. Not to her own child.

Her child….the despair spread through her like a cloudy storm. It shook her to the core, and her head lowered to her chest. The black weight remained on her chest, crushing her. She had to be strong. Somehow, she had to survive this.

Headlights pierced the gloom below her. On the invisible road, a car appeared. The twin yellow orbs of light looked like the eyes of a monster. The car disappeared from view, and she knew he was parking. Clara stomped her feet on the ground to get back circulation to her frozen toes. She tightened her arms across herself, but couldn't stop the shaking. After what seemed an interminable wait, she heard his steps.

They came up slowly but surely. She knew he would've been careful to note if she had come alone.

They had been here before, under happier circumstances.

When the man's silhouette appeared, she frowned. That wasn't…a new fear jolted in her blood, freezing her body. The tall figure stood there, watching her in silence. His coat tails flapped in the breeze, but he didn't seem to care.

"Who…who are you?" Clara said, finally. He said nothing. He stood still, but she could sense his eyes moving over her body. Fear seemed to have driven nails through her feet, she was rooted to the spot.

Clara repeated her question, but she heard only the whining of the wind. She couldn't get past him to reach the path that would take her down to the car. She could try, but chances were she would slip and fall. She could go further up, but that led to the edge of the cliff, and the sheer drop below. She was trapped.

"Look, I don't know who you are. It's time for you to leave." Even as she said the words, she wondered how this stranger had known she'd be here. Calming her rapid breathing, she took a step forward to go past him. He sidestepped, blocking her way.

Then he came closer, swiftly. She could make out his features now, and recognition dawned. She grimaced.

"You? What are you doing here?"

He remained silent as a gravestone. It was clear he was going to block her way, and she had enough of this game.

"Move," she shouted, and tried to go past him. His outstretched arm was like a block of wood that hit her in the chest. He moved like lightning, finger gripping her throat, moving her back. His feet slipped on the wet gorse, but he recovered quickly. She tried to move past him again, but he grabbed her by the waist, and slammed her to the ground. Pain mushroomed in her chest, and breath exploded, emptying her lungs of air.

She called out his name, her voice wobbling with tears. "Why are you doing this? What have I done to you?"

"It's what you will do to the Brotherhood," he finally spoke, his voice quiet with menace. He was on top of her now, holding down her arms as he sat astride her chest. The pressure was immense, and she heard her ribs crack as he leaned forward. She screamed in agony. His face blurred, then became bigger as he leaned forward.

"I am the Guardian of the Brotherhood," he said. "I will protect them."

His hand lashed out, striking her face with savage fury. As the blows rained down, she tasted metallic blood, filling her mouth. Her hands rose to protect herself, but they were like straws in the gale of his violence, and he flung her feeble resistance away. She screamed again, and then heard his deep throated laughter, rising above the moaning wind.

CHAPTER 2

Detective Inspector Rita Gupta stared unblinking at the man in front of her. Sweat plastered the man's forehead. He looked around him like a cornered rat.

"Mr Oswald," Rita said, forcing the man to look at her. "Your DNA was found on the victim's body. You were seen by witnesses entering and leaving the house.

Mr Oswald gulped, his face a deathly white colour. His eyes were wide, bulging. His expensive lawyer, Mr East, leaned over and whispered in his ears. Rita hated these solicitors with a passion. This case was open and shut, but this man would try everything to get his client off the hook.

"No comment."

"We have you on CCTV, driving to your house. She lets you in. You emerge an hour later. You planned this, as you knew she would be home alone."

"Hearsay," Mr East calmly said. "You do not know what my client's plans were."

Rita ignored him. Mr Oswald was looking like a fish out of water, gasping for breath. Rita drilled her eyes at him.

"If your wife died, her entire estate would be left to you. You had a string of affairs. The marriage was broken. I can understand that," Rita said. Mr Oswald looked at her. Rita knew how valuable sharing a little sympathy with the criminal could be. Get them on your side. Rita's twenty-two years as a detective had taught her a trick or two.

"No one is blaming you for walking away from the marriage. But its not just a marriage you broke. You killed a woman in cold blood. Do you agree?"

Mr Oswald licked his cracked lips. "No comment."

Rita smiled. "We have all the evidence, apart from the cameras inside the house, which were not working for some mysterious reason. You say another intruder entered the house after you left. The CCTV doesn't show anyone. You were the only person in the house when your wife died. Your fingerprints and DNA are all over her body, including her throat."

Mr East sighed. "They had sexual relations. Any judge will expect that, DI Gupta."

Again, Rita ignored him. She dropped her voice, and made sure Mr Oswald was focused on her.

"Shortly after you left, your children returned home. Your two boys. 12 and 14 years old. Your 14-year-old son found their mother dead on her bed. Can you imagine what that did to your son?"

Mr Oswald was turning a shade of green, and it looked like he might vomit. He leaned to the left, and his solicitor whispered in his ear, but he wasn't listening any more. Rita moved in for the kill.

Rita leaned forward, putting her elbows on the desk. "Think of how your sons will remember you. They will know what happened. This is already in the papers."

Mr Oswald opened and closed his mouth. Words appeared to have deserted him.

Rita said, "Imagine the future where your sons look behind their back, and suspect you. Imagine lying to them your whole life. They knew, don't they?"

Rita shook her head. "Or you can set them free. Admit to what you did, say sorry to your sons, and move on. Think about your boys, Mr Oswald."

The man's face cracked liked a stone thrown at a mirror. He covered his head in his hands, and sank down to the table.

"Mr Oswald," Rita said, "Did you kill your wife?"

The man nodded, without lifting his head. Then he spoke up. "Yes. I did."

Rita's sergeant, Dean, stirred. She glanced at him, and saw the triumph in his eyes. She didn't feel any sense of victory. But she had achieved justice for the dead woman, and that was all she cared about.

Her radio beeped in her pocket. Dean whispered, “I’m okay to finish up here. You can answer that.”

Rita nodded, and left. She stepped outside the interrogation room in the basement of the Finchley Police Station in North London. She rang her boss, DCI Thomson, who had messaged her three times already.

“Come up to my room right now,” Thomson said, in his low, gravelly voice.

CHAPTER 3

Rita walked down the green, linoleum-covered corridor, her flat shoes making a barely audible squeaky sound. Her long black hair fell past her shoulders. The whitewashed walls had turned grimy with age and needed a new lick of paint. Photos and mugshots of criminals were pinned on bulletin boards as she walked past them. A couple of uniformed officers walked by, and she acknowledged their greeting.

She took the stairs up to the third floor and rapped on the brown mahogany door that said "Detective Chief Inspector Adrian Thompson." A barking voice asked her to enter. She shut the door behind her and stood. The office was spacious as far as the London Metropolitan's offices went. Through a window at the rear, she could see the trees of the neighbouring park and the council estates next to it.

Thompson was a slim, wiry man with intense, dark eyes. His sunken cheeks and sparse hair spoke of many hours at the helm of a cash-strapped police force. He was a quiet man and seldom raised his voice, Rita knew very well that stress had eroded his sense of well-being, and he kept a bottle of whiskey locked in the lowest drawer of his desk.

"Sit down," Thompson said.

"If you don't mind, sir, I'll stand."

There was something about Thompson's gaze that unsettled her. He looked away, and a sigh escaped his lips. That was unusual for him. He was normally a straight-talking man who didn't waste any time. Rita stepped forward until she was close to his desk.

"Is anything the matter, sir?"

When he looked back at her, she saw resignation on his face, mixed with something else she hadn't seen before. Regret, perhaps, or something best left unspoken.

"A woman's remains were discovered in the North York Moors, outside the seaside town of Scarborough." Thompson paused and looked at her.

Memories, visions, screams, and words collided in Rita's heart with the force of a sledgehammer. She forgot to breathe, and her body went rigid.

Ice-cold numbness spread to her fingers and toes, and her legs suddenly felt weak. Her nostrils flared as the past flooded her mind like a wave, a tsunami threatening to engulf her senses.

Her mouth opened, but she couldn't breathe. From a distance, she heard Thompson's voice, as if it was coming down the end of a long tunnel.

"DNA tests and dental records have shown a positive ID." Thompson paused once again, his jaws flexing. He didn't break eye contact with her. "A 32-year-old Caucasian woman called Clara Winters."

A buzzing sound was growing in Rita's ears, drowning her thoughts. She stepped forward again, and her groping hand found the reassuring backrest of the chair. She pulled it up and sat down, glad it had been close by. Her head lowered onto her chest for a few seconds, then she snapped straight to look at Thompson.

She had to clear her throat before she could speak. Even then, her voice was a bare whisper. "Are they sure?"

Thompson nodded. "I don't think there was any other Clara Winters of that age in that area in 1998. Carbon dating has pointed to that year, but the month is uncertain as yet. They're working on it." The corners of his eyes softened, and the tension left his jaws, having delivered the news. "I'm sorry, Rita."

Words had disappeared in the fog of Rita's mind. She stared at Thomson like he was a ghost, then her eyes flickered downwards. She felt the ground slipping beneath her feet, but instead of falling, she was holding on to the edges of a precipice with her fingertips. Strange whispers rose up from the depths of her soul, like bubbles from an unseen beast in the ocean's depths.

She fell back on her rational brain, her mind of a detective. Her fingertips, holding her above the void.

"Can I see the file?" she asked, her voice barely above a whisper.

"Yes, of course." Thomson picked up a folder from the table and handed it to her.

Rita held it in her hands like it was a thousand-year-old antique document. The words "North Yorkshire Police Department, Confidential Report" were written in black letters against a light brown surface. She felt the rough texture of the folder under her fingers.

Could she open it?

Could she really see what was inside?

She had to, but her hands seemed to have stalled and wouldn't listen to what her mind was saying. She swallowed and took a deep breath. The black weight lodged in her throat wouldn't budge.

She opened the folder and moved through the pages. The papers made a rustling sound like bones being dragged across the street. It was all there: photos of the crime scene, descriptions of what had been found.

Breath constricted in her chest until her lungs were made of steel. Her nostrils quivered. She could see the remains of the blue jacket. She saw the blue topaz ring. The flesh had succumbed to the earth, never to return. The bones were slowly going the same way, but the skeleton was mostly intact. She flicked through the forensic photos quickly, unable to look at them for long. And there it was. The DNA match from the National Crime Database. The dental records.

They all pointed to the victim, whose photo, name, date of birth, and last known location were printed on the page.

Printed on her soul.

Clara Winters.

Her mother.

CHAPTER 4

Rita closed the folder slowly, like she was putting back the pin in a hand grenade. She rested both her hands over it, watching her pink-painted nails, the blue veins on the back of her hand. These little details seemed important now, grounding her. She wanted to hold onto this folder, hold it close to her chest like a newborn mother clasping her baby. She felt the paper warm beneath the palms of her hands.

Questions were shooting across her mind like stars in the night sky—the why, where, and when that had plagued her for thirty years. The sense of incredulity seeped back, overcoming her again.

She opened the folder and checked all the information, her eyes quickly scanning the final report and summary, then the photos. She shut the folder quickly, embarrassed all of a sudden. She sensed Thomson's eyes on her. She glanced at him, self-conscious, and couldn't hold his gaze. There was understanding in his heavy-lidded eyes and the sombre expression on his face.

"What would you like to do?" he asked in his heavy, low voice. "I can arrange for you to go up there and take part in the investigation."

He settled back in his chair, and she heard it creak. His face changed, his jaws relaxing as a new light appeared in his eyes. "As it happens, in Scarborough the serious crime branch is going through a reshuffle. One of their senior inspectors has relocated to Scotland. There is a vacancy."

Rita blinked a few times, her mind grappling with the implication of Thomson's words. He noted the confusion on her face and smiled.

"I can speak to the superintendent there. Would you like to lead the investigation?"

Rita's heart hammered painfully against her ribs as she leaned forward. "You mean, go up to Scarborough and…" She stopped, realizing how stupid her words sounded. Of course she would have to go up there. "I mean, I've got a case I need to close here. And my work…"

She stopped when Thomson raised a hand.

"You're close to charging the guy downstairs, aren't you? Is he going to confess?"

"He has confessed," Rita confirmed, with a small sigh of relief. "We will have a strong case for the Crown Prosecution Service." The CPS oversaw all criminal prosecution cases in the UK.

"I can get someone to take over from here," Thomson said. "You've done the hard work. You could do with a break, anyway."

Rita stared back at Thomson, her brain clicking through gears rapidly. She lived alone and didn't have a family. Work was her life, and if truth be told, she lived for little else. She didn't have a man in her life at the moment. And even if she did, her work still came first.

"Are you sure, sir? I know the department's stretched as it is. I could be gone for a few weeks, at least. But I can commute."

She remembered the long journeys she took with her mother, visiting relatives in London. They had family in Wimbledon. Those days of summer suddenly flashed in her mind—the sun angling across the windshield, '90s pop music on the radio. The glint of the blue North Sea as it dipped behind the hills of Scarborough. The fading cry of seagulls. A lonely, forlorn sound, a call that took her back to hazy days of sunshine, and to everlasting regrets.

She blinked again, her mind slowly coming back to the present.

A little smile creased the corners of Thomson's lips before they vanished, replaced by the usual firm flatness. "It's typical of you to try and do two things at once. You can't do it all, Rita. It's time you learned that."

From anyone else, she would have taken it wrongly. She reacted too quickly to words. From Thomson, who had known her right from when she had been a constable fresh out of detective course exams, it was constructive criticism.

"Clear your desk," Thomson said. "If you want to liaise with Richard for the prosecution's case, then do so." Richard Smith, or Bob, was the legal go-between for the police department and the CPS. It was their job to make sure all the investigation and evidence would secure a conviction and not be a waste of time and money. Rita nodded.

"I'll do that, sir. We should be done in a day."

"Good." He pointed to the folder. Rita realized she was gripping it tightly with both hands. Like she was afraid to let it go. Like it might disintegrate and vanish into the ground like her mother had, three decades ago. She relaxed her hold on it, afraid she might damage the folder.

Thomson said, "You can keep that. It's a copy. Very confidential, as you know. No sharing. Information governance," his lips twitched without humour. Rita grimaced as well. These days all police officers had to do the same compliance training as the rest of the civil service. As if the government could teach a senior police officer how to maintain confidentiality.

Rita stood, holding the folder against her chest. She locked eyes with Thomson. "Thank you, sir," she said and meant it. "I'll be back."

Thomson, more than anyone else, knew the pain of unsolved cases. The lack of closure that kept detectives awake at night. It nibbled away in the back of their minds.

And if it was your own relative?

Your own mother, brother, or sister? The pain was unimaginable.

Rita had lived with it her whole life. It almost seemed beyond belief she might be able to get some answers now. Or she might not. But at least she had the option now to try.

"Good luck," Thomson said. He went back to a folder on his desk, and Rita walked out of the room. She closed the door with a soft click, then leaned against the wall and closed her eyes.

A few deep breaths stabilized her. She opened her eyes and looked down at the folder, as if to make sure she hadn't lost it. Then, swiftly, she went down the stairs.

CHAPTER 5

Rita spent the afternoon packing her stuff. There wasn't much, to be honest. She packed her suits for work and the sensible rubber-soled shoes issued by the London Metropolitan force, leaving her heels and other dresses behind.

She doubted she would have a social life in Scarborough. Scarborough was the main base in that region, and that was where she would meet the detective superintendent of North Yorkshire Police's local branch. She expected hostility. She knew what people were like in the smaller towns; she had grown up in Scarborough and Whitby, after all.

Rita stuffed some clothes into her suitcase, and her hands stilled as the memories struck her again. A shaft of sunlight slanted in through the window, warming her face.

In the days before her mother vanished, she seemed distant and preoccupied. Rita blinked, and the days went into fast forward, looping through her mind.

All she was left with were memories of those terrible days: waking up alone in that cold, silent house; the grey clouds outside, like the belly of a dead fish; the cold wind blowing in from the North Sea; thc cry of the seagulls, lost like her. When her mother didn't turn up that day, she took herself to school and told the teachers.

It was funny how the small details stuck in her mind. The blue and yellow uniforms of the police who came to see her at school. The ride back in the police squad car, sitting next to a kind-faced female officer. She remembered the looks on the children's faces. For the first time, they seemed impressed that she was getting a ride in a police car.

The next few days were a blur. She was sent to a children's home in Scarborough. A foster family adopted her, and she did six years of her schooling there. But she moved between three foster families.

The first one was a drunk couple who used to beat her up. She ran away to the police station and had another stint in the same care home where she had started. The second foster parents kept a filthy house full of foster children, which was a business for them. She ran away again when one of the boys in the house tried to grope her.

Finally, for the last three years of secondary school, she found a quiet couple in their 60s, Mr. and Mrs. Rutherford. They never had any children, and they gave Rita the home she had longed for since her mother disappeared. They didn't mind her long, jet black hair and light brown skin, for which she had been teased sporadically all her life.

Mr Rutherford died ten years ago. Rita stayed in touch with them and spent a week in Scarborough after her foster father's funeral. It had been strange to go back. Scarborough had changed a lot, but the old things remained: the wide blue expanse of the North Sea, the castle at the top, the sting of sea salt, and always, the lost cries of the seagulls.

She shook her head as the memories came and went like waves on an empty beach. Eight years ago, she had made inquiries again into the disappearance of Clara Winters. Scarborough had been turned upside down the first time, and again, she drove around the hills and cliffs around the North Yorks Moors that surrounded Scarborough like the ancient mouth of a dark monster facing the North Sea.

She found nothing again.

North Yorkshire police had closed their books on the case and didn't appreciate her meddling. That's when she had come into contact with the same detective superintendent, she was going up to see now, Nicola Perkins. Her first impression of Nicola was that of an arrogant woman who didn't like outsiders like Rita, butting their nose in where it wasn't required. Now, she would have to work with Nicola, not just meet her.

Rita sighed. She wasn't looking forward to that, but she hoped Nicola's outlook on her mother's case had softened now with the new discovery.

She packed the photos from the mantelpiece and desk. She was taking a leave of eight weeks, which should be enough, she thought. Questions niggled at her mind.

Did her mother go for a walk and get lost? She doubted it. Clara was a North Yorkshire lass, and she knew the area well.

Her father was Indian, and physically, Rita took after her dad, but she had her mother's eyes, shape of face, and slim build. She knew she had to get in touch with her father, with whom communication had been difficult all her life. Jayesh, his name was, and Rita had inherited his family name, too. Clara used to call him Jay.

Initially, Jayesh didn't want to know about her, but then he made visits to Scarborough, from where he had settled with a new partner in Swansea, Wales. It was a long distance, and as the years had dragged on, the distance had become longer, until her father's memories were like a speck on the horizon of a desert. She wanted to get to know him better, of course, but it wasn't possible.

Regrets rained down on her like a blizzard from a sunlit sky. Unwanted, undesirable, soon to be forgotten. That's what she had felt like after her mother died.

Her father did come to see her then and even stayed in Scarborough for a few days while she had been in the care home. But he refused to take her in, and she knew it was due to his present family. That had hurt her, but she had no choice. No say in the matter.

She looked at the photos of her mother and herself with some of her mother's friends on a cliff in Scarborough, overlooking the sea. They were all smiling, happy. Rita put the photos in her suitcase, not even sure why she was taking them. She had to close this chapter of her life. It yawned like an endless chasm, and she was tired of getting lost in it. But once it was over, she intended to come back.

She finished packing, then made sure she had her warrant card and extendable steel baton. Her one-bedroom flat in Primrose Hill was small but tastefully furnished and in a nice area. She rented it still, and on her salary, she would never be able to afford to buy a flat here.

She locked the door and went down to her decade-old VW Golf. She started the car and checked the time. It was just past 7 PM, and summertime, so she hoped the traffic would be okay.

She joined the great flow on the M1 and went steadily up north. It was midnight by the time she arrived in

Scarborough. She checked into a hotel next to the police station. She was exhausted after the drive and fell asleep as soon as her head hit the pillow.

CHAPTER 6

Thirty Years Ago

It was late at night, and a wind howled outside the window. Eleven year old Rita was waiting for Clara to come and read her a bed time story. The room was dark, but she could see shapes on the walls. A dragon's mouth, belching out smoke. It was scary, and she wanted Clara to be here. She got up, and opened the door. then she padded down to the stairs, and stopped when she heard her mother's voice downstairs.

"Don't call me again. Do you hear me? How did you get this number?"

Rita could tell her mother was stressed. Clara kept her voice down to a whisper, but it was forceful, like the hissing sound from a pressure cooker. She was on the last step of the staircase, knuckles white as she clutched the phone to her ear. Her body was taut with tension.

"I don't care. Never call here again."

Clara listened as the other person spoke for a while. Then her spine jerked straight, and she stood up, pacing the landing.

Rita drew back into the shadows so Clara couldn't see her. She could see her mother's face now. Patches of red had appeared on Clara's cheeks, and her lips were taut with fury. Rita saw something else in her mother's eyes that she hadn't seen before. A wide-eyed fear. It made Rita feel scared.

"You wouldn't dare," Clara whispered. She closed her eyes as she listened, and her head drooped down on her chest. She massaged her forehead with one hand and sat back down on the stairs. When she spoke again, her voice was broken.

"Okay," she whispered. "Okay. Tell me when." She listened for a while, then hung up. Her head remained bent, then lowered to her hands. Her back shook, and Rita could tell her mother was crying. She padded down the stairs and stopped halfway.

"Mummy? Are you okay?"

Clara wiped her face, sniffed, and turned around quickly. Rita caught a glimpse of her mother's red-rimmed eyes, and then Clara was next to her, drawing her close in an embrace. Rita inhaled her mother's familiar scent, the smell of clean clothes, and the woodsy perfume. A comforting, reassuring smell that she would remember for the rest of her life.

Her mother took her up to the bedroom. Rita lay down, and Clara tucked her in. Clara took out the book and started to read, but Rita could tell she was distracted.

"It's okay, Mummy. I want to sleep now." Clara sighed and kissed her daughter's forehead. She checked the windows were shut and lingered by the curtains, looking out. She did that every night, ever since they had moved to Scarborough. Then she turned out the lights and made sure the door was firmly shut when she went out.

Rita didn't know what woke her up, but she sat upright in her bed. She thought she could hear voices. She got out of bed and listened against the door. She thought she heard her mother's voice again. She opened the door a crack. A light was on downstairs. Her mother's bedroom door was open. Rita went out into the small landing and peeked inside her mother's room. Like the rest of the landing, it was sunk in darkness. She could tell her mother wasn't there.

She went downstairs and saw her mother putting her coat on. The wind shrieked outside, lightning flashed in the sky, and thunder rumbled. Rita sat down on the stairs and put her arms around herself. She shivered.

"Mummy, where are you going?"

Clara snapped her head around and saw Rita. Shock appeared on her face, her eyes wide with the same fear that Rita had seen earlier. A sudden coldness spread inside her body, and she shook, a panic gathering in the pit of her stomach.

"I thought you were asleep. You should be in bed!" Clara swore softly under her breath so Rita couldn't hear. She took her jacket off and came up the stairs. This time, Rita wouldn't budge.

"Where are you going?"

"Nowhere. Come on, you should be in bed."

"If you're going somewhere, I want to come with you," Rita whined.

Her mother said nothing. She took Rita back into the bedroom. This time, Rita wouldn't let go of her mother's hand. She gripped it tightly. She could be strong when she wanted to be.

"Don't go, Mummy."

She saw sudden tears tremble in Clara's eyes, and then Clara brushed them away. She smiled, but Rita could tell her mother was sad. She felt lonely and scared, and she thought Clara felt the same way. Clara hugged her, and Rita held her tight.

"I'm not going anywhere, silly," Clara said. "A friend just called. Do you remember Angela?"

Rita nodded.

"Her car's run out of petrol, and she's got no money. I need to go and give her some money, then I'll come back."

"Why can't she take the bus to come here?" Rita asked, with the unwavering logic of a child.

Clara hesitated. "Because she is too far away and its easier for me drive over to her. You sleep, and I will be back in an hour's time, I promise."

But Rita wouldn't let go. A strange fear was rippling through her body, shaking her soul. She felt something really bad was happening, and her only protection was her mother. She wouldn't let go, no matter what happened.

"No," she whispered. "I'll come with you."

"Stop being silly," Clara said, her voice firm. Rita shook her head and tightened her grip around her mother's waist.

Clara sighed. "Okay. Move over and I'll lie down next to you, okay?"

Rita was happy now. She nodded eagerly and shifted across the bed. Clara got in beside her, still fully dressed. Rita felt her mother's arm across her, warm and snug. She held it, and within minutes, she was asleep.

***

Morning light slanted in through the curtains. The storm had abated, and although it was a cold December day, the sky was blue. Rita could see it through the crack in the curtains. Then she realized Clara wasn't next to her. She must be downstairs, making breakfast.

Rita got up and checked her mother's bedroom, and then the bathroom. They were empty. She went downstairs. Their small terraced house had a tiny kitchen, and a small lounge and dining room. They were all empty. There was no sign of Clara. There was no breakfast, and the kettle hadn't been boiled.

Rita went to the rear door and looked out into the tiny garden. The grass had overgrown, and weeds sprouted between the cracks of the patio stones. Clara wasn't there. There was no sign of her.

Panic grew inside Rita's chest, and shivered down her spine.

"Mummy?" she called out. She ran around the house and looked under the beds, feeling foolish even as she did so. Clara wasn't the type to play hide and seek first thing in the morning.

"Mummy?" Tears sprouted in her eyes, as bitterness squeezed her chest in its iron grip.

"Mummy?" she screamed.

Rita woke up, breath heaving in her lungs, tearing out from her gasping lips. Sweat plastered her forehead and soaked the bed sheets. She didn't recognise where she was, and the old panic returned, surging through her. Then she realised she was in Scarborough, in the hotel room. She squeezed her eyes shut, and rubbed a hand across her face, but she still felt restless, on edge.

Damn it.

It was the same nightmare, all over again.

She went into the bathroom and splashed water on her face. Then she looked at her bedraggled face in the mirror.

A pretty face, she'd been told. Men liked her. Right now, she saw the tear stains down her cheeks, a heaviness in her eyes, and that stone cold deadness in her heart. She looked, and felt, ugly. Just ugly.

She shook her head, and sank down to the floor. She needed to get a grip on herself.

CHAPTER 7

Rita got ready and checked herself in the mirror. She liked to leave her hair open, but this was a new place, relatively speaking, and she didn't know what to expect. She tidied it up in a ponytail. She clutched the folder Thomson had given her, and her warrant card. She left her bags in the hotel room, knowing she would be returning.

She hailed a cab from downstairs and took the short ride up to the Scarborough police station. She had last been here eight years ago. She wasn't welcome then, and she wondered what sort of reception awaited her this time. She thanked the driver and got out. Wind tugged at her coat, and even here, further inland from the sea, she could smell the salty twang in the air.

The police station was close to Scarborough Castle, on the hill that looked down towards the bay. It was a beautiful view, she had to admit. There were some perks to being back in Scarborough. She could see the harbour with the green, black and white boats bobbing up and down in the water. They contrasted with the vivid blue of the sea, which stretched out endlessly until it blurred with the horizon. Clouds played hide and seek with the sun, and shafts of sunlight lit up patches of the sea.

She had a good view of the South Bay Harbour and promenade, overlooked by the long ramparts of the castle. It was just how she remembered Scarborough.

She turned back to the station. The place had a facelift since she had last seen it. It had a sloping metallic roof and a dark glass front. The letters "North Yorkshire Police" were emblazoned in big red letters, with the logo beneath it. The large car park had numerous squad cars and unmarked police vehicles.

She went into the lobby and presented her warrant card to the duty sergeant at the desk. He was a big, chubby, wide-shouldered fellow, and his bushy eyebrows climbed on his forehead as he examined her warrant card.

"Have a seat, guv," he said hastily. "I'll inform the super that you're here. Would you like a cup of tea or coffee?"

That was more than she was expecting. She smiled and thanked the sergeant, declining the offer. She sat down on one of the blue plastic chairs, the same as in all police stations in England. A couple of drunks were slumped against each other in one corner, and a man covered in tattoos sat still, his eyes watchful. He glanced at Rita once, and she averted her eyes. The sergeant came back and gestured towards the side door. He pressed the buzzer, and the door slid apart.

"Top floor," the sergeant said. "Turn left, and you'll see the super's door three doors down."

Rita thanked him and walked through the sliding doors. The corridor had the same grey-blue lino on the floor, but this was a new building and in much better condition than her North London station. She saw inquisitive glances as police officers and detectives walked past her. She was a stranger here.

Rita took the lift up to the fourth, and top, floor. She knocked on the door that said "Nicola Perkins, Detective Superintendent."

Nicola looked up from her desk as Rita entered. She was a small and wiry woman, no more than five feet three. The steely, uncompromising look in her dark eyes permeated down to her small, pinched nose, and the firm line of her lips. The angles of her jaw were sharp, giving her face a pointed chin, resulting in an angular look that made her seem more severe. Glasses rested on her nose. She didn't smile as she put down her pen, took off her glasses and sat back in the chair. She indicated the chair opposite without a word.

They knew each other from eight years ago. Occasionally, they had exchanged emails when Rita had asked for updates. There was no point. The cold case into her mother's disappearance was never revived. Until now.

"Thank you, ma'am," Rita said as she took a seat. The office was large, and behind Nicola, there was a large window that let in ample sunlight. She could see the building compound and, beyond that, streets of houses.

Bookshelves flanked the window on either side. On the shelves, she saw photos of Nicola with various dignitaries she didn't recognize. Rita didn't dwell on them. She sat straight, her palms resting on the folder on her lap. Nicola drilled her with a gaze that seemed to penetrate her eyeballs and roam inside her skull. Rita didn't flinch.

"I'm sorry to hear about your mother," Nicola said finally. Apart from her lips, no other muscle on her face moved. If there was any emotion behind her words, Rita couldn't see it.

"I'm glad we found her, though. Forensics are pretty clear on the identity."

"Yes, I read the report. Thank you."

"I spoke to DCI Thompson, your boss. I know you can do the job. But we need to get a few things straight."

There was a glint in Nicola's eyes now. Rita stiffened because she knew what was coming. Nicola glanced to her left, to where a brown manila folder rested on a stack of papers. She opened the folder and flicked to a page.

"Your psychiatrist's report," she said, glancing down at the paper, then at Rita.

Rita frowned. She hadn't been expecting that. Nicola continued, her face as blank as stone.

"You are seeing the force's occupational health psychiatrist, Dr Maguire. You have twice-weekly checkups with him. But you didn't attend the last one. Is there a reason?"

Rita blinked a few times. Over the last five years, she had better control of her anxiety. She had learned to deal with it, and with the panic attacks. They didn't affect her like before. And she didn't think a psychiatrist's review was necessary anymore. But she didn't want to say that to Nicola.

"I've always had a clean bill of mental health from Dr Maguire," she said softly, composing herself. "I was taken off the medications two years ago. The last meeting was a formality. Yes," she carried on quickly before Nicola could interrupt her. "I should have attended it, but Dr Maguire wasn't really bothered. I spoke to him on the phone later, and he was happy to discharge me."

Nicola stared at her with the same x-ray vision. Did the woman never blink? There was a strange, almost catlike quality about her continuous gaze.

“I’m concerned that you’re too personally involved in the case, and that will affect your judgement.”

“I understand your concern ma’am, but I will treat this as another cold case. There is no need for you to worry.”

“I hope so, for your sake,” Nicola said. The warning behind her words were clear. Nikki was little taken aback by the frank hostility. What did Nicola have against her?

Then Nicola’s lips parted, and the tension relaxed from her jaws. The corners of her eyes softened, and it was the first indication that she was mollified by Rita's words. She nodded and closed the folder. She put it back on the pile of white papers. She folded her hands and looked back at Rita. The hardness in her eyes returned.

"I will introduce you to the team. You will have a sergeant and two constables. As you know, we are lacking an inspector, and you will slot into that role. Apart from investigating the cold case, you will be required to fulfil on-call duties. Is that okay?"

"Of course, ma'am." Rita knew she had to be the senior investigating officer on duty as her rota demanded. "Is it one in four weekends? Or the whole week?"

"Weekends, but one in two," Nicola said. "If there is a serious crime or a homicide, I want a report the morning after. Is that understood? I don't want the cold case interfering with your duties when you're on-call. You have a job to do here, and I expect you to pull your weight."

"I will, ma'am, you don't have to worry."

"Good." Nicola opened a drawer on her desk and took out a small see-through zip lock bag. From inside it, she took out an identity card on a lanyard and a warrant card. She slid both across the desk to Rita. Then without a word, she rose.

"Come with me to meet the team." She strode out the door without looking to see if Rita followed.

CHAPTER 8

Rita followed Nicola's diminutive figure as she went rapidly down the stairs. Nicola didn't look back or pause to check. Rita got the feeling the woman resented her being here. She wouldn't say it in as many words. But her attitude spoke volumes.

Nicola strode down the corridor and then opened an office door on her left. The office was open-plan, with several desks placed around the room. The floors had blue carpet, and the walls were painted white. In one corner, printers and fax machines rested on tables. There was a big whiteboard on a wall and a map of Scarborough and the North Yorkshire coastal region next to it.

Two men and a woman were seated at their desks, and the other three desks were vacant. All three of them looked up as Nicola and Rita entered. Nicola shut the door behind them.

"This is Detective Inspector Rita Gupta. She is on a sabbatical from the London Metropolitan force and will be working with us for a while. She will be the SIO on the Clara Winters case. She will also be leading the serious crimes department for now," Nicola announced.

She turned slightly, angling her eyes to Rita. "Her role is not permanent."

That was not necessary, Rita thought, and only served to undermine her authority as the leader of a new team. But she kept her thoughts to herself.

Nicola turned back to the three detectives who were still gaping at them. "Any questions?"

Three pairs of inquisitive eyes swept over Rita. One of the men was older, in his late 30s or early forties, Rita thought. The other two seemed to be in their late 20s. Nicola proceeded to introduce them. She pointed to the older man first.

"This is Detective Sergeant Richard Staveley." The man nodded at Rita, and she acknowledged with a tight smile. "And this is Detective Constable Rizwan Jaffer and Detective Constable Maggie Long." Both the detective constables murmured a hello, and Rita smiled back at them.

“I’ll leave you to get acquainted. The canteen is further down the corridor on your right. The forensics department is upstairs, and the cybercrime laboratory is next to it. The lab is still being set up, and we send most of our electronic evidence to Sheffield and Leeds. I'm sure the others can fill you in.” Nicola glanced at Rita again.

“No problem, ma'am, thank you.” Rita held Nicola's eyes; the older woman nodded once, her face still impassive. She ran out the door and shut it firmly. Rita heard her heels click down the corridor and then fade away. She turned to the others and rubbed her hands together.

“Right, nice to meet you all. Now let me introduce myself properly. I'm Rita, and I grew up in Scarborough. I went to university in Sheffield, studied criminology, then found myself in London doing a job I didn't like. I applied for the police, and the rest is history.”

She stepped forward and extended her hand towards Richard. He seemed a little uncertain, Rita thought. He was a short, stocky man and got to his feet slowly. The smile on his lips was forced, and she detected a wariness in his eyes. His short-cropped brown hair was receding in the front. His navy blue suit was crumpled and needed ironing. He shook Rita's hand and maintained the forced smile.

“Richard. Nice to meet you.”

The two detective constables seemed more at ease. They stood and shook hands cheerfully. Rizwan was about her height, with brown skin and a well-trimmed beard. Maggie was tall, close to five ten, Nikki thought, a shade taller than herself. Maggie bubbly and blonde, her blue eyes sparkling as she pumped Rita's hand.

“Nice to have you here,” Maggie said. “It gets tiring with these two lads in here.” She grinned, and Rita agreed with a smile.

“Nothing like balancing the scales. Right, who wants a tea or coffee?”

The others nodded, but Maggie wanted a coffee. “I'll come to the canteen with you,” she suggested. Together, they walked out of the office and down the corridor. A couple of uniformed officers walked past them, and Maggie said hi to them. The officers looked inquisitively at Rita, as she nodded at them.

“So, how was your journey up here?” Maggie asked.

“Long, as you can imagine. I arrived late last night and went straight to sleep.” Rita had spruced up the best she could, but she knew she looked tired. She was trying hard to be normal, but she felt on edge. She wondered how much Maggie and the others knew about her real reason for being here.

“I haven't been down to London since last year,” Maggie said. Her accent was Yorkshire, a comforting sound for Rita. It reminded her of Clara, and her heart clenched suddenly.

Maggie was still talking. “It was my friend’s wedding. Like you, she moved down south for a job. She's been there for almost 10 years now. It was a really nice wedding at some old hunting lodge in Surrey; I can't remember the name of the place now.”

Rita smiled at her, nodding absentmindedly. They got to the canteen. It was small, as befitting the size of the local force. North Yorkshire police covered a large area, but a lot of it was the wilderness of the Yorkshire moors. There was a queue for coffee, and they joined it. The smell of fried bacon was heavy in the air, but Rita wasn't hungry.

She asked, “Is Richard okay? He seemed a little quiet.”

Maggie sighed. “Don't mind him. He can be grumpy sometimes. He was close to the old guvnor, Inspector Iain Robson, who took early retirement for PTSD. Richard thought he was going to get the inspector job, but then he learned that he wouldn't.”

Light dawned in Rita's mind. “So he's not exactly happy that I'm here,” she said.

Rita didn't like the fact that Nicola hadn't warned her about this. Nicola would have known of Richard's aspirations.

Rita knew how Richard must be feeling. He wouldn't be the first detective sergeant waiting for a promotion, only to be denied by news of a new arrival.

They got to the head of the queue, and Maggie ordered for them while Rita insisted on paying. Maggie got some biscuits, which Rita looked at enviously. Maggie caught her eyes.

"Do you want some?"

"No," Rita waved a hand. "At my age, I can't afford biscuits."

"You look good," Maggie said. "A couple of biscuits won't hurt. Temptation?" She held up the packet of biscuits and they both laughed. They walked down the corridor, carrying their drinks.

Rita said, "For me, it's all or nothing, unfortunately. Unless I go cold turkey, I'll keep having biscuits and cakes every day." Rita smiled, but her mind wasn't on casual conversation. Her thoughts lay on the windy slopes of the remote hill where her mother's body had been discovered.

Once they got back to the office, Rita put her coffee down at the same desk where she had left her warrant card. The desk faced the whiteboard and large map of the North Yorkshire coastal region, from Middlesborough in the north, to Bridlington in the South.

She cleared her throat, getting everyone's attention. Richard glanced up once, then his eyes went back to his phone.

Rita said, "Can we please get started with the Clara Winters case?" I want a timeline set up from the date of her disappearance. I've read through the notes. Can I please have your thoughts?"

She watched as Richard sighed and put his phone in his pocket. He folded his hands over his ample belly but said nothing. Rizwan spoke up.

"A group of ramblers found the body in a shallow grave about 15 miles outside Scarborough. It's in the moors, and it's a well-known walking spot. One of the ramblers' dogs had sniffed out the grave and was digging at it with his paws."

Maggie said, "There's been rain recently, and the ground was soft. That probably exposed the grave."

Rita felt a chill on her skin, and she flexed her jaws. "Anything else?"

Rizwan said, "The ramblers called 999. Uniforms responded, and arrived promptly. They set up a perimeter and protected the crime scene. Scene of crime officers have examined the area, and they are still visiting it daily. The woman's remains are on site, and the pathologist is working on them."

Rita said, "Have any of the remains been sent to CAHID?" From the three blank faces, she knew they didn't know what she was talking about. For the first time, Richard seemed interested. He frowned at her, then looked away again.

"Centre for Anatomy and Human Identification, or CAHID," Rita said. "It's the U.K.'s biggest centre for identifying victims from their skeletal remains. It's based at the University of Dundee. I take it the skeleton hasn't been sent there as yet?"

Maggie and Rizwan shrugged, and Richard raised his eyebrows. Rita scribbled on her notebook to set a reminder for herself. Then she pointed her pen at Maggie and Rizwan.

"Can one of you please ring the pathologist and ask them if it's in the pipeline? We might have an ID, but for in-depth evidence about how this woman died, we need feedback from CAHID."

Maggie and Rizwan nodded. Rita rose and went to the whiteboard. She wrote Clara Winters in big letters. She turned to the team.

"Where did this woman live? When was she last seen?"

The answers were engraved in the pits of her soul, but she wanted to check if the team had done their homework. She took a deep breath to compose herself.

Maggie said, "She lived on Oak Road, near Falsgrave Park. It's on the south side of town, a long stretch of residential houses that goes down to the beach. She was reported missing by her daughter, who told the teachers at school. Her body was never recovered. She was last seen in the early hours of the morning when she put her daughter to bed. After that, there are no eyewitnesses. No one saw her leave home or where she went. The search went on for eight weeks."

"CCTV?" Rita asked, feigning nonchalance.

Rizwan said, "Unfortunately, she lived in a CCTV dark spot. Her car was seen going up Scalby Road, the A171, then she took a country lane up into the North York Moors. After that, she wasn't seen. ANPR wasn't active in 1994, unfortunately."

"Good," Rita pointed a finger at the young constable, who seemed visibly pleased with the compliment.

Automatic number plate recognition, or ANPR, was used extensively by the police in UK to identify a car by its number plates. Numerous criminals and terrorists were caught that way. But it started in 2002.

"There was a national appeal in the papers and also on Crimewatch," Rizwan continued. "Like Maggie said, no witnesses came forward. It happened in the winter when Scarborough's quiet anyway. The hordes descend in the summer, don't they?" She grimaced. "If this woman went missing in July or August, someone might have seen her."

"You don't know that," Maggie said. "She left late at night, like she didn't want anyone to know where she was heading. No one would see her even in the summer. I do find that weird. Why would she leave her daughter alone at home? She was 11 years old."

"Good point again," Rita said. She was trying to hold it together, but she could feel the broken edges of her mind slowly giving way. It felt surreal, listening to Rizwan and Maggie.

Her jaws ground together, and her nostrils flared once. Had this been a bad idea?

It was too late now. She fought the panic that suddenly rose up inside her, sending her heart rate into a clear frenzy. She forced a smile on her lips. "Excuse me," she said. "I need a loo break."

CHAPTER 9

Rita all but ran to the bathroom. She almost barged into a female uniformed officer, emerging from the toilet. She excused herself, went in, and locked herself inside a cubicle. She sat down and held her head in her hands.

She forced herself to do the slow breathing exercises that she had been taught in her yoga class. They helped more than any amount of counselling or distraction techniques. She breathed in slowly through her nose, counting to four, then let go even slower, counting to six, through her mouth.

She put a thumb over her left nostril and breathed in through the right, repeating the same process three time. After a few minutes, her heart rate had slowed down, and she felt more in control. The storm was slowly receding from her mind.

She opened her eyes and stared at the grey door of the cubicle. She came out and checked herself in the mirror. Then she walked back to the office. She noticed Richard giving her a funny look, a frown on his face. She ignored him. She went back to the whiteboard and picked up the black marker.

Under her mother's name, she had written one and circled the number. She wrote down the date and time from memory – digits that were imprinted on her brain.

22nd November, 1994.

Under number two, she wrote occupation. She looked at the others. "What did the victim do for a living?"

Saying the word victim sounded alien on her tongue, like raindrops in a desert.

"The police interviewed her friend, Angela. The victim worked at the tills in the local supermarket. Her employers were interviewed. CCTV was checked at the supermarket. Nothing suspicious was found. She didn't get into any arguments with customers. She seemed to live a pretty uneventful life," Maggie said.

Rita asked, "Did she have a partner or boyfriend? Was she married?"

Maggie said, "No one came forward. Her neighbour said she lived alone with her daughter. The daughter had not seen anyone come to the house. The victim had an ex-partner from last year, but she didn't have a boyfriend at the time of her disappearance."

Rita knew her name had not been disclosed in the report, which was in keeping with the law. She had never been so relieved.

Maggie was still speaking. “The daughter was taken into care and then adopted by foster parents. Poor girl," Maggie sighed.

Rita let out a soft exhale and composed herself.

Rizwan said, "The victim’s car was last seen on the A171, like I said. The body was discovered near a peak called the Raptor Viewpoint. It's a place where people go to watch eagles." He shrugged and spread his hands to show his ignorance. "Birdwatcher's paradise, apparently. But only in the winter, when the large eagles appear."

"How far is that spot from where the victim lived?" Rita asked.

"About 20 miles," Rizwan said. "But its not just the distance. The terrain is hilly. It's part of the moorlands, and the roads are hilly and narrow. At night, it would be a cold and remote place."

Maggie was looking at her laptop screen, and read from it. “I’m looking at the map. It says from Pickering head east on A170 turn left at sign for Anvil inn, sawdon. Go on sawdon lane through sawdon, pass the inn onto yederick road which becomes cockmoor road and follow road round to the raptor viewpoint.”

“Are you Miss Satnav?” Rizwan chortled.

“Are you Mr Useless?” Maggie fired back.

Rizwan grinned. “You’re so easy to wind up.”

Rita smiled at the constables. They clearly knew each other well.

She said, “The route Maggie mentioned goes from the A170. But the car was last seen on the A170. Maybe she used a different route.”

Maggie looked at the map on her screen again. Then she nodded. “Yes she could’ve gone up and cut left, through Low Road.”

"Was her car ever found?" Rita asked.

It was a question that had been gnawing at her mind for three decades.

She knew the car was still missing, and she was playing devil's advocate to see if the team knew anything. A discovery of the car would be a major breakthrough in the investigation.

Rita now suspected that if her mother was killed, the murderer would have disposed of her car. But it wasn't easy, and there wasn't a large lake where the body was discovered, from her reading of the map.

The two constables shook their heads, and Rita looked at Richard. He caught her eyes and looked away, shrugging. He remained cold and indifferent, and his attitude was beginning to irritate Rita.

"Do you have anything to add?" Rita asked him. "I'm sure you've read the case files." It was a statement, not a question.

There was a quietness in the room as Richard sat up straighter in his chair. "I looked through the scene of crime report. The body was in a shallow grave, and the ground must have been soft, and presumably it was the work of one or two men. The victim's clothing or drops of blood were not found leading up to the spot where the body was discovered. It seems she died at the viewpoint."

Rita didn't show it, but she was pleased with his assessment. She nodded at him, and their eyes met again briefly before Richard looked away. "Anything else?" Rita prompted.

"We don't know how she died. But she was buried with her clothes on. They didn't find a phone or her car keys. She didn't have any identification."

"But her clothes and remnants of the underwear provided DNA," Rita said. She kept her voice stable and remained resolute, despite the tension in her heart. "That provided the positive ID, along with the dental records. They didn't find any evidence of a murder weapon or the shovel used to dig the grave, did they?"

Richard and the two constables shook their heads. Rita glanced back at Rizwan.

“Questioning her employers didn't reveal anything of significance. She did her job and came back home. That was all, wasn't it?”

Rizwan nodded. "She had CCTV footage from when she walked around in the town centre, in the days before her disappearance. She had been alone, all with her daughter. There are also photos of her dropping her daughter off to school and picking her up. Again, she was always alone."

A veil of memories dragged itself across Rita's eyes. For a few seconds, her mother's face, a kind smile, her soft hair loomed so large she couldn't see anything else. She blinked furiously, dispelling the images.

It was true, she didn't remember her mother having a boyfriend or partner in the days and weeks before she disappeared. She recalled a man coming to the house when she was younger. He was Robert MacFarlane, a garage mechanic. Rita had known him as a child. She had a few memories of Robert coming to their house. He was a kind, nice man. She remembered playing with him in the garden. He had a motor boat, and on weekends, he took Rita and Clara fishing in quiet corners of the harbour.

When Rita joined the police, she got in touch with Robert, who had been questioned extensively by the police. For many years, she thought he had a role to play in her mother's disappearance. But her memories of Robert were pleasant. He had always been sweet to her, and a gentleman to his mother, as far as she could recall.

And nothing was ever found to connect him to that fateful night. He had not been in touch with her mother for more than a year before she disappeared. He still lived in Scarborough, but he was with another woman, who had provided him with an alibi. Rita knew Robert name was mentioned in the report, and she asked the team about him.

"Yes, Robert McFarlane lives here, on the north side, close to the hills," Maggie said. She had a tablet device in her hand and was flicking through the pages. She stopped at one and concentrated.

"Mr. MacFarlane is now 61 years old. He used to be a garage mechanic, and then became a property maintenance and repairs man. He is now more or less retired, and we were thinking of getting in touch with him." Maggie looked at Richard. "Haven't we?"

Richard nodded. "Yes. He knew the victim two years before she disappeared. Although he had an alibi, he lived close by, I wouldn't disregard him completely."

"Why not?" Rita asked, intrigued.

"The relationship had ended a year before, and he was with someone else. And this woman gave him an alibi. They were together that night."

Richard continued. "In the report, it says they went to bed together, and after that the woman only remembers waking up at 8 AM the next morning. If Mr. MacFarlane had slipped out of the house at night, she wouldn't be aware. There is no CCTV on the street where they live."

Rita thought for a while. "Does he have any police record? Or have members of the public or previous girlfriends complained about him?"

"No," Richard said. "No PCNs and the victim had never complained about him when they were a couple." Richard shrugged. "I would keep him as a person of interest, now that we are reopening the case."

"That makes sense," Rita agreed. "At this point, we need to treat everyone as a suspect until we can narrow down the list as more evidence emerges. Cast the net wide."

She spread her hands and then drew them into the centre slowly. "By asking everyone and anyone connected to the disappearance, we might be able to connect the dots later on. We are guided by the evidence, but an absence of evidence does not mean evidence of absence."

She stopped and looked at them, letting her words sink in. "Agreed?"

Richard looked at her, and for the first time, he seemed impressed. He nodded, along with the constables. "If we are to assume that she was murdered, for which there is a strong possibility, we need to think about means, motive, and opportunity."

Richard said, "Mr. MacFarlane had the opportunity, I believe. He was a strong man, and he could have strangled her to death or used a weapon like a knife. As for the motive, that's where I draw a blank."

Maggie said, "A jealous lover? I know they broke up, but what if he still had feelings for her?"

Rizwan said, "But was she seeing anyone else at the time? Why would he be jealous?"

Maggie said, "Well, there was no evidence she was with anyone else. But that doesn't mean she wasn't seeing anyone."

Rita pointed at Maggie, encouraging her. "Exactly. That's what I mean by an absence of evidence. Just because a man didn't show up with her on CCTV doesn't mean that man doesn't exist. We need to ask around, again, to see if the previous investigation missed anything out."

Her mind shuttered and clicked like the lens of a camera. She had lost count of the nights she had spent poring over the reports, trying to find gaps in the investigation. North Yorkshire police had questioned everyone her mother knew: the people she worked with, her friends, her neighbours. Now, Rita knew it was time to go back to that investigation and pull up that list again.

"Okay, so her closest friend was Angela," Rita said, writing down the name on the whiteboard. "Her neighbours were the Paynes and the Thackers. Is that right?"

The team agreed, going through the pages of the report. Rita noted with satisfaction that Richard seemed more engaged now. He had opened up his own tablet and was looking at the screen.

"There was also the house where she lived," Richard said. "It was checked out thoroughly by scene of crime at the time, obviously. They are meant to head down there later on today to see if they find anything. The house isn't occupied. It was a council property, and tenants have lived there over the years. But it's been empty for the last three months."

Rita steeled herself, her fists clenching behind her back. "Then that's where we start," she said quietly.

CHAPTER 10

Rita didn't have a car, so all four of them got into a black Ford in the car park. Richard drove, and Rizwan sat next to him. Maggie got in next to Rita in the rear.

The clouds had dispersed, and the sky was clear now, with the sun making a rare appearance. It was still cold outside, and Rita kept her window up. The sea had changed colour, now a more vivid blue, reflecting the sky.

As they drove down the hill, Scarborough Castle loomed to her left, its ramparts blotting out the sky. The stone castle occupied the entire hilltop, and despite its age of almost a thousand years, it was well maintained.

It was built in 1156 by King Henry II, and its architecture was borrowed from the parts of France Henry II ruled over. But Henry II was relatively late to Scarborough. The town's name originated from "Scars Berg," a Danish settlement started by the Viking king Skarthi Thorgil.

Thorgil and his band of vicious Viking raiders settled here just before 1000 AD. King Henry II might have been 200 years later, but he left the castle behind and granted the town royal charters. He also allowed an annual Fair to be held, which became famous throughout the region.

The song that made the fair famous came to her mind briefly. She shook her head, a wan smile fading on her lips. As school kids growing up in Scarborough, they twisted that song into various rude improvisations. She hadn't been to Scarborough Fair for three decades.

As the road went through a grimy block of council estates, with unemployed youths hanging around on the street corners, Rita realised things hadn't changed much around here. But she still held happy memories from her childhood, going down to the beach in South Bay just outside the tourist season, picking shells and clams when the tide was low.

She remembered playing with her mother and going on picnics with her friends. By the harbour pier was also where she first kissed a boy, a 16-year-old called Jack Branford.

The memory jolted her. She still remembered Jack's name, and the smile returned to her lips. They became an item, and she went out with him until she was 18 years old. They were teenagers, and he had been her first love.

She recalled his face now, his blonde hair falling over his forehead, the strong square jaw of the boy who slowly grew into a man. When she left for university, so did Jack. He went off to Edinburgh to study law. They visited once or twice, but the magic slowly dissipated, and then it ended. It was funny now, thinking about Jack. She wondered where life had taken him.

As they got closer to Falsgrave Park, the roads became even more familiar. She went past Manor Hill School, where she did her A-levels. This building also had a facelift, with a new metal and glass frontage replacing the hideous black and white art deco building.

Briefly, she recalled her school friends. She had lost touch with all of them, and she wondered if her girlfriends were still around. Julia, Vicky, and Nina. Her three best friends, with whom she had lost touch. She wondered what happened to them. She remembered their last names and planned to look them up.

The car slowed as it took the left into Oak Road. Finally, it stopped in front of her old house.

There was no hiding anymore. There was no golden memory here, no respite from the sudden, harsh reality that had ripped her life apart 30 years ago. She got out of the car, blinking in the sunlight. A fresh wind blew over the housetops, skittering dry leaves. It was a terraced house, small and compact, two up and two down.

Richard had a set of keys. The front garden was overgrown, and the faint smell of wasting vegetation crept into her nostrils. Her breath caught when she saw some garden gnomes under the hedge on the right. They were old and discoloured, and she recalled when her mother had bought them. A fist seemed to punch her in the abdomen, and the pain almost doubled her over suddenly.

She didn't want to be here.

She didn't want to relive the terror of that night.

But she had no choice.

Maggie stood by the door, waiting for Rita. The men had already stepped inside.

"Coming, guv?" Maggie asked.

There was no point in delaying the inevitable. Rita nodded and pushed the rusty, creaking gate to one side. She stepped on the stone path, the grass overgrowing at the edges. Then she stepped inside her childhood home for the first time in three decades.

CHAPTER 11

The place looked different. The narrow hallway walls had been painted a pale lavender colour, and she didn't see any trace of the floral wallpaper she remembered.

To her right, the living room was just big enough for two sofas and the TV by the bay window. But the room was completely empty. The carpets had also been changed. The lavender coloured curtains, matching the light carpets, looked new and were drawn. The constables pulled them apart.

Sunlight flooded through the net curtains, dust motes flying in the rays. There was no smell of old, decaying floorboards. There was no sound, even their footsteps were hushed by the carpets. A faint trace of new paint smell entered her nostrils.

This house had been renovated; Rita could tell that much. Even the bookshelves were painted white and bare.

Her childhood – erased and redacted. Consigned to the dustbin of memories. Was it like this for everyone returning to where they lived as children? Perhaps it was better this way. Cold, clinical and austere – to contrast against the wild emotions tugging at her heart.

Richard was standing behind her. She knew he had looked in the dining room and kitchen already.

"This place has been empty for three months. The previous owners complained it was in a state. I guess the council renovated it."

Rita nodded in silence. She turned, and Richard moved back so she could walk out into the small landing. She looked at the staircase, at the dark, invisible landing above.

Memories assailed her, flooding her mind. Her jaws flexed as she tried to swallow the black weight lodged in her throat. She didn't succeed. She walked into the dining room. Again, the carpets felt new, the walls with the same new paint as in the landing. The room was empty. She walked to the end, where the small patio door looked out into the tiny garden.

The council clearly hadn't sorted out the grass. Weeds grew everywhere, and the tiny shed had its windows smashed in. She remembered how she stored her bike there. How Clara taught her to ride the bike in Falsgrave Park. The sense of elation, the pure joy that shot through her the first time she could cycle without help. Clara used to run behind her, shouting to keep her eyes on the road. The visions came and went, sliding across her heart like snapshots of an old Polaroid camera.

Rita walked into the kitchen. The cupboards had remained the same. They had been repainted white. She touched a cabinet, and her hand stilled. It was warm, she could feel the grain of wood under her finger.

Slowly, as if she were sliding a gravestone to one side, she opened the cupboard door. It was empty inside. She repeated the process with the other cupboards. Everything had been cleared out. The dishwasher and washing machine were also empty.

Rizwan had opened the side door in the kitchen and stepped outside. Rita recalled how she used to run through the door while her mother was busy in the kitchen. Clara used to scold her for scurrying around, and Rita heard her mother's voice, faint, like it was coming from the end of a long tunnel.

Suddenly, it was too much. She felt that piercing pain again, slicing through her heart, cleaving it in two. She exhaled and whipped around, heading out to the landing. She went up the stairs quickly to hide herself from the others.

The small bathroom and the two bedrooms next to it remained the same, as she had expected. The bathroom had been cleaned, and the shower curtain was new. But the bath basin and commode were in exactly the same place.

She took a deep breath and went inside what used to be Clara's bedroom. She stepped inside, her feet sinking in the new carpet. The room was dark, and she turned the light on. Then she shut the light off and opened the curtains. The room was empty and looked bigger without any furniture.

It all looked so sterile, in sharp contrast to the mess of jumbled-up memories in her mind.

Her room was smaller, enough space for a single bed, wardrobe, and desk and chair. Rita pulled the curtains apart, and dull light flooded into the room. There was nothing here. Even the marks she had drawn in the wall were now covered in new paint. She had so many memories of this room, but it seemed like her memories existed on a different planet. This used to be her bedroom, but nothing here was hers, anymore. The laughter, tears, birthdays – it was all gone.

A futile nostalgia constricted her lungs all of a sudden, like she couldn't breathe.

Was there any point in being here?

That heavy black weight in her throat wouldn’t budge. She went outside, into the narrow landing.

She was about to go downstairs, one foot on the step, when a distant memory struck her. She looked up and saw the hatch door for the loft. She remembered Clara going up the stairs.

Rita looked in the airing cupboard and found the stick retractor to release the latch door. Rizwan came upstairs and stood on the landing, watching her. Rita pulled down the loft door and found the staircase. It still worked. She released it down to the floor and tested it.

Rizwan came forward. "I've got a flashlight. There should be light up there as well, but we don't know if it's working."

"Only one way to find out," Rita said. She gripped the ladder and started to climb.

She remembered where the light switch was. And it was still there, on her right. She flicked the switch, and the light came on. She got up slowly and stood. The loft had not been touched, just like the garden.

It was still a mess of cobwebs, and here she did smell rot, probably from some damp wood. She had seen a few tiles missing when she looked at the roof. With Rizwan's torch, she looked around. She found some boxes, which made a hollow sound when she kicked them gently. A head poked above the hatch, and it was Rizwan. He pulled himself up into the loft and stood.

"Anything interesting?"

“Let’s have a look.”

The torch beam cut through the darkness and picked up two rolled carpets against the partition wall. She called Rizwan, and with his help, unrolled the carpets. They were old and decaying, but there was nothing inside them.

She was about to go downstairs when she noticed a couple of loose bricks on the chimney stack. It could be wear and tear, she thought, and the bricks just needed pointing. But when her torch beam swept up and down the chimney stack, she found the rest of the chimney stack in good working order.

Only two bricks that were badly damaged, like someone had chipped at them with a hammer. Intrigued, she leaned closer. With a gloved hand, she was able to move the bricks.

"Come here," she called to Rizwan, who had moved to the other side. "Hold the torch so I can see."

Working with both hands now, Rita was able to pull the two bricks loose. Her breath caught when she found a box inside. It was made of black leather and had a zip. She reached inside, and a couple of spiders skated past her hand. She grimaced, withdrawing her hand; she hated spiders.

Then she pulled out the small leather bag. She could feel something inside. She put it on the floor, and Rizwan trained his torch beam on it. Inside the bag, there was a video camcorder, the compact ones that were used in the 1990s. It seemed to be in good condition. Rita pulled it out.

Another fleeting vision zoomed past her mind. Her mother, attaching the battery on this camera, and looking through the eyepiece. Rita wanted to have a look, but her mother declined. The memory came and went like a blazing comet. Rita didn't see the camera again until now. But was it the same device?

She pressed a couple of buttons, but nothing happened, as expected. Flicking the detach switch, the battery fell into her hands. She clicked it back into place, then put the camera back into the leather case. She stood, an odd excitement now spiking in her bloodstream.

"Let's get this back to forensics," she told Rizwan.

CHAPTER 12

Rita came out of the house, her mind working overtime. In an evidence bag, she held the black leather bag with the camcorder inside it.

Did Clara hide the camera in the loft? Through the clear evidence bag, she glanced at the black leather bag again. Clara hadn't been the kind of person to keep secrets. But what did Rita really know of her mother's life?

Rita didn't doubt her memory of the camera, but she wondered if it could have been a different device. Her analytical mind also told her this black leather bag, and the camcorder inside it, might predate the times when she and her mother lived here. That would mean 41 years ago – and she discarded that thought. Small Camcorders like these had not appeared in the eighties.

She looked around the street. The houses looked the same, and she saw net curtains flutter in the house opposite. She wondered if the neighbours were still the same.

She turned to Maggie, who stood beside her.

"Have the uniforms done a door-to-door? I mean, only the old residents would remember anything. It might not be anything of value, but still." Rita shrugged.

Maggie shook her head. "No one's told the uniforms what to do. To be honest, until you arrived, we just looked at the reports, that's all."

"Okay." She instructed Richard and Rizwan, "Start at opposite ends and work your way down. Maggie and I will tackle the houses nearest. We'll meet in the middle." Richard looked hesitant, then nodded.

Rita knocked on the door of the house to her right. She didn't know what to expect. This house had also been renovated, it seemed. A woman opened the door, a child in her arms. She blinked at them in confusion. Rita showed her warrant card. The woman peered at it, then frowned.

"What's happened, like? Not seen the police round here for a while." Her accent was strong North Yorkshire, a comforting sound that hearkened back to Rita's childhood. It almost made her smile.

"No, it's all fine," Rita reassured the woman. "How long have you lived here?"

"Moved in four years ago. Why?" The frown remained on the woman's face.

“We are just following up leads on the investigation of a cold case,” Rita answered. She needed to put the woman's mind at ease. “A woman in the house next door went missing 27 years ago. We are just following up on new evidence, that's all.”

The tension cleared from the woman's face. The toddler started to cry, and she bounced him a couple of times until he stopped.

“Thanks for your time,” Rita said. Maggie joined her on the pavement. “I asked the man on the right,” Maggie said. “He doesn't know anything. He shares the house with another man, and they're both renting.”

“Let's carry on,” Rita suggested. She took the houses opposite, and Maggie stayed on the same side.

Rita walked past a green door that looked familiar. She stopped and looked at the faded, peeling paint on the door, and the old brass calling bell. A young family used to live here, and she used to play hopscotch with a little girl. The bay windows looked the same, and she could tell this house hadn't been renovated, at least not on the outside. She pressed the doorbell, her heart thudding. There was a delay, then the chain locks slid, and an elderly woman's face appeared.

Her hair had gone white, but it was still plentiful. Age had left deep marks on her face, and the wrinkles around her eyes were pronounced. Rita stared at her for a while, then the memories surfaced. Yes, she knew this woman. Suddenly, she was very glad Maggie wasn't with her. She tried to remember the name, but despite searching her mind, she came up with a blank.

She showed her warrant card. “Detective Inspector Gupta, of North Yorkshire Police,” Rita said. “I'm asking about the woman who lived at number 53, opposite.” Rita pointed at the house across the street. The woman's eyes followed her gesture, and a frown appeared on her face.

“Do you remember a lady called Clara Winters, who lived there?”

The older woman peered closely at Rita, and her heart fluttered with sudden panic. Did the woman recognize her?

“Yes, I do. Why?”

Rita asked, “What's your name?”

“Harrington. Susan Harrington.”

Yes, now Rita remembered her even better. Her daughter was called Emily, and fleetingly, Rita wondered what happened to her.

“We found new evidence about Clara Winters,” Rita said, trying her best to sound plain and matter-of-fact. “She went missing thirty years ago.”

“I... I remember that well. What have you found about her?” Susan's posture was keen now, and an inquisitive light shone in her eyes.

“Some new evidence, which I cannot disclose as the matter is under investigation. I'm sure you understand. Is there anything you can tell us about the woman who lived there?”

“I remember the police coming round, like you have now, asking questions. They did it a couple of times. I remember the little girl being taken away. She was crying, the little one. It was so sad.”

The words seemed to reach out and curl around Rita's heart, shrinking it slowly. Susan's eyes flicked to Rita's jet-black hair, and back to her face. The corners of Susan's eyes crinkled.

“What did you say your name was again?”

“Detective Inspector Gupta,” Rita said quickly. “Is there anything you can tell us about Clara Winters, maybe something new you've remembered since the last time?”

Susan stared at Rita for a while, like she was trying to guess who she really was. She seemed to give up after a while. She shook her head. “No, I can't. It was a very sad business, I remember that. Are you sure you can't tell me what you found?”

“Not as yet. But we will keep you informed. Do you live here alone, by the way?”

“I do now. My husband died a few years ago. My daughter lives in Sheffield now. She knew the little girl. Rita, I think her name was.”

Rita felt Susan's eyes hold her captive, like she suspected something. Rita stepped back and shrugged, trying to act nonchalant. She felt stupid all of a sudden. She shouldn't have knocked on Susan’s door. What was she thinking?

“Thanks for your help. If you remember anything, please give the Scarborough police station a call.”

She walked away, feeling Susan's eyes on her back. She bumped into Richard, who had now joined Maggie. Rizwan was still knocking on doors, she assumed.

Richard said, “Most of the families here have moved in in the last decade. Or thereabouts. There's one old man, but he doesn't remember Clara Winters. His wife might have, he said, but she's dead.”

“Okay,” Rita said. “Maggie, help Rizwan. Let's finish this quickly and head back to the station.”

CHAPTER 13

It was midday by the time they got back to the station. Rita's tummy was rumbling, but when she was busy on a case, she could ignore the pangs of hunger. She asked the others if they wanted to go for lunch, and they agreed.

She joined them but got herself a coffee, then took the evidence bag and headed up to the second floor, to the Scene of Crime office. She took the lift, sipping her coffee, clutching the evidence bag tightly in her hand. The second-floor corridor was exactly the same as the ground floor: blue lino and whitewashed walls.

Rita knocked on the door that said "Scene of Crime, No Entry" in big white letters. There was a glass panel, and the cover over it slid to one side, exposing the face of a black woman. She stared at Rita for a few seconds, then opened the door. Her hair was braided, each neat ribbon coming down to the nape of her neck. Her chestnut brown eyes were large and liquid, and she was pretty. Her expressive eyes focused on Rita. She wore a lab coat over a blue dress.

“I've not seen you here before,” the woman said. “But I'm assuming you are new, and you must work here.”

Rita showed her warrant card, and the woman nodded. An ID card hung from a lanyard on her chest. She raised it so Rita could see.

“My name is Shola Adebayo. But everyone calls me Shola.”

“Nice to meet you, Shola,” Rita said, extending her hand. They shook hands, and Rita walked inside.

There was a cool hum inside the lab. Long desks were placed at regular intervals, with microscopes and other instruments on top. Rita showed the evidence bag and explained where it had come from. Shola took it from her and sat down at her desk. On the desktop computer, she inserted the serial number from the bag. Then she stood and went to one of the long examination desks.

A man wearing a similar white coat appeared from another door at the rear of the office. He walked up to them. He was tall, with a thin face. His blue eyes swung from Rita to Shola, then back to Shola again. He had a light blonde stubble on his cheeks. His shoulders were stooped, and his hand came up to stroke the stubble, then went down to his sides again. Large hands, Rita noticed. His skin was pasty white, like the man had stayed inside a laboratory most of his life and not seen much sunlight.

"Henry," Shola introduced them. "This is Rita Gupta, a new detective inspector who just joined us."

"How do you do," Henry said. His voice was a whisper, and he had to clear his throat to speak louder. Rita shook the large hand, feeling a faint trace of moisture in the palm. She refrained from the urge to wipe her hand against her trousers and turned around to Shola.

"Shall we take a look?"

"Of course." With careful, practiced hands, Shola removed the camcorder from its leather bag. Before she did so, she lifted the bag to the light and examined it carefully. Her gloved finger traced around the edge of the chain. Lights hung over the desks, and Henry grabbed one, shining it down on the camcorder. Shola murmured her thanks. She put the camcorder on the desk.

"Where is the battery charger?" Shola asked.

"It wasn't in the leather bag, and we searched for it, but the house was empty."

“It's strange the charger is not here,” Shola said. “But I'm sure we can find something to charge the battery.” She clicked the battery off and examined it.

Henry said, “This is an old device, and it might be difficult to find a charger. But we can certainly look.”

“It's a Panasonic.” Shola turned the device around, and on the back, in black letters against a metallic surface, Rita could see numbers and letters. The serial number, she guessed.

“I'm hoping we can find where this item was bought, and by whom, from that serial number,” Rita said. “As far as I can see, I can't see a tape inside it.”

Shola and Henry hunched over the camera, examining it closely. Then they both shook their heads. Shola said, “It's best to charge the battery up, or see if we can connect it to the mains. Once we open it and have a look inside, we'll have a better idea. Did anyone else touch this?”

Rita shook her head. “No. Thanks for your help. By the way, I am the SIO for the cold case. Have you been to the site?”

“Yes, we have. Going there later today again, as it happens. Lots of samples there.”

Rita nodded. “Who ID’d the body?”

“The pathologist did. The crime scene is an excavation site. We've not removed the remains. Just a few items of clothing that weren't fully degraded.

We got the DNA and dental records, and the pathologist did the rest."

"Where is the pathologist? And what's his name?"

"Dr Das. He works at Scarborough General Hospital, and you'll find him in the morgue, in the hospital basement. I can ring him and let him know you're coming."

"I'll see him later in the afternoon," Rita said, taking out her phone. "But first, I want to visit the crime scene. Maybe see you there later?"

Shola smiled and Rita reciprocated. "Look forward to it," Shola said.

CHAPTER 14

Rita came down the staircase to the ground floor and walked down the corridor. A man caught her eye. He wore a sharp blue suit that showed his athletic, lean body to perfection. His brown hair was cut short, which matched his dark eyes. He was ridiculously handsome, and as Rita watched him, a sudden memory triggered. She stopped dead in her tracks.

The man had clearly noticed her as well, because he slowed down. They stood there, staring at each other.

"Rita, is that you?" the man said, stepping forward. His eyes held hers and then roamed around her face. He blinked a few times, as if he was trying to make sure he wasn't making an embarrassment of himself.

"Jack," Rita said, frowning. That single word was a statement, not a question. Jack Banford. Her boyfriend from what seemed like a lifetime ago. They had lost touch in their mid-20s, and it had been close to 20 years since she had seen him. His hair was thinner, and his face had lost the slight chubbiness of his youth. He looked in good shape.

"Yes, it's me," he said slowly. A look of wonder passed over his face. He shook his head, as if he couldn't believe what he was seeing. Then he smiled. "I can't believe it's you. What are you doing here?"

Rita realized that she was smiling too, and she felt a little unsure of herself. "I'm a Detective Inspector for North Yorkshire Police. I'm here to lead an investigation."

The corners of his mouth relaxed, and his eyebrows rose upwards. The smile faltered on his lips, and she sensed a stiffness in his features now.

"Oh, I see," he said. "I'm a criminal solicitor. I was just with a client in custody downstairs." He inclined his head. He didn't say anything for a few seconds. They both knew policemen and defending solicitors didn't always see eye to eye.

For Rita, that was putting it mildly. She hated lawyers with a passion—men and women who kept criminals out of jail, all in the pretext of fake justice. The smile on her lips had also shrunk and become a tight, forced line. Perhaps it was for the best that they hadn't crossed paths until now.

"Oh, nice. Do you practice here? Are you a duty solicitor?"

Jack shook his head. "No. I'm a partner in a firm in Scarborough. Our office is on the south side, near the town centre."

Rita digested that slowly. So, Jack had returned from Edinburgh University and settled back here. "Are you doing well?"

"Getting along, I guess," he said, his shoulders lifting a touch. "How about you?"

"Yes, carrying on." She stopped, and they stared at each other, silent questions darting around their minds like balls on a billiard table, but neither able to utter them.

There was so much of their lives that they didn't know, and they were different people now, but still… It was funny, Rita thought. She never would have thought in a million years she would bump into Jack.

She had noticed already he didn't have a wedding ring. And she also knew he had noticed the lack of hers.

"Are you settled down here?" she asked, regretting the words as soon as they left her mouth. She didn't want to sound eager, and the truth was she didn't really care.

"Divorced," he said simply. "I've got a daughter, six years old." He smiled warmly then, and she saw his youthful features suddenly appearing like the sun behind clouds.

She smiled as well. "What's her name?"

"Maya." He grinned.

Rita nodded, then looked at her watch. "I'd better get along. Nice to see you."

"Sure," he nodded swiftly. "Catch you later sometime, maybe? I'll be here over the rest of the week."

"Sure," she smiled. As she walked away, she wondered what he thought of her. It wasn't important, she thought. It was just a chance meeting, and she might never see him again.

In the canteen, she didn't see the others. Her tummy rumbled again, and she decided to pick up a porridge, and another cup of coffee. She took it back to the office and found Rizwan and Maggie there.

"Where is Richard?"

"He had to take a call. He should be back soon."

"Okay." Rita sat down on a chair and started to eat. She pulled a laptop out of her bag and checked emails. "I'm going to the crime scene after this," she informed the two constables. She noticed Rizwan and Maggie look at each other.

Maggie said, "Do you want us to come with you?"

"Are there any uniforms at the scene?"

Maggie nodded. "There's someone on guard till nightfall. A scene of crime officer might also be there. Did you meet them?"

"If you mean Shola and Henry, then yes. Are there any others?"

"No, it's a small department, just like ours."

Rita nodded. "I need to see the pathologist after visiting the crime scene, so I'd love to get a move on. One of you can come with me."

CHAPTER 15

Maggie drove, with Rita sat next to her in the passenger seat. The sea sparkled to her right as they sped down the hill. Some of the streets looked exactly the same, but the sea views were blocked in several places with modern high-rise flats. These apartment complexes had sprung up in the last eight years - when Rita had last been to Scarborough. The land they now occupied used to be designated green land, but clearly, Yorkshire Council changed their minds. Big money from a developer tended to do the trick.

They left the traffic behind and took the A161 that headed out to the hills. The road dipped and rose, and the flat moorland appeared, with the hills rising in the distance. After half an hour, they climbed steeply until the road flattened out at the top. A gravel drive had been turned into a car park. A sign proclaimed the Raptors' Viewpoint to be a 10-minute walk from here.

"On foot from here," Maggie said, unbuckling her seatbelt. “Raptor’s sounds American, doesn’t it?”

“Yes, it does.”

“Apparently it means all birds of prey. The big eagles, and owls, basically. But no one round here calls them raptors anymore.”

They got out of the car. "Glad to get some fresh air," Rita said. She stood and stretched. The air was fresh and scented, and she smelt the heather and gorse, with a tinge of brine that blew in from the sea.

They crossed the car park into the woodlands and started to go up the path. The trees were dense and close, and the ground seemed to absorb all sound except their soft footsteps. Rita looked up, and she could barely see the sky due to the dense foliage.

She thought about her mother, thirty years ago, walking down this path in the dead cold of night.

Was she killed here and then brought here? The latter idea made more sense. Clara went out to meet someone, and then she was brought to this remote location. Unanswered questions raised their heads like snow peaks out of the mist. She had no answers, only a fog of confusion, and no closure.

They finally arrived at a break in the trees, and the view was breathtaking. The cliffs fell off into a ravine, giving way to a deep valley. The thin silver ribbon of a river snaked along the bottom of the valley. After dense woodlands, the hills started again, rising up into the clouds.

Benches had been laid near the cliff edge, and another sign said this was indeed the viewpoint for the winter predator birds.

Rita had done her research. The sign, and these benches, did not exist in 1994. The place was known to birdwatchers, but that was about it. The car park didn't exist either. Although this whole area was designated as an area of outstanding natural beauty, it didn't attract the tourists like it did now. Besides, the tourists only came in the summer. Clara had disappeared in late November. The 22th, to be exact—a date that was engraved in the darkest corner of her heart

They trudged on further, the land sloping slightly downhill and plunging deeper into the trees. After another ten minutes walking, they came into the main clearing. Two white tents had been erected on either side of the crime scene. The excavation was now complete.

The original grave had been carefully extended on both sides, and to the front and back. Rita knew this was standard procedure in forensic investigation. The old soil hid valuable clues. Objects could sink in soft soil, and further evidence was often unearthed in new digs.

She had waited thirty years for this. But now that it was time to finally look at her mother's remains, she felt a tremble in her spine. She had to be the detective, the clinical investigator who was inured to such sights. She had to be. Slowly, her eyes skimmed across the ground, and fell on the skeleton inside the exposed grave.

CHAPTER 16

When Rita saw the bare bones, the skull, and the limbs, she couldn't help but wonder at how well-preserved they were. It wasn't her mother. It couldn't be. All those words, songs, memories of her. And this…this was just cold bones lying in the bare earth.

Sudden emotion clogged her throat, and her lips trembled. The tips of her fingers turned red, and she blinked furiously to keep the tears at bay. She couldn't. She turned away quickly so Maggie wouldn't see her.

With the grief, she also felt anger. Furious, uncontrolled rage that someone would dare do this to her mother. Her own flesh and blood. And to think she hadn't been able to do anything to stop it.

No, she wasn't thinking straight.

She took out a handkerchief and dabbed at her eyes. Maggie had given her some space, and she was glad. She walked ahead, to where a man wearing a white spacesuit was kneeling by the skeleton's head. Another man was standing in front of one of the white tents, staring at her. A uniformed Inspector came up to them, and he seemed to know who Rita was.

"Excuse me. Are you the new DI from London?"

"Yes, I am," Rita said. Her voice was remarkably steady. She felt hollow inside, like her soul had been scooped out, excavated like the ground where her mother lay.

She took out her warrant card and held it for the uniformed Inspector to see. He examined it, then held out the clipboard. Rita signed her name. The man was tall, and looked big in his high visibility overcoat. He had a brown beard, and he wore his peaked blue cap. He smiled at her.

“I’m Inspector David Botley. Nice to meet you.”

Rita forced herself to smile, and shook Inspector Botley’s warm hand.

“Found your way here okay?” Botley asked, as they walked towards the crime scene.

“Maggie got us here. Nice views,” she was grinding the words out, trying to be normal.

“Aye, that it is. Shame about what happened here though.” Botley down turned his lips. Rita felt his eyes on her, and she looked up once and shrugged.

“Let’s see what we can find out.”

Botley led her to a small station by the white tent where he handed her shoe coverings, a plastic apron, and a mask. There was also a hair covering, and Maggie helped her put it on, then did the same for herself.

Walking softly, Rita manoeuvred to the edge of the excavation, then slowly lowered herself into the hole. The man who was kneeling by the skeleton looked up at her. His skin was brown, and he wore black-rimmed glasses. A mask covered his face, and he stared at her inquisitively. An Indian man, Rita could tell that much. She introduced herself. The man got to his feet slowly. He was much older than her, and only slightly taller than her 5 feet seven.

"Dr Samir Das, the pathologist. Nice to meet you, DI Gupta." He gripped her hand.

"Likewise." She hooks his gloved hand, then her eyes fell back on the skeleton.

Her earlier shock still remained, but it was slowly receding, leaving that forlorn emptiness she knew so well. She tried to be dispassionate and forced herself to look for evidence. From her casual look, she could not see any breaks in the bones. Items of clothing that had survived had already been removed. She could see the white circle marks where the clothing had been found.

She looked at Dr Das. "Anything interesting?"

"Everything is interesting," Dr Das said, spreading his hands. "It's not very often we get something like this." He squatted down, and she followed.

Rita asked, "Do you have an interest in forensic anthropology?"

He glanced at her. "I don't have any formal training in it. But every pathologist learns a few things." She couldn't tell if he was offended by her remark. He looked down at the skull and pointed. "Check the skull fissures. They are fully joined and firm." He reached out a gloved hand, and with forefinger and thumb, pressed over the skull fissures that ran horizontally. The skull bone was solid.

"That only happens after the late teens. Till then the brain and the fluid around it can still expand, hence the skull is softer. This woman was definitely an adult, we can tell that much. From her nose, jaws, and cheekbones, and the size of the teeth, it's also clear this is a female. A Caucasian female, as the African and Eastern Asian races have quite different bone structures."

Rita was impressed, but she tried not to show it. Dr Das rose, and shuffled over to the middle of the body, and indicated the pelvis. "You can tell by the brim this is a woman. It's what we call a gynecoid pelvis. It's rounder, more spacious than a man's. Her long limb bones are fairly thin, and her feet are also small."

"When I first saw the skeleton, I knew it was a Caucasian woman, and an adult one."

"Thank you," Rita said. Dr Das was clearly good at his job. She knew forensic anthropology was a specialized branch of pathology. "I hope you didn't mind when I asked if you knew about this stuff. I can see that you do."

For the first time, the corners of Dr Das's eyes crinkled as he smiled. "No offense taken. It's a legitimate question. As it happens, I did some skeletal work during my pathology training."

Rita nodded. "Anything else of interest?"

The doctor agreed gravely, in silence. He squatted down again, and carefully lifted up the right hand.

"Look closer," he said holding the hand up slowly. "Can you see those marks on the knuckles? You have to come closer. I had to use a magnifying glass."

Rita did as the doctor told, and after a while, she could see the light, very faint depressions on the right hand knuckle bones.

"Those were made by a sharp object that cut through her flesh. It wasn't just a small knife, more like a machete, or an axe. This poor woman was attacked, and she used her hands to shield herself." He put the hand down, and Rita stared at it, her blood running cold. Breath was frozen in her lungs, and her chest hurt.

The doctor pointed at the collarbone. "It's broken," he said simply. "So is the left humerus, and the right distal radius, where it joins the wrist." He pointed at them, and Rita had to look closer to see the arm bones. She had completely missed these on her casual inspection.

"From the fractured edges of the bone, you can see a heavy sharp object sliced through them."

Dr Das maintained a soft, low voice, but his words smashed against Rita's ears like cannonballs. "This woman had nothing but her bare hands to fight back. She was no match against the sharp instrument. It was wielded with some force, and I think it was a man attacking her."

CHAPTER 17

As Rita listened to Dr Das's words, she shivered in the cold wind that filtered down through the pine trees. She forced herself to remain objective. She noted the fractured bones and took some photos with her phone. She noticed how the body lay: the left arm was folded inwards, and the legs also pointed to the left. But the figure lay on its back, looking upwards. She stood, and her eyes closed momentarily.

She could feel the soft earth beneath her feet. It was black and granular but still compact. The earth her mother had lain in for so many years. Without thinking, her face drifted upwards, and she met the waving green branches of the palm trees. They seemed to close in together, the wind whispering secrets as it brushed through them. The sky above was darkening, grey clouds starting to blot out the light.

Before her life became extinct, this is the view her mother would have seen. Emotion grabbed her again, closing her throat, and she turned her back to the scene and looked at the dense forest beyond. A few deep breaths did not calm her nerves. Nothing would take the pain away, and she had to work through it.

"I'll be back in a minute," she told Dr Das over her shoulder. The veteran pathologist gave her a thumbs up. Rita walked around the perimeter to the edges of the blue and white tape. She ducked under it and went a few steps outside the clearing. The forest was dark and deep here, absorbing all sounds. Rita leaned against a tree, composing herself.

How did Clara get here? She drove obviously, her car was caught on CCTV, but only on the main road. She must've walked a while to reach this spot. She wondered where her mother's car was. Did her killer drive it somewhere and then dispose of it? That wouldn't be easy, Rita knew.

She walked back to the crime scene and joined Maggie and Inspector Mark Botley who were standing next to each other, talking in hushed tones.

"Has there been a drone search of the surrounding area?" Rita asked. "We need some aerial views to search for more evidence. The victim drove a car that night, and it was never recovered."

From the blank faces of Maggie and Mark, Rita had her answer. Maggie said, "I'll look into it, guv. Do you want me to ask Rizwan now? He's at the base."

"Yes, please. Is it the crime lab who would organize it?"

Maggie nodded. "Drone surveillance is a new thing for us, but we did use it last year." She smiled wryly.

"A boat got lost at sea, and we managed to find it, caught against one of the wind farms."

"There is a wind farm at the sea?" Rita was surprised. Things had definitely moved on in Scarborough. She had never imagined her remote, childhood coastal town was now getting into green energy.

"Oh yes," Maggie nodded. "You can see it on a clear day. It's not visible from the castle or the station, as it's on the other side."

Rita realized now why the wind farm had not been visible. She was glad these initiatives were taking place; Scarborough needed jobs for its youth like a desert needed rainfall. Maggie walked off to call Rizwan.

Rita asked Mark, "Has anyone else been here? Any members of the public?"

"Apart from the group of ramblers who found the body, no. But we don't have anyone here overnight. However, a squad car patrols the area. They come up to the crime scene once at night. There haven't been any reports of visitors."

Rita thought about that. Scarborough was a small town, but she knew the media was still active. While it wasn't a big city, it was a popular tourist area. It was well known, not just in Yorkshire, but in England as a whole. The discovery of a skeleton, and a murder, would definitely stoke the interest of the local press. She knew that one of the ramblers would leak the news. It was inevitable.

"Any sign of the press?" she asked. Mark shook his head. He grinned and held up a hand with crossed fingers.

"Let's hope not."

Rita wasn't so sure. "It's only a matter of time. We are lucky this area is remote. Anywhere else, they'd be swarming all over us now. At the first sign of a reporter, increase the number of uniformed officers here. I don't want the media taking unauthorized photos, and those images turning up in the papers, or even worse, on social media."

Mark nodded solemnly. "Understood."

Rita hated the fact her mother's remains might be under media scrutiny. It was just the kind of thing a reporter would love to take photos of. A scoop, in their words. More like a travesty of personal dignity, she thought.

She went back to the dugout and joined Dr Das. Behind his glasses and mask, and the sterile suit that covered his head, she could see the lines around his eyes. She guessed he was an older man, probably in his mid to late sixties.

He nodded at her, and then continued to use a small brush at one of the toes. Rita crouched by his side, and examined the feet. Dr Das said, "The left ankle is twisted. But there's no break. I think it was her upper body that took the brunt of the blows."

Rita nodded and walked up, examining the pelvis and the other bones carefully. Then she looked at the ground around the body. She knew this area would already have been searched already. But a fresh pair of eyes wouldn't hurt.

She took her time, leaning over and sometimes squatting. She used her extendable baton to poke the ground and turn over clumps of dirt. Her breath was warm against her mask, and beads of sweat collected on her forehead. She stopped suddenly as her eyes caught something.

It looked like a leaf that was sticking out of the ground. It had become dark brown, like the earth. And it wasn't unusual for leaves to be on the ground. But something about it grabbed her attention.

She got closer, and from the breast pocket of her jacket, she took out a pair of plastic clippers and an evidence bag. She cleared the ground around the object, and her breath came faster when she realized it was a photo. She pulled it gently out of the ground with the clippers. Most of the photo was damaged. Only the extreme right side remained, showing what looked like the spire of a church. A sky with clouds was visible behind the church spire. Rita shook the photo gently, releasing the dirt sticking to it. She inserted the photo inside an evidence bag and stood.

She walked back to Dr Das and showed it to him. He squinted at it through the evidence bag. "That looks interesting. Where did you find it?"

"About 10 feet away to the right of the body. I'm surprised the scene of crime officers didn't find it when they did their search."

"They might have focused on the remaining clothes fragments. This is the kind of thing that's easy to miss. The excavation might have buried it by mistake."

That made sense, Rita thought. "I'll have a look around to see if I can find anything else." She straightened and waved at Maggie.

The detective constable came down into the pit. Rita showed her what she'd found, and together, they started searching. After more than half an hour, Rita was starting to get tired. Maggie and she were squatting, and moving around on the earth wasn't exactly easy. They moved around the body and met by the head.

Maggie lowered her mask, breathed, then wiped her forehead. "I can't see anything else, guv. How about you?"

Rita shook her head and stared at the skeleton, reflecting. "Has anyone had a look *under* it?"

Maggie shrugged. Rita went up to Dr Das. The pathologist narrowed his eyes.

"No, but I guess now that the majority of the evidence has been gathered, there's no harm in us trying to do so."

Rita steeled herself. A film fell across her eyes, removing herself to a clinical, cold space. She had to do this and get it over and done with. She grit her teeth and followed Dr Das's instructions.

The ribs separated easily from the ribcage, as if they wanted to merge into the earth and disappear. The rest of the body followed in quick succession. Dr Das asked them to leave the pelvic bones untouched. Rita turned away, letting out the breath she'd been holding. It came out in a rush, as she put her hands on her hips, leaving over. She closed her eyes. She couldn't do this much longer. She needed a break.

Dr Das squatted by the pubis and took out a magnifying glass and a torch on a rubber strap that went over his head, directing the beam at his examination. He leaned close, looking at the convex curve of the pubic bone.

Then he straightened and called to Rita. His attitude was different now, a stiffness in his posture, and a firm set to his lips.

"There are indentations in the pubic bone. It's not smooth. I had noticed it before, but now I'm sure."

There was a quietness in his voice that made Rita pause. She could hear her pulse thrumming against her ears. "What does that mean?"

"It means the ligaments and muscles that attach to the pelvis were stretched. That means something heavy was resting on the pelvis."

Rita felt the air getting sucked out of her lungs, and the hollow emptiness returned. Her throat was parched dry. She couldn't speak. Maybe the words weren't necessary.

Dr Das's voice was low. "I think the victim was pregnant when she died."

CHAPTER 18

The Guardian was watching from his safe spot on the hill, hidden behind dense foliage.

He had a perfect bird's-eye view of the crime scene. He could see the two white forensic tents on either side of the excavation. Ever since he heard the whispers in town, he had come to visit. He wanted to see how far the police would get. He wasn't worried. If anything, a new excitement churned in his blood. It had been many years since he killed Clara Winters. She would always be special to him. She was his first kill, after all.

He still remembered that night vividly. How he stood there and watched her, and then saw recognition flash in her eyes when he came close. She probably thought he was too young to be a threat. She tried to brush past him. How dare she?

A light smile played on his lips as he remembered the shock on her face when he pressed her against the rocks and his hand closed around her throat. The look of disbelief as he thrust her on the floor and tightened his grip around her neck. Then the blood suffusing her face, the veins standing up on her forehead, her legs thrashing around, hands clawing at his grip. Laughing, he had let her go.

He shook his head, grinning. The memory was as charming and pleasant to him as a walk on a beautiful beach during sunset. That night, she had tried to go past him again, and again he subdued her. Played cat and mouse with her until he drew out his weapon. She fought him still; he had to give her credit for that. But she was no match for his long, sharp weapon. A few blows from that, and she had lain still on the ground, never to rise again.

He closed his eyes and breathed in deeply. The smells of the surrounding forest were so fresh and pure. Invigorating, like the smell of Clara’s blood when it flowed. He remembered that, still.

He knew then he had found his life's mission, and he would do it again, at any cost. The feeling of power was like an electric jolt to his brain. He was like a god, able to take a life at his whim. Life was so precious, wasn't it? Wasn't that what everyone said? Life is a gift that can be taken away at any moment. So always preserve it.

Stupid people, those mediocre men and women who knew nothing. They filled their bellies with junk food and watched crappy game shows in the evening and led boring lives that led to nothing.

How were their lives precious? What did they add to this world? He asked himself that question all the time. He didn't understand why so many people needed to live. More human beings should be like him. Rising above the rest, not content with being average.

The blood of these sad people should wash the earth clean. Only then would there be happiness for the few chosen ones. Like him and the Brotherhood. The Brotherhood would always remain, and one day, they would rule the earth. He was their Guardian, and he would make sure that would happen.

The people who called life precious had no idea how powerful death was. Death was demonized by the great religions and by everyone in general. But death was actually the greatest liberator. It freed the hapless, boring individual from a life of servitude.

Clara Winters had it coming. She had acted too brave, tried to do things beyond her means. While he respected her for that, she had to pay the ultimate price.

The Guardian had enjoyed playing cat and mouse with the police after her death. He even submitted a witness statement, saying he saw her in town that day. It wasn't a complete lie because he had, but only from a distance as he followed her around.

Did the stupid police pay any attention to his comments? He doubted they had. And if they did, they might well have seen him on CCTV.

He smiled to himself. The game was starting again, and he couldn't wait to take part. He walked around the hills frequently, coming to visit the graves of his chosen ones. And Clara would always be the first of the chosen ones. He liked coming here. It was peaceful and tranquil, and he could get his thoughts in order. He could plan how to get to the next chosen one.

He saw two women walk into the clearing of the crime scene. He looked closer, but his eyesight wasn't as good as thirty years ago. He took out his binoculars and trained them on the women.

The taller one was clearly in charge. She wore a long, dark blue jacket and black shoes. Her hair was jet black and tied up in a ponytail. She seemed to be of a different race, but he couldn't be sure. Her skin was olive, like an Italian or a Middle Eastern woman. Or maybe she was mixed race.

Something about her struck him as familiar, and he observed her closely. She walked up to the uniformed Inspector and appeared to be giving him an order. The blonde detective constable he had seen before. He watched as the woman got inside the excavation pit and spoke to a man in a white suit. They seemed to have a conversation.

Over the next half hour, the Guardian watched the woman. From the way she spoke, it was clear she was issuing orders. Could she be a new detective inspector he hadn't seen before? It was possible. The thrill of a new adventure started to pound in his heart. His mouth opened and his breath came in short gasps. He licked his lips. He sensed the smell of blood in the air. The blood of his next chosen one. That black-haired woman, down in the excavation pit.

CHAPTER 19

Rita watched the varying shades of emerald as the landscape slipped past the car's windows.

Her mind was a blank; she didn't want to think. Maggie was driving and left Rita alone. The radio had squawked a couple of times, and Maggie dealt with it. Rita felt the constable's eyes on her, but she remained silent and kept her face averted. She realized her behaviour seemed odd to Maggie, but in her present mood, she didn't really care. She didn't allow any feelings to enter her heart, which felt cauterised, stitched up after an injury.

If she allowed a single drop of emotion, it would turn into a deluge that would catapult her out of the car's window, screaming like she'd been cast out of the mouth of a cannon.

No, she couldn't do that. She wouldn't go there, try to process, or try to understand.

She just had to face the reality, which was the case of a woman murdered thirty years ago. She had to solve it. A woman who had been assaulted with a large knife, and who had been pregnant. Those were the facts, and nothing else mattered.

And yet…her chest seemed to cave in suddenly, the ribs pressing on her, crushing her lungs. She couldn't breathe, and the light swam in her eyes, fading. The car was hurtling down the slope, and she opened the window, letting the cold air blast in. She breathed heavily, eyes closed.

She heard Maggie's concerned voice. "Guv, are you okay?"

She blinked, trying to get back to her senses. She looked at Maggie and made a miserable attempt at a smile. "Fine. Running on empty isn't doing me any favours." She patted her tummy. She didn't feel any hunger, but it seemed like an appropriate excuse.

Maggie was frowning, worry in the lines of her forehead. Rita couldn't hold her eyes. She repeated her question. "Yes, I'm fine. I should be eating more, to be honest. Let's get back to the nick." She smiled encouragingly, and Maggie nodded.

Rita called Richard, who didn't answer. Rizwan did, and she asked him about the drone surveillance. "I've spoken to the super, and she has authorized it," Rizwan said.

"I gave you authority, didn't I?"

Rizwan hesitated, and Rita didn't like it. She was the SIO, and her orders shouldn't be questioned. Was Nicola trying to micromanage? Or had she told her team to keep tabs on her and give feedback to Nicola? Rita sighed. She didn't have time for office politics right now.

"She rang and asked for an update," Rizwan said. His voice and words sounded defensive.

"Let's make sure the drones are up today. The light will be fading soon."

"Yes, guv. I'm waiting to hear back from Shola, who is dealing with the company that operates the drones. It's a third-party service, and they're based in Leeds."

"Keep me posted." Rita hung up.

Back at the station, Maggie parked the car and they walked through the rear doors. A couple of the uniformed officers were smoking outside, and they said hi to Rita, who acknowledged the greeting with a smile. She was still a stranger here, but the sooner she got to know the staff, the better it was. No one liked being given orders by an outsider.

They were walking past the canteen, and Maggie stopped. Rita read the inquisitive look in her eyes. She didn't feel hungry, but she realized it was for her own good. She picked up another coffee and a hummus wrap, while Maggie got more coffee for Richard and Rizwan.

The two men looked up as the women entered. They sat down at the table and sipped on the drinks. Rita left her food untouched. Instead, she accepted a biscuit from Maggie and dunked it in her coffee.

"Any news?" Rita asked, focusing on Richard. If Nicola was keeping an eye on her, the D Sup would have asked Richard. Rita sensed Richard was close to Nicola. This might explain the detective sergeant's strange attitude. He cleared his throat and pressed his lips together, as if considering his words.

"Shola called. It's about the camcorder you found in the victim's loft. She wanted to speak to you about it. She's found something interesting, she said." A look of irritation appeared on Richard's face, then faded.

His lips pressed tightly together. "She wouldn't tell me what it was."

Rita suppressed a smile. She was starting to like Shola. She picked up her phone and called the head of forensics.

"So you're back from the crime scene?" Shola asked.

"Yes," Rita said shortly. She didn't want to talk about it. "You found something about the camcorder?"

"Well, it's more about the black leather bag. It had a flap on the inner cover, which was disguised. Inside it, I found a piece of paper with numbers written on it."

Rita frowned. "What sort of numbers?"

"It looks like a serial number. It starts with the initials MDB and then there's a string of 12 digits. I can read it out to you if you want."

Rita took out her black notebook and wrote the numbers down. "MDB 09614239201253." She tapped her pen against the piece of paper, staring at it.

"I wonder what that is," she said softly.

"That's your job," Shola said, her voice light. "But to my untrained eye, it could be a bank's serial number."

"You're right," Rita agreed. "But it could also be a person's initials and phone number, especially as it starts with 09. We'll have a look and let you know." Before she hung up, a question struck her. "By the way, do we have cryptologists here?"

"Cryptologists?" Shola laughed. "We're not a big city department, Rita. You're lucky we have drones. But in the station, we're quite small, and we like it that way. Do you want someone who can break codes?"

"Yes, exactly. If there is a code in these numbers, I want to know. Do you know of any third-party service providers? I could call North Yorkshire HQ; they might know."

"That would be a good idea. Sorry I can't be of more help."

"No problem, what you've done so far is great. Were you able to track down the serial number of the camcorder?"

"Henry is working on it. As soon as he gets something, I'll let you know."

CHAPTER 20

Rita stared at the initials on the number she had just written down in her notebook.

MDB sounded like someone's initials, but she had to keep an open mind. She wondered why her mother would have written this down on a piece of paper and hidden it inside the bag. It had to be important; otherwise, she wouldn't have made the effort.

As for the camcorder, Rita wondered where the tapes were. What was the point of hiding the camcorder without the videotapes? She made up her mind to go back to the house and have a look around the loft again. Maybe she had missed something.

She also had to catch up with her mother's friend, Angela. She checked her phone and sent her a text. Then she told the team about Shola's findings. She read out the numbers, and Rizwan wrote them down. So did Maggie. Richard sat motionless, hands folded on his lap, listening to her. She glanced at him and he averted his eyes. Was he sulking? Rita thought so.

"What do you think?" Rita asked him.

Richard blinked a few times, then cleared his throat. "I'm not sure about the numbers. But MDB could be someone's name, or an institution, like a bank or building society."

"What sort of bank did you have in mind?"

"Well, Midlands Bank, which had several branches in Yorkshire and the North, used to go by the initials MDB."

A distant memory flared in Rita's mind. She remembered seeing checkbooks with those initials. It seemed like a lifetime ago. "That's right," she narrowed her eyes. "The bank's logo was a blue circle with the letters MDB in yellow."

"Exactly," Richard said, nodding. His face remained as impassive as before. He looked away from Rita, not meeting her eyes.

Rita said, "What happened to Midlands Bank? I've not seen any branches around lately."

Maggie and Rizwan shrugged, professing their ignorance. Richard glanced at Rita again before lowering his eyes. He said, "They got bought out by HSBC. They ceased to exist. All the Midland Bank branches became HSBC."

Rita nodded slowly. "Okay. Richard, can I please ask you to contact HSBC and find out if they have records of the Midland Bank accounts that were taken over from the Scarborough branch? And from the North in general. There will be a lot of accounts, but they should be able to run a search against our number."

Rizwan said, "That's assuming this is a bank account number. We should check for that first."

"Yes, we should," Rita agreed. "But something tells me this is a bank account number. Unless it's a code for something else."

Rita continued. "Can we please call up Leeds and Sheffield and ask them if they have a cryptologist we can use? These numbers can be fed into artificial intelligence code-breaking machines to see if there's a pattern. I suggest we do that sooner rather than later."

Rita knew Sheffield and Leeds were part of Yorkshire police. Sheffield was more South Yorkshire and would have a different leadership. Leeds, however, came under North Yorkshire police, and it might be easier to send them a request. She explained her reasoning to the team, and they nodded. She pointed at Rizwan and Maggie.

"You two get busy with the cryptologist request." She turned her focus on Richard. "Can you please call up HSBC?"

Stone-faced, he nodded. He didn't look happy at all. He opened up his laptop and stared at it.

Rita's phone pinged, and it was Angela. She tried to call her once and left a text. Rita excused herself and went outside. She walked down the corridor, past the canteen and the staircase, and turned right towards the rear entrance. Outside, she went behind the entrance, where there were a couple of trees by the fence. She stood there and called Angela.

"Rita, is that you?" Angela's voice came down the phone. Rita had told her she would be coming up.

She remembered Angela well. The woman was close to her mother, and sometimes Angela used to pick Rita up from school and take her back to her house. Clara finished work and joined them for dinner. Rita still remembered those days, and it brought a smile to her lips.

How simple life had been. The golden halo of memories brightened her mind for a few seconds before fading into the harsh reality. She couldn't hide the truth from Angela. But neither could she disclose confidential information right now.

If Angela told someone... Rita remained ambivalent. She needed Angela's help, so she had to tell her sooner or later.

"Yes, it's me," Rita said. "How are you?"

"Getting by, my love. So you've come back up here to work? Missing Scarborough, were you?" Rita could hear the laugh behind her words. It made her smile.

"Well, I guess you can take the girl out of Scarborough, but can't take Scarborough out of the girl."

"Not heard that one before," Angela said. "Most people who leave this old town don't come back. Missing us, were you?"

There was a degree of skepticism in her question that made Rita pause. What did Angela know? Had the Ramblers who found Clara's remains already talked about it? Scarborough remained a small community, and word could spread quickly.

"I needed a break from my job in London." There was an element of truth in that. The constant grime and dust of the big city, not to mention the massive bureaucracy of the Metropolitan Police force, was beginning to weigh heavily on her shoulders. At least she didn't have to deal with that over here. There would be less box-ticking and form-filling, and she was looking forward to that.

"Aye," Angela said. "Well, it's good to have you back. Any of your friends still up here?"

"To be honest, I've not had the time to get back in touch with them. I only arrived yesterday. I will call them at some point." They chatted for a while. Angela was now in her sixties, and she lived with her husband. They got married 12 years ago, and it was Angela's second marriage. Rita got the invite for the wedding, and she had attended. It was a pleasant affair at the church near Whitby Abbey, by the sea.

Rita paused. She had to think about her next question. "I wanted to ask you about me mum," she said. Her voice took on the North Yorkshire accent without her noticing.

"I was driving past the house, and I thought of a few things. Can I come and talk to you sometime?"

Angela paused too. Static in the phone line filled the silence between them. Then Angela spoke in a quieter voice. "Yes, of course, my love. Come round any time."

Neither of them had to speak, but they both knew what each other was thinking. Clara's voice, her smile, and words loomed large in their minds.

"I know it's late notice, but is tonight possible?"

"Yes, sure," Angela said. "Why don't you come down for dinner?"

"No, that's okay," Rita said quickly. "I don't want to cause any hassle. I could meet you tomorrow afternoon."

"Nonsense," Angela said firmly. "Come round this evening. What's the time now?" She went offline, then came back. "It's just gone past four. What time will you be free from work?"

"Not till seven or 8 PM. It might be too late."

"That's fine. Come for 8 PM, and I'll have some dinner ready."

“Are you sure?”

“Yes love, I’m positive.

Rita thanked her and hung up.

CHAPTER 21

Rita went back inside. From the office, she collected the evidence bag with the old photo she had discovered at the crime scene. Maggie was on the phone, and Rizwan was busy on his laptop. Richard was not there.

When Rita asked about him, Rizwan said he had just popped out.

He called after her as Rita turned to leave the office. "Can I please have a word, guv?"

"Yes, of course." They went outside, and Rita leaned against the wall. Rizwan looked apologetic and looked down at the floor, shuffling his feet.

"What's the matter?" Rita asked.

"It's just that my girlfriend's coming to our house this evening. Kind of like a big deal because it's the first time. I need to get back home to help me mum. Is that okay?"

Rita smiled. "Yes, of course, you can. You can shoot off now if you want. Is the drone surveillance thing all sorted?"

"Oh yes, it is. They won't get the drones up tonight, but they will be first thing tomorrow. Is that okay?" He looked anxiously at Rita.

"This is fine," Rita said, uncrossing her arms. "Can I ask you something?"

A guarded look appeared on Rizwan's face. "Uh, yes, sure."

"This will stay between you and me. But the D Sup must have told you about my arrival. Did she mention anything else?"

Rizwan looked unsure. "Like what? Yes, she said you were coming up to take charge of this case. You'd be the SIO. She didn't say much more than that."

"She didn't ask you to keep an eye on me? Report back to her about how I was doing?"

Rizwan's mouth opened and closed as understanding dawned in his eyes. Then he spoke quickly. "No, nothing like that. I mean, as you know, there's feedback forms and so on about all staff members. At some point, she said she wanted us to fill those out about you. But nothing else, like."

Rita stared at him for a few seconds and realized he was speaking the truth. She thought he would be too scared to hide anything from her. She smiled, trying to put the young man at ease. "Thank you," Rita said.

"Actually, I remember one thing." Rizwan pressed his lips together. "The super asked Maggie and me to step outside while she spoke to Richard alone. We went back to our desks, and Richard came and joined us a bit later. I'm not sure what the super told Richard."

Rita had suspected as much. Did Nicola ask Richard to monitor her? What for?

"Thank you, Rizwan," she said, and meant it. "If you've finished up, then go off and have a good evening with your girlfriend and family. See you tomorrow."

Rizwan grinned at her and gave her a thumbs up. Rita went upstairs to the scene of the crime office, clutching the evidence bag. Shola was still there, working alone at her desk.

Rita waved the evidence bag gently. "Got something for you to look at."

Shola raised her eyebrows. "Keeping us on our toes, are you?" She grinned.

Rita laughed. "You better believe it."

Shola put on sterile gloves and used a pair of tweezers to take the photo out carefully. She checked the back and front and pointed at the rear before she said anything.

"The name of the film company is written there. Polaroid."

She put the photo gently on a tray and looked at it carefully. Most of the photo was destroyed. As Rita had seen before, the church spire to the right was visible against the darkening sky and now she could see the sea waves below it.

To the left, she saw a street scene, with a couple of house chimneys. The entire middle of the photo was obliterated, only wet white paper remained.

"Not much to go on, is there?" Shola said, examining the photo intently. She opened the drawer and pulled out a magnifying glass. She let Rita have a look with it. In the bottom right corner, Rita saw people's legs as they walked.

"This is clearly a residential street somewhere," Rita said. "Could it be in Scarborough? The sea suggests it's somewhere on the coast. And the photo was taken from a height, looking down at the sea."

"Possible, or very close to the sea." There was silence for a while as they looked at the photo.

Rita wished she could perform some magic, bring the image back to life. The photo looked back at her, tantalizing her mind, whispering of a deadly secret. This photo had remained close to her mother's body. The killer either didn't discover it, or her mother managed to hide it.

Could Clara have been holding it in her hand? Rita thought the killer would have searched her clothes and emptied her pockets. No keys or phone were found at the crime scene.

But somehow, the killer had missed this. It was the one mistake he made, Rita thought.

"We could magnify the image a lot more using electron microscopy," Shola said. "You never know, we might find something that gives us a clue about the location. Leave it with me. That will take a few days. We don't have an electron microscope here, so I've got to send the photo to York University."

Rita nodded. York was a beautiful medieval town not far away, and it had a well-known University. "How long do you think?"

"Three to four days if I put in an urgent request. You think this is important, right?"

"Yes, definitely. We need to find where this place is." Her mind was telling her it was somewhere along the coast, if not in Scarborough. But she knew there were hundreds of small towns and villages along the North Yorkshire coast where this photo could have been taken. She thanked Shola. "Is there any update on the camcorder?"

"Not yet. The serial number should tell us which store it was bought from. Depending on when it was bought, there might be some CCTV from the shop. We just have to get lucky. By the way, you didn't find the tapes?"

"No, but I'm going to search the loft space once again to see if I find anything."

CHAPTER 22

By the time Rita arrived at her childhood home, light was fading rapidly from the sky. The distant cries of the seagulls were louder in the early evening, that same haunting, lonely sound.

Orange and yellow lights were flickering to life in the streets and houses below. The sea was visible far away, the waters turning grey, mirroring the sky.

Rita looked at the house and steeled herself. She had to get this over and done with quickly. She pushed open the small, broken iron gate. She put her gloves on and took the keys out. When she shut the door behind her, the silence seeped back, settling on her skin like an invisible cloak.

She moved forward into the landing. She looked at the edges of the carpet carefully – none of them had been lifted near the skirting boards.

She went into the lounge and, on her hands and knees, checked the fireplace and tried to pull the carpets up at the edges to see if any of the floorboards were loose. She repeated the process in the dining room and checked the cupboards in the kitchen. Finding nothing, she went upstairs.

A quick but thorough search of the two bedrooms didn't reveal anything either. She took out a torch and lowered the ladder from the loft trapdoor.

In the loft, she resumed her search. The two bricks were still loose, and she had a good look inside with a torch beam. Nothing.

She looked around every corner of the loft as well as she could. Again, there was no sign of anything remotely similar to a box or videotapes. She stood there for a while, smelling the dust and faint damp, frustration mounting inside her.

She got down from the loft and then went outside and locked the door.

A fresh wind blew in from the sea, shrieking over the chimneys. She shivered in the sudden gust. This house still made her feel spooky; it seemed to be calling out her name as the wind moaned between the houses. She walked back to the street and walked to the end, where Maggie was waiting. It was nice of the constable to give her a lift.

"Did you find owt?" Maggie asked in her Yorkshire accent.

"I found *nowt,* to be precise," Rita said. "No sign of the videotapes. No sign of anything else, to be honest. Let's go."

As Maggie started the car and drove, Rita's mind was drawn back to the camcorder and the missing tapes. If her mother hid that camcorder, then she would have hidden the tapes as well.

Rita got an uncomfortable, prickly feeling. Had someone been to the house, found the camcorder, and taken the tapes? It was possible. The bricks were loose when she found the camcorder. Someone might have found the hiding spot and taken the evidence that mattered.

But what was on the tapes? And why would they leave the camcorder?

Her mother worked in a supermarket; she wasn't anyone important. What could Clara have known that was worth stealing? The question circled her mind like a dog chasing its own tail. She sighed and opened the window, letting the cold air filter in. It cooled her fevered brow.

Maggie said, "Are we going back to the nick? Or somewhere else?"

Rita glanced at her watch. It was almost 6 in the evening. "Drop me off at the nick," she said. "I'll sort out some paperwork, then go home."

"Do you want me to stay?"

"No," Rita said firmly. "Thanks for your help today." She glanced at the young constable and smiled. "I mean that."

"No bother. Good to have you here."

"Thank you. Have Richard and Rizwan gone home?"

"Yes. Richard hasn't got hold of the right person at HSBC as yet, but I'm sure he will tomorrow."

Rita nodded. Maggie dropped her off at the station car park and waved as she drove off home. Rita went back to the office. It was empty, and she was glad to be alone. She opened her laptop and wrote a report on the day's activities, then sent it to Nicola. Then she sat back in her chair, her mind refusing to let go of what she'd seen today.

Her mother's final resting place. Rita knew she couldn't allow Clara's remains to be forgotten on a remote hilltop. She had to give her a proper burial. But most importantly, she couldn't forget Dr Das's words.

Clara had been pregnant.

She couldn't have been that far along, or Rita would have noticed. How many weeks?

Rita never had children, so her knowledge of childbearing matters rested on what she'd seen her friends go through. She knew that after 16 weeks, the show would be obvious. She cast her mind back to her final days with Clara. She couldn't have been any more than 10 or 12 weeks pregnant, Rita thought. Or was she wrong about that? She was only eleven at the time.

Her fingertips pressed against her forehead, as if trying to suppress the macabre visions that raised dark shadows in her mind. Her head sank down on her chest. Who could have done this to a pregnant woman? Did they know she was pregnant? Is that why she was killed?

Rita couldn't think anymore. Her breath came in gasps again, and the air in the office suddenly seemed to close in, reaching out hands to cover her mouth, suffocate her. She knew the signs of a panic attack now before they started. She got out of the office quickly and all but ran down the corridor to the rear car park.

She took out her phone to check for messages, put her earphones in, and started to play some music. She walked past the car park barriers and pressed her fob key at the gates, which swung open silently.

She walked down the street, listening to the calming music, and slowly, her breathing returned to normal. The meditation music channel kept on playing as she circled around the block and returned to the office. It was close to 7 PM now. She gathered her stuff and called a cab and, when it arrived, gave them Angela's address.

CHAPTER 23

Angela lived on the outskirts of Scarborough, not far from the main road that connected Scarborough to York. It was a nice little village called Hedley, with pretty stone cottages with thatched roofs. A river gurgled through the centre, and Rita's taxi crossed the bridge over it.

Rita remembered spending many happy hours here. It was dark now, but she could still see the outlines of the village green, ringed by trees, and the cricket pitch in the middle. The cab went over the bridge and stopped in front of a detached house with a nice front garden. Rita thanked the driver and got out.

She stood there for a few seconds, enjoying the fresh air and the quietness. She could hear the river rushing in the background, a soft, gentle sound in the night. Lights were aglow in the houses all around, but the streetlights were not very frequent. Angela had lived here for many years. She got the house after her first divorce, and then her second husband had moved in with her. Rita had seen the man only once, at the wedding. Derek, she thought his name was.

She went in through the gates, smelling the dahlias that were neatly arranged on the flowerbeds by the stone path that led up to the door. There was a wooden porch, and she stepped on it, then pressed the bell.

A light went on in the landing, and then the door opened. Angela was a small, sprightly brunette. She opened her arms, and Rita leaned in for a hug. The faint smell of food came from inside. The landing was lovingly decorated. There was a nice rug on the floor, and the parquet wooden floor was varnished. Photos of family and pets hung in frames on the walls, with a couple of paintings of the Yorkshire moors.

Rita took off her coat and hung it on one of the pegs.

"Come in," Angela said, steering her inside. "What would you like to drink?" she asked. "Glass of wine? Tea or coffee?"

Rita had a long day, and a glass of wine sounded like just the thing she needed. She also wasn't driving. She accepted the glass of Chardonnay from Angela with a murmur of thanks. They sat down on the sofa. They talked for a while, with Angela inquisitive about why Rita had accepted a job in Scarborough.

"I just felt like coming back. I needed a break." Rita looked down at her glass. Sooner or later, she had to tell Angela the truth. There was no way around it. She had thought about it on the way here. Angela was the only person who might know things about her mother that she didn't. “But there’s also something else.”

"There's new evidence about Mum," she said. When she looked up, Angela's face was very still, her eyes fixed on Rita's.

"What sort of evidence?"

"She was up in the moors, near a village called Sawdon. There's a hill there called Raptor's Viewpoint." Rita looked down at her glass. "She was spotted there by a witness. Do you know why she would go there? It's quite remote."

A deep frown was rippling across Angela's face. "Near Sawdon? The Raptor's Viewpoint? Yes, I've heard of it. Never been, mind." Angela paused.

Rita repeated her question. "Do you know what mum might've been doing there?"

Angela shook her head, and her eyes drifted down to the brown and white rug on the floor. "No, love, I wouldn't know. When was she seen there?.I mean, was it day or night? And who saw her?"

Rita put her glass on the table, elbows on her knees, then clasped her hands together. This was going to be harder than she had imagined. She had to tell Angela; there was no way around it.

"You need to keep this very confidential. It's a police matter investigation. I could get into trouble. Do you understand?"

Rita knew the news was probably out there already. One of the ramblers had told their friends or relatives. It was only a matter of time before the rest of Scarborough knew.

"A skeleton has been found in a shallow grave by Raptor's Viewpoint. DNA samples and dental records show it was my mother. Carbon dating points to 1994. That's when she disappeared."

When she looked up at Angela, the woman's lips were parted, her eyes round and fixed as if she was staring at a ghost.

"You can't tell anyone," Rita repeated. "Do you understand?"

In silence, Angela nodded. The slight movement of her neck seemed forced, as if she was worried that if she inclined her head too much, it might snap off and break. She blinked furiously and finally found her voice.

"Is this confirmed? There's no doubt it was Clara?"

"No, there's no doubt."

With shaking hands, Angela put the glass of wine on the glass coffee table. It made a loud sound. She covered her mouth with a hand, then stared down at the floor.

Rita said, "Robert Macfarlane. The man who used to be Mum's boyfriend. His girlfriend gave him an alibi for the night of Mum's disappearance. Do you know anything about him?"

Slowly, Angela raised her head. She seemed to be lost in another world, her eyes glazed and unfocused. "Angela, are you okay?" Rita asked. She shuffled closer to the edge of the sofa and put a hand on Angela's knee. The older woman's hand found hers, and they gripped each other's hands tightly.

"Yes, my love, it's just such a shock, you know." Angela's eyes reddened, and moisture gathered in the corners. She wiped her eyes with a sleeve, and the tip of her nose turned red.

"Robert Macfarlane," Rita repeated. "Do you remember him?"

"I... I do. I saw him in town a couple of times after your mother broke up with him. But I had nowt to do with him, obviously. He was a builder, wasn't he? Not sure where he is these days."

"He still lives around here. On the stouh side, not far from the hills. I'll visit him tomorrow. But I just wanted to ask you first, to see if there was anything else you remembered about him."

Angela shook her head. “Nowt, sorry.” Then she gazed at Rita, her eyes full of torment.

Rita could tell she was bursting with questions. "Who did that to her?" Angela asked. "And why?"

"We don't know," Rita sighed. "That's why I'm here, trying to piece it all together. It's tough, as you can imagine."

Angela gave her hand a squeeze. There was silence for a while, then Rita looked at Angela.

"How was Mum in the last few days and weeks? You've told me this before, but try to think if there was anything you might have missed."

Angela folded her hands on her lap and looked at the opposite wall, lost in thought. "She seemed distracted, definitely. She wouldn't tell me why. She was quiet as well and kept to herself, if you know what I mean. That was unusual for her."

A familiar emptiness was spreading in Rita's heart. "Did she have money problems? Or was she in any sort of trouble?"

"She was a single mother with a low-paid job. Of course she had money problems. Your mother was proud. She wouldn’t go on the dole." Angela smiled ruefully.

"But she wasn't in any other kind of trouble, if you know what I mean." She stopped suddenly, the corners of her eyes narrowing. Rita sensed a change in her posture. She leaned forward. "What is it?"

CHAPTER 24

"In the weeks before she disappeared, Clara had started a new job," Angela said. "It was hard work. She wouldn't say where and wouldn't talk about it."

Angela turned to look at Rita. "That's all she said. When I asked about it, she clammed up. I can't help thinking that was the reason she was stressed."

Rita stared at her for a while, an odd feeling surfacing in her mind. "Why didn't you mention this before?"

"I did, to the police. I thought you knew about it as well." Was there a defensive note in Angela's voice now, or was Rita imagining it?

She stared at her mother's old friend, the woman who was like an aunt to her. Angela held her gaze. Rita was the first to blink. It had been a long day, and it was possible her mind was playing tricks. She had skimmed over Angela's original police statement. She needed to read it again.

"I think I mentioned it to you in the past as well," Angela said and shrugged. She reached for her glass of wine and took a sip. There was something different about her attitude now, the earlier sadness, and then the tension, was replaced by... evasiveness? Rita couldn't put a finger on it, but it bothered her.

She looked at Angela again, and something told her Angela knew more about this than she was letting on. But why would she even mention it if she was holding a secret? That didn't make any sense.

"Please think carefully, Ange," she urged. "Mum told you nothing about this new job?"

"No," Angela shook her head firmly. "I got the impression she didn't want to tell anyone. She let it slip by mistake."

"That sounds dodgy to me," Rita said, frowning. "I wonder what she was mixed up in."

New fears and suspicions were now knocking on the doors of her mind, darkening her thoughts. She thought of the old photo at the crime scene. She wished she could show it to Angela. She made up her mind to bring it next time.

Her mind also grappled with telling Angela about her mother's pregnancy. Would Angela know anything about it? Surely her mother would've told Angela…or maybe she didn't. Maybe she wanted to keep it a secret from everyone. That sounded very odd, even now. There was no reason Clara would keep *that* a secret, even from her best friend.

Her sixth sense was humming, a low but insistent buzz she had learnt not to ignore. Her instinct told her Angela should know about the pregnancy.

"I need to tell you something," Rita exhaled, then closed her eyes. "Mum was pregnant when she died."

The sudden gasp was audible. Rita opened her eyes. Angela was frozen, a rictus of shock gripping her face.

"Did you know?" Rita asked gently. She knew the answer from Angela's expression. There was no way Angela was acting.

"No, of course I bloody didn't," Angela blurted. "How did you know? Was there…

"The doctor could tell from the pelvis of the skeleton. Pregnancy stretches the ligaments, which leaves marks and indentations on the bone."

Angela covered her mouth with a hand. Her forehead contracted, and she shut her eyes. Rita gripped her shoulders. She could see Angela was blaming herself.

"You didn't know. It's okay."

A sob escaped Angela's lips. "She was different those last few weeks. I should've known something was up."

"There was nothing you could've done."

Angela shook her head, as if negating Rita's reassurance. Her neck lowered, and she remained like that for a while.

"Are you sure mum didn't have a man in her life back then?"

Angela wiped her eyes and sniffed. "Well, if she did, I didn't know. Look like she did, clearly. Or maybe it just happened." She looked at Rita, who nodded in understanding.

"Maybe she met someone at this job," Rita mused. "And something happened there." She glanced at Angela. "Mum was killed. Murdered with a knife. A man slashed at her so hard there's still cuts on her hands."

Angela looked like she was going to faint. Her face was turning a shade of green. She stood up. "Excuse me."

Rita watched her go into the landing, and to the toilet. After a while, the toilet flushed and Angela came back. Her eyes were red rimmed, cheeks pale.

"So you're sure you don't remember anything else about the last days?" Rita probed again. "I mean, for someone to do that to her, she must've made some bad enemies."

"Or it was some psycho. You know, like a serial killer," Rita added. "Either way, we need to figure out what happened in those final weeks of her life."

"Yes," Angela said. Regret lined every corner of her face. "I can't believe this," she whispered. They sat there in silence for a while.

"Are you okay love?" Angela asked eventually. "You know you can come and stay with me if you want, don't you?"

Rita looked at her, and saw genuine concern in her eyes. She smiled. "Thank you. Yes, I'm fine. And also hungry. The smell is delicious." She patted her tummy.

"Aha. Let's go and eat then."

****

It was past 10 o'clock by the time Rita finished dinner. Angela had made a lamb roast and potatoes, and it tasted heavenly. Rita was famished, and she tucked in with gusto. She felt a little self-conscious, but Angela kept heaping her plate with more until Rita had to tell her to stop.

"Leave some for Derek," Rita said, referring to Angela's husband.

"He's gone down to London for a business trip for a couple of days," Angela said. "This is all for me and you. I don't really eat red meat anymore, doctor's orders. Same for Derek. So tuck in, and take some back with you."

"Thank you," Rita said. After their heavy conversation, dinner had provided a nice distraction. They had chatted about the old days and about Rita's school friends. One of them, Nina, still lived in Scarborough and was married to one of the town councillors. Angela had her husband's number, as he was friends with Derek. She gave Rita the details.

"Nina Potter, she's called now. She's got a son, and he's five years old. She’s doing well." Angela looked at Rita, and she realized the meaning behind her look. It was bound to come up sooner or later.

"No, I don't," she said. "A man takes up too much time, and my last relationship didn't really work out."

"That bloke called Charlie? He was a banker, wasn't he? Did well for himself, from what you said."

Rita rolled her eyes. "He also wanted me to sit at home, bear his children, and be a good little housewife." She raised both hands and made a square shape in the air. "If I didn't fit into his box, then it wouldn't work."

"I see, shame that." Angela didn't say anything more, but she didn't have to. They both knew Rita's childbearing days were over. She was forty one now, and unless something changed pretty soon, she wouldn't be having children.

Most of the time, she tried not to think of such things. It didn't get her anywhere. She had chosen this life for herself, and she had learned to be happy in her own skin. She had stopped thinking what the world thought of her.

She knew her mother's disappearance had shaped her life. That's what made her become a detective. To find the lost ones, to seek closure. Finally, that ending might be in sight.

She said goodbye to Angela, and they waited on her porch as the cab pulled up. Before Rita got into the cab, a flicker of movement in the darkness opposite caught Rita's eyes.

A shadow detached itself from under a big tree. It was a man's figure. He stood there for a while, watching her.

Then the shadow retracted into the depths behind the tree and disappeared from view. Rita frowned and stepped to one side to get a better look. There were a lot of trees on the other side, and darkness consumed them into indistinct, vague shapes. She didn't see the man again, but she had a funny feeling he had been observing her. Casting one last look at the dark street, she got into the cab.

As the cab drove away, she turned back. She could see nothing in the darkness behind the lights of Angela's house.

Back at the hotel, she got changed, and then stood in front of the mirror. It had been a long, bruising day. Tomorrow, the journey would continue. She had waited for this moment all her life, and now that it had arrived, she hoped her heart was strong enough to deal with it.

She gripped the sides of the sink, and her eyes closed as she leaned forward and her head rested against the cold glass of the mirror.

Voices started whispering in her ears, little tears and cries that rose like tentacles from the vast blackness inside her. She kept it bottled up, deep in the dungeon, but the stone had slid, and the tentacles were rising, crawling all over her.

She thought of the skull, where her mother's face had once been. The rib cage, where she had once listened to the heart softly beating. She thought of her mother's arms coming around her like a benediction, shielding her from the unforgiving world.

And then she thought of the child her mother had carried, a sibling that she would never see, a little life gone to waste.

The dam broke inside her, and the waves surged like a tsunami. A guttural scream ripped out of her throat, tearing into the walls, destroying everything in its wake.

Her fist pounded against the wall, and her feet kicked at the wall and the pipes. Then she was on the floor, her fists hammering uselessly on the tiles, harsh sobs shaking her whole body.

She heaved, but only bile came out of her throat. She curled herself into a tight ball, like a discarded foetus, and wrapped her arms around herself and cried. She wept for the mother she had lost, for the little life Clara had carried inside her, and she wept for the fact that she had not been able to do anything about it.

CHAPTER 25

Loud beeping from the alarm woke Rita up. Her head remained buried in the pillows as she reached out a hand to slap the offending device into silence. That didn't work. Something rolled off the bedside table and landed on the carpet. It was her bottle of water.

Sighing, Rita opened her eyes. It was six in the morning, and she hadn't slept well.

There was a lot to deal with today, and she had to get a move on. But the drowsiness wouldn't leave her. She managed to shut the alarm off and then flopped back in bed, clutching her forehead with both hands. She rubbed her eyes and realized sleep wasn't coming back. Not that she wanted it to. Last night had been filled with familiar demons, nightmares she had forgotten. The care homes and foster parents she had to deal with as a teenager. No, she definitely didn't want to go back to sleep. She got off the bed and went straight into the shower. She stood under the steaming shower, and washed her hair. Slowly, she began to feel better.

She put on her usual dress clothes: black cotton trousers, a white blouse, and a black jacket. She got breakfast from a café outside the hotel – a coffee and a muesli bar. Her stomach couldn't tolerate much food until later in the day, and besides, she didn't feel hungry. She was preoccupied with her list of jobs.

She had to see Nicola to get clearance to bury her mother's remains. The bones were now in the morgue, and Rita felt uncomfortable about having to discuss this with Dr Das. Maybe Nicola could help her remain anonymous.

The photo next to her mother's body remained in her mind. Did the killer drop it, or was her mother carrying it? Either way, that photo was critical to finding out what happened to Clara.

It was close to half seven when Rita got to the office. What Angela had told her the last night stayed on her mind. She opened up the case report and looked at the witness statements from thirty years ago.

Angela Peacock had mentioned that the victim, Clara Winters, was stressed because she started a new job. That relaxed Rita somewhat. Angela wasn't lying. But still, she thought Angela's behaviour was odd when she discussed it with Rita last night. Or maybe her overwrought heart was reading too much into it. Rita moved on through the report, her forefinger dragging down the page, skimming the lines.

There was no evidence that Clara had started a new job. There was no payslip, no contract, no money in her account from another employer apart from the supermarket.

Rita checked Clara's bank statements once again. She didn't find anything unusual apart from the usual grocery shopping, rent and bills. Her mother hadn't been abroad. She also noted the bank account details. The bank's name was Royal Alliance, and she wrote down the account number. There was no similarity with the suspected Midland bank account details.

Rita looked at her watch. The door opened at that precise moment, and Richard walked in. He froze when he saw Rita, then smiled stiffly and went to his table. He wore the same crumpled dark blue suit as yesterday, and the stubble remained on his cheeks. He looked tired.

"I was just thinking about you," Rita said. "Not a good sign. You'll have a long life." She smiled, trying to drag him into a conversation.

Richard merely looked up, smiled stiffly again, then averted his eyes to his laptop. Rita sighed. She wanted to have a normal professional relationship with team members. But Richard still preferred to remain distant.

"Richard," Rita said, "did you look into Midland Bank? Do those numbers belong to an account?"

Richard stared at her for a few seconds, unblinking. Then he nodded. "Yes, I got through to HSBC. They managed to put me through to their historic accounts department. Those digits do correspond to an old account. The account holder is a company. The account is closed, and they don’t have any further information on it."

Rita was listening intently. "Maybe that's why the forensic financial data didn't show a second bank account on the victim's record. What's the name of the company?"

"Blue Rise Holdings."

On her laptop, Rita went to Companies House, the UK database for all registered companies. When she typed in Blue Rise Holdings, she got several hits, and they were all current. She had advanced disclosure as a detective, and she could unlock the records of companies that had shut down. She scrolled down to 1994 and found only one Blue Rise Holdings Inc. But the records weren't in digital format, and they had to be requested in paper form from Companies House. That would mean a wait, which was frustrating. Rita told Richard what she had found.

"Looks like we have to wait then," Richard said.

An alarm bell was ringing in Rita's mind. Her mother hid the details of this account with the camcorder. She had to keep an open mind, of course, because she might be barking up the wrong tree. It might be someone else who had hidden that camcorder, for whatever reason.

But a little voice in her head told her that wasn't the case. Clara and Rita had lived in that house for more than a decade.

Rita couldn't explain it, but she felt a strange pull when she pried open the chimney bricks and pulled out that black leather bag. Like it had been waiting there for her to find. It didn't make any sense, but she couldn't ignore the dark, inchoate feeling.

She picked up the phone and called Companies House. A woman called Verity answered.

"Good morning. I am Detective Inspector Rita Gupta of North Yorkshire Police. We are investigating a historic murder case where the victim is associated with a company called Blue Rise Holdings. Your online records indicate the company was active in 1994 when the victim died. But there are no digital records prior to 2005. It will take five working days to send us paper records. However, this is a fast-moving investigation, and we need the records sooner than that."

There was silence at the other end, filled by the sound of fingernails clicking on the keypad. "What's the name of the company again?”

Rita told her and waited. She drummed her fingers on the table. After a few moments, Verity's voice came back on the line.

"I've got it here. Yes, you're right. The company did exist in 1994. It was incorporated in 1989, and it was shut down in the year 2003. Like you said, I cannot see any other records."

"I need to know the names of the people involved, please. Can you provide that?"

"Not really." Verity sounded hesitant. "The names will be in the paper records, which will be sent out to you when you request them. As this is a police inquiry, we will treat it as urgent. You might get the records within three working days."

Rita pressed her lips together and drummed her fingers on the table again. "I'm afraid we cannot wait that long." A thought occurred to her. "Where are your paper records held?"

Verity was silent again, as if she was considering her next words carefully. "In the main office, where I am."

"Then is it possible for you or someone there to check the paper records while I hold on?"

Verity was silent, and Rita didn't hesitate. "If you cannot do it, then can I please speak to your supervisor or your line manager? As I said, this is a murder inquiry and an urgent matter."

Verity sighed. "Let me see what I can do. Can you call back in 10 minutes?"

"I'll give you longer than that. Please ask your manager to get the paper records. They can be faxed to us or scanned and emailed. I will call back in half an hour."

Rita sat back in her chair after she hung up. She did an online search for Blue Rise Holdings. She didn't find anything useful. She looked up at Richard.

"Thanks for that. I hope we get some leads from this." Richard shrugged and went back to his laptop. Rita realized she had tolerated his behaviour for long enough. It was close to 8:30 now; Rizwan and Maggie would be arriving soon. She stood.

"Richard." He looked up at her, clearly recognizing the firm tone in her voice. Rita opened the door. "Can I have a word with you outside, please? Now."

CHAPTER 26

Richard stared at her for a while, as if she was speaking in a language he didn’t understand. Then he stood stiffly, like a man who had the hands of a 300 kg gorilla pressing down on his shoulders. They went outside and walked down the corridor. Rita opted to go inside one of the interview rooms just before the staircase. She pressed her fob key against the door, and it buzzed open.

The door had a glass panel with a shutter, which she pulled down. This was an informal interview room, and it had a two-seater sofa and a table with chairs on either side. Rita indicated the sofa and asked Richard to sit. He still looked like a man who was being dragged along the ground, hands and feet tied. He sat down, spine straight, eyes focused on Rita like he expected her to pull out a knife any minute.

Rita clasped her hands together and stared at him.

"Look, I'm sorry you didn't get my job. I don't know if you applied for it, but if you did, then I know it's not ideal. But we need to move beyond that. You're an experienced detective, and I can use your help. It would be good for the investigation. However, if your attitude towards me doesn't change, and you see me as someone who got the job you deserved, then we have a problem."

She paused. Richard didn't say anything. But his breathing rate had kicked up a notch.

Rita continued calmly. "If you don't want me here, that's fine, but that's your problem. I have a job to do, and I definitely intend to do it as well as I can. Like I said, I value your experience and your input. But if we're going to keep having a problem, then perhaps you need to move to another team." She stopped and waited for Richard to answer.

He took a deep breath, like he had forgotten what oxygen felt like in his lungs. He exhaled, and then his head dropped as he stared at his twisting hands. After a while, he spoke, his words slow, like they were taking time to form in his brain.

"I was close to the previous guvnor, Ian Robson. He worked here for 15 years. He taught me everything I know. He wasn't in a good state at the end. He was suffering with PTSD."

Rita said, "Were you a detective constable under him as well?"

Richard nodded. “Yes.”

Some of his behaviour made sense to Rita. A closely forged bond had been disrupted, and then she had suddenly appeared, taking over where his previous mentor had been.

Richard said, "And yes, I was looking forward to being given the inspector grade. I felt it was my time."

"I'm sorry," Rita said. "I know it's not easy for you. For what it's worth, I have been in the same situation. Being a woman, I was passed over for promotion six times. Finally, I put in a complaint. The London Metropolitan is a big force, and it's only recently that women are getting senior ranks. I finally got the job after applying for the seventh time. But I shouldn't have to complain. I earned the job with merit." She stopped, and they held each other's eyes.

"So I know how you feel," Rita said.

Richard wore a resigned look his face. He spread his hands. "Thank you."

"I'm not going to be here for long," Rita said softly. "And when I leave, I'll put in a good reference for you." She smiled. "Depending on how we get along, of course. No pressure."

The flickering ghost of a smile appeared on Richard's lips for the first time. Rita said, "There's something else. Did the Super ask you to keep an eye on me?" She raised a hand to clarify her statement. "I don't mean to pry. But whatever you tell me remains confidential between us. I won't tell the super, and you have my word on that."

Richard's eyes snapped shut, and suddenly he looked wary. His jaw relaxed, and the tips of his shoulders went down, like the invisible strings that had been holding him up had been cut. He shook his head once and rubbed a hand over his forehead.

"The Super is like that. She likes to control everything. Maybe I fell into her trap. Yes, she did tell me to report on you, and I don't just mean the normal staff feedback." He spread his hands. "I'm not even sure what she meant, to be honest. But I told her that I would."

Rita nodded. So Rizwan was right. She was glad she got to the bottom of the matter and just as important - cleared the air with Richard.

Rita thought carefully before uttering her next words.

"What did the Super tell you about me?"

Richard blinked at her. His face remained neutral, and she didn't think he was trying to hide anything. "Not much else," he said. "She said cold cases were your specialty, and you had caught a couple of serial killers in the south. I read about one of them. The hair collector? The guy who was a hairdresser, and he shaved his victims' hair after he killed them. I forget his name now."

"Chris Mason," Rita said grimly. "Nasty piece of work. Yes, I'm glad he'll never be released again."

"That job made you famous. Your name got in the papers. That's all I knew about you. In a way, it was good that you came up here. We haven't had a case like this for years."

Rita stared at Richard for a while, and he held her gaze. If Richard had known that Clara Winters was her mother, she would have felt something, either in his posture or in his expression. But Richard wasn't lying.

If Richard didn't know, that meant Nicola had maintained her confidentiality. She sighed and focused on Richard again.

"Are we okay then?"

Richard looked much more relaxed. He sat back on the sofa, his hands resting by his side and on the sofa handle. Unlike before, his hands weren't moving. His body was still, and the gaze in his eyes was softer.

"Yes, guv. I'm sorry. Just a few things on my mind, that's all."

Something in the way he said it caught Rita’s attention. "You're married, aren't you? Family all right?"

A dark shadow slipped across Richard's face again, and his eyes clouded. His gaze flickered down to the floor.

"Just between you and me, it's not going well. My wife and I have been pretty much leading separate lives for the last few months. We're staying together for the sake of the children."

"How old are they?"

"10 and 12. Brian's younger, and Melissa is getting taller every day." He smiled, but Rita could see the sadness.

"I'm sorry. I've never been married, but I've seen friends go through it." She thought for a few seconds.

"Look, if you need to take some time off, that's okay with me." Richard went to speak, but she raised a hand. “Talk to someone. Don't hit the bottle. Don't go on a bender. None of that will help."

Richard stared at her for a while. "Yes, I know," he said softly. "Work does provide a good distraction. My wife and I don't talk anymore, really. We're both just playing our parts, to be honest. But sooner or later, we need to have the discussion."

“Do you have friends you can talk to?”

“Yes, I do.”

“How about Occupational Health? The Force will provide a counsellor for you.”

Richard took a deep breath. “You know what its like, guv. I don’t want the Chinese whispers to start. I’m alright, like. I can deal with my own mess.”

“But you need to look after yourself. I can see the strain on you, if you don’t mind me saying.” Rita smiled. “I don’t know you Richard, but you can come and talk to me anytime you want.”

“Thanks, guv. I mean that.”

“No problem. I’ve been there myself. Not with relationship issues, but mental health.” Rita tapped the side of her skull and grinned.

“And I won't mention this to Maggie or Rizwan. Do they know?"

Richard pressed his lips together in a tight line. "I think they've heard me arguing with my wife on the phone a couple of times. Seen me angry. I mentioned it to Rizwan once."

"I've got a feeling Maggie might know as well, not that she told me anything specific. In any case, I won't tell them anything."

"Thank you."

"Good," Rita smiled, and got to her feet. "I'm going upstairs to see the super, just to give her an update about everything. Don't worry, I won't mention our conversation. Does she know about this, by the way?"

"Nope."

Rita nodded. Richard was struggling, she could see that. She felt sorry for him.

"It's going to be alright. You, the girls and their mother, will be fine. These things take time. Just trust me on that."

"Time is a healer, as they say, guv."

"Exactly." Rita smiled at him. "Feel free to chat to my if you need to. Alright?"

"Thank you." Richard appreciated their conversation, Rita could tell. She sighed, her mind returning to work.

"Would you mind coordinating the others to catch up with Shola and see if the pathologist has anything more?"

"No problem, guv," said Richard, reaching for the door handle.

CHAPTER 27

Detective Superintendent Nicola Perkins was in her room and asked Rita to enter when she knocked. She didn't look up as Rita went inside and shut the door. Nicola was signing a document, and her attention seemed absorbed in the piece of paper. Rita came forward to the desk but remained standing. Eventually, Nicola put the paper to one side and looked up. She didn't seem surprised to see Rita, as if she had been expecting her.

"I got your report this morning. Looks like you've made some progress. Any suspects as yet?"

Rita shook her head. "Not yet. But we're working on it. We might have something very soon." She coughed, putting a fist in front of her mouth. "I'm going to ask Dr Das, the pathologist, to release my mother's remains. I want her to get a proper burial. After they come back from CAHID, of course."

"I can't see a problem with that." Nicola raised her eyebrows, her demeanour suggesting she didn't understand why Rita was wasting her time.

"I don't want Dr Das to know the victim was my mother," Rita said plainly. She held eyes with Nicola for a while, and eventually, the super nodded. “I don’t want to sign the release documents as next of kin, but I want the remains to go to the undertaker.”

Nicola stared at her. “Just tell him there’s no next of kin.”

Rita felt uncomfortable with the lie. She didn’t want to say that, and she could tell Nicola had guessed it. Rita knew sooner or later she would have to disclose her relation to Clara Winters, but she didn’t want others to know just yet. This was still intensely raw, deeply private. She needed time to deal with it.

“I won’t tell Dr Das that,” Rita said flatly. “I will ask him to release the remains to the undertaker, and the NOK will pick up from there. It’s not like there’s a body to identify.”

Nicola had the same implacable, unfriendly look on her face. Rita didn’t know what she had done to displease her. But she sure as hell was going to stand her ground, and not get pushed around.

“Okay,” Nicola said finally. Her eyelids fluttered, and her gaze lost its hardness.

"Thank you," Rita said, relieved. "I'm going to see Dr Das in any case, to see if he's got anything else regarding the remains. I'll let you know."

Nicola nodded curtly, then pulled the paper back towards her. She picked up her pen and became engrossed in the document, indicating their conversation was over. Without a word, Rita turned and left the room.

***

Back at the office, Maggie and Rizwan had arrived. Rizwan smiled widely at her and got up from his table. He walked over to Rita's table, at the far end of the room. Maggie was busy on the phone.

Rizwan lowered his voice. "Thanks for letting me leave early last night, guv. The dinner went well, and my parents really like my girlfriend. It's not been easy, you know," his expression grew heavier. "Katie's not Muslim, if you know what I mean."

Rita understood. "Your parents want you to marry a Muslim woman? Or they want Katie to convert?"

"Katie doesn't want to, and that's fine." Rizwan shrugged. "That's her decision, and I'm happy with it. But my parents aren't. Despite that, they welcomed her, and we had a good evening." His face clouded over, and his eyes lost some of the sparkle. "Until my dad started talking about religious stuff, and Katie got a little uncomfortable. Luckily, my mum changed the discussion."

Rita studied the earnest young man in front of her. He was a good man, trying to be true to his parents while also living his own life. It wasn't easy, and she had friends who had been through the same process.

"Do you love her?" Rita asked simply. The bluntness of the question surprised Rizwan. His eyes snapped open, then blinked several times. He seemed to weigh up something in his mind.

"Yes, I do, guv."

Rita smiled. "Remember that's the only important thing. I'm not saying don't be true to your religion, or your parents. Listen to them, but follow your own heart. Explain that to your parents, and because they love you, they will understand."

Rizwan looked as if he was listening to an oracle delivering a sermon. His mouth opened, but he couldn't get the words out. Finally, he spoke. "Thanks… Thank you." He smiled. "That makes sense. But it's not easy."

"I know," Rita said. "But ultimately, you can only do what makes you happy. And happiness often means a compromise and finding a new way to make things work."

Rita watched as Rizwan went back to his desk and sat down. He looked deep in thought.

Rita picked up the phone and called Companies House. A different receptionist answered, but she asked for Verity, who came on the line shortly.

“DI Rita Gupta. We spoke this morning.”

“Ah yes, I remember.” The sound of rustling papers came down the line. "I've got some details for you. I can fax you the paper records if you send me a number. And I've got the names of the directors and shareholders."

"Excellent, please give me the names first."

Rita opened her black notebook and wrote the details down. Then she gave Verity the station's fax number and thanked her.

She looked at the names she'd written down. Alfred Northallerton and Edward Salt were named as directors of Blue Rise Holdings. There was no company secretary, and there were no shareholders. She circled the names and put a question mark next to it. She searched for the name on the Internet, but it came up with a number of random hits.

She scrolled down the list and finally came across something interesting: an article from the Scarborough Daily, dated July 7, 2016. Scarborough Harbour had been shut down that day due to a fire at one of the fishing factories. The factory was owned by a company called Northern Ventures. There had been a police investigation, and the chairman of Northern Ventures had also been interviewed. His name was Edward Salt.

Rita looked up from her laptop at the two constables. As she did so, the door opened, and Richard walked in.

After Richard sat down at his table, Rita asked them if they had heard of Edward Salt. The constables drew a blank at first, then Maggie spoke up.

"Isn't he the guy who owns all the properties in town?"

Richard said, "He's a well-known businessman. He's got properties all over the North-East. Scarborough, Hull, Leeds, even up in Newcastle, I've heard. He owns some fisheries as well, and shipbuilders. Why?" He looked at Rita.

"He was one of the directors of Blue Rise Holdings, the company whose bank account you confirmed," Rita said. "Another man called Alfred Northallerton was the other director."

"Northallerton?" Rizwan said. "As in Lord Northallerton?"

Rita raised her eyebrows. "Is he a Lord?"

"That's the only Northallerton I know of."

Maggie answered, "They're an aristocratic family who are big landowners in the northeast. They've got a big manor house in the Yorkshire Moors, don't they? They're one of the sponsors of the annual Scarborough Fair."

"That's right," Richard said. "They're quite well-known in this area. Alfred Northallerton is the scion of the family.

Rita searched on the internet and came up with several hits for Northallerton. She saw his photo – a short, pot bellied man in a tweed jacket, posing for the cameras at Scarborough Fair, smiling in the sunshine.

She checked his date of birth – it was the same as in Blue Rise company account filings. It had to be the same person.

Rita frowned. “So Mr Salt is well connected. He formed a business with Lord Northallerton. But why did the victim have their bank’s account number?”

Maggie asked, “And how did she get hold of it? Rich people aren’t in the habit of giving their bank account numbers away, are they?”

“Maybe the victim had some financial dealings with them,” Rita thought aloud.

Richard frowned, sitting upright in his chair. "What did Blue Rise Holdings do?”

"The paper records were faxed should be arriving very soon." She looked at the constables, and Maggie got to her feet.

"I'll go and check."

She came back soon, with a stack of papers in her hand. She handed them to Rita. They were the filed accounts for the company.

It seemed like the company had bought a number of houses. Their addresses were scattered across Scarborough, Whitby, York, and in smaller villages and towns.

Rita counted eight properties in total. The company made a healthy profit after the deduction of all expenses. In its final year, which was 2003, the company was £464,000 in the black. Twenty-four years ago, that was a hefty chunk of money, Rita thought.

An uneasiness was settling into her bones. Why did her mother have the bank details of this company? Was she getting money from them?

Was this the job that Angela was referring to?

"I'm looking for Mr Salt's contact number," Rizwan said, his fingers tapping across his laptop keyboard. He stared at the screen, then looked up at Rita.

"I can call the company secretary."

"Go ahead," Rita said.

He spoke, introducing himself. "DC Ahmed from North Yorkshire Police. Can I please speak to Mr Salt?"

The others listened as Rizwan spoke. He had a conversation with someone who clearly not Mr Salt.

"And when will he be free?" Rizwan asked. Eventually, he agreed a time of tomorrow morning, at 11am.

When he hung up, he looked pleased. "Mr Salt will see us tomorrow. I didn't tell the secretary what it's about."

"Good."

“The company is based in York, but they have an office in Scarborough as well. She asked me what it was about, but I said I'd only speak to Mr. Salt. She didn't sound very happy." Rizwan grinned.

Richard was busy on his phone, and hung up soon. “Lord Northallerton is abroad on business. I just spoke to his secretary. He’s not back till late tomorrow.”

“OK,” Rita said. “Make sure we speak to him as soon as he’s back.”

Richard nodded, and picked up the phone again.

Maggie said, "By the way, guv, the drones are going to be up over Raptor's Viewpoint, this morning. If they see anything, we will be alerted ASAP. Traffic are dealing with it. They have used drones in the past."

“I want the drones to look out for the ruins of a car. The victim drove there, but no car was ever found. That should be their priority.”

Maggie gave Rita a thumbs up. “I’ll tell them now, guv.”

Rita stood, and glanced at Richard, then the constables. “I’m going to see Dr Das. Call me if you hear anything.”

CHAPTER 28

As Rita left the office and went down the stairs, her phone beeped. She had a call from switchboard.

"DI Gupta," she said.

"A call for you from Dr Das, the pathologist," the switchboard operator said. "Can I connect him?"

Rita stopped at the landing and leaned against the wall. Through the long windows, she could see an outline of the castle and the sea in the distance. Seagulls floated in the air, diving and rising. "Yes," she said. She clutched the phone tightly to her ear.

The pathologist's warm voice came down the line. "Hello. Is that D.I. Gupta?"

"Hello, Dr Das. I was on my way to see you."

He chuckled. "In that case, you will have a long life. I was thinking of you, so it must be a good omen." He cleared his throat, and his tone became serious. "I've uncovered a few more things. Shall I wait until you get here, or do you want to hear it now?”

“Tell me now, please.”

"Beneath the bones, we found a fragment of a necklace chain. Not sure how we missed it the first time. In any case, it's a gold chain, and it seems to have a name on it."

Rita straightened. "A name? What does it say?"

"X-ray microscopy showed it as Riley. It was the clasp of the necklace, and the tie section is about 5 cm long. There was nothing else. We did another excavation after we found the necklace chain."

"So, the clasp of the necklace said 'Riley's'? What does that mean?"

Rita's mind was working overtime, reaching into the dim recesses of her past. As far as she knew, her mother didn't know anyone called Riley. Why would Clara be wearing a necklace with someone's name on it?

"I don't know," Dr Das said. "I'm just telling you what we found. I've sent the necklace off for analysis. A chromatography of the metal might reveal useful clues about its composition. That might indicate the manufacturer, if we are lucky."

He paused to cough once. "There are microscopic metallic fragments where the bone was fractured by the sharp instrument. That means in her collarbone and on the wrists. Again, these fragments have been sent for analysis."

Rita felt excited. She didn't want to get her hopes up, but this could be a breakthrough.

"I'll pop over now, if that's okay. You can show me the new evidence."

Dr Das agreed. Rita hung up and went rapidly down the stairs. She waved at the desk sergeant on duty, and took a right to head for the main gates. She had called a taxi already. By the time she went down the main stairs and into the front car park, she had been allocated a car. But the wait was 15 minutes. It seemed cab drivers in Scarborough liked to take their time.

Frustrated, she waited by the gates, pacing. She thought about what Dr Das had discovered. Her thoughts collided and spun like bullets ricocheting around a metallic chamber.

She stopped, and her eyes narrowed. A distant memory surfaced.

A gold chain.

She recalled her mother getting ready for bed, with Rita hanging by the door. Clara was irritated, asking her to go to bed. Her poor mother had probably come back from work and was exhausted. All she wanted was for Clara to go to sleep, but instead, Rita was being the difficult daughter.

As if in a movie, Rita saw her mother take off the gold necklace from her neck and fold it inside a little box on the makeup table.

Could this be the same necklace?

Rita put her hands on her hips and thought hard. Her face lifted up to the sunlight. As she did so, she saw movement across the road.

Trees were planted at regular intervals, and the street was nice and shady, a change from the barren streets of London. She saw a man's shape appear from behind a tree. It was clear that he was observing her. And if he wanted to remain hidden, he wasn't doing a very good job.

A spasm of tension twisted in her guts. The man's shape was similar to what she had seen outside

Angela's house. Now she knew it wasn’t her mind playing tricks.

The man stepped behind a tree and then started to walk away. He walked briskly; the gait of a man who knew he had been spotted. Rita went after him. She quickened her pace, then called out, "Hey, you. Stop."

She could now see the man was of slim build and medium height. He had brown hair and wore a dark jacket and blue jeans. His trainers were white. She couldn't tell his age from behind, but he wasn't old. He clearly heard her because his pace got faster, then he broke into a run. Rita swore and sprinted after him. The man was quick, and he was near the street corner. He took a left and vanished.

Rita pumped her legs and skidded to a stop at the corner. A few cars went by, two women walked past her, chatting and observing her curiously. She couldn't see the man anywhere.

She ran forward, then slowed down to a walk. This road was busier, with pedestrians and shops. She went inside a newsagent and had a quick look around. She repeated the process with a couple of cafés. She came out on the road and whipped her neck sideways, feeling the frustration surge inside her.

The man was nowhere to be seen.

CHAPTER 29

Wiping the sweat off her forehead and taking her jacket off, Rita walked back to the main gates of the station. Her taxi still hadn't arrived. The frigid, cold air felt chilly, even though her shirt was sticking to her back.

Rita looked at her phone again. The app said her driver was delayed by eight minutes. She swore, and looked behind at the front car park. Perhaps one of the squad cars could give her a lift.

A sleek black BMW pulled up in front of her. She was on the opposite side of the driver's seat and at first, she was confused, then a little alarmed as she saw a man smiling at her.

Then she recognised Jack Banford. He pulled up, and got out of his car. He was wearing a brown suit today, as sharply cut as before. His cheeks were smoothly shaven, showing his strong jawline. His large, dark eyes rested on her, inquisitive.

"You alright?" The hint of a smile played on his lips, and she responded. He said, "Looks like you're stranded, unless I'm mistaken. Waiting for someone?"

“Kind of. I'm going to the Scarborough General Hospital's morgue to see the pathologist.”

“I can give you a lift, if you want.”

Rita hesitated. She didn’t want to keep Dr Das waiting, but neither did she want to take advantage of Jack’s offer. It didn’t feel right to get close to him again. On the other hand, she had a job to do. He seemed to read the hesitation on her face.

“It’s alright. Just thought I’d ask. I’m not following you around, promise.” His smile reappeared, and he was the same old Jack, in many ways. Well, what harm was there in getting a lift in his car?

“Ok, fine.” She looked into her phone and cancelled the taxi.

“I hope the hospital’s not too out of the way for you." She got into the front passenger seat and strapped herself in. The leather interior was warm and soft, and her seat had heaters, which was nice. The powerful engine purred smoothly as the car zoomed down the road.

“Nice car.”

“Thank you.”

She angled her eyes at Jack as he drove. His large hands gripped the steering wheel. A faint trace of aftershave hit her nostrils.

"How's it going?" Jack asked. Rita averted her eyes as he glanced at her.

"Early days," she sighed. "But yes, I will settle in soon, I guess. After all, nothing here is new to me."

Jack was silent for a while. They drove towards the town centre, and traffic got busier. To their right, the road sloped down the hills to the grey and red brick houses. The sea glittered in the distance.

"Where are you staying?" Jack asked. "If you don't mind me asking."

"It's alright. I'm at the Wayfarer Inn, close to town. The Force got me a room there. Hopefully I get my own flat in the staff quarters soon. Or I might have to sign a tenancy agreement for a short term let."

"You won't be here for long then?" He smiled at her. "Sorry for the questions. I'll shut up, shall I?"

That was one thing she had liked about Jack – he was a gentleman. Despite his nice suit and car, he didn't have an ego to match, either. Well, she didn't know if he had changed.

"No problem. My life's not that interesting." She shrugged. "I need to wrap up this case, and then I'm back down again."

He nodded. "If you stay for longer and need a place, I can recommend someone. A client of ours runs an estate agency. We helped him win a court battle against a competitor. I can put you in touch with him if you want."

"Thanks."

They stopped at the lights. He hooked an eyebrow upwards. "No, really. It's no bother. Nothing to do with me. He's a good bloke. As far as estate agents go, anyway." He grinned in that boyish way. Rita smiled and then looked away, out of the window.

As they went down the hill, Rita saw the streets below, on their right. There was a street with a gap in the middle, looking like a toothless cavity. On either side of the gap, detached Victorian houses stood, all big, and reasonably well maintained. The area of the gap was cordoned, and grass had grown in the middle. In the distance, the sea glimmered, and birds chased each other over the waters.

"What's that?" Rita pointed, as they had stopped in traffic.

Jack looked to his right. "Oh, that's Sawyer's Hill. Old houses there, some were demolished years ago."

The car moved again. Rita took one last look at the odd space, not seeming to belong in a row of handsome houses. Like the street had been struck by a bomb, and the building destroyed. For some reason, the street reminded her of a place she'd seen before. She searched the corners of her mind, but came up with a blank.

A silence fell between them, but it wasn't uncomfortable. She didn't feel the need to talk, and when she did, it was because she was intrigued about his life. Jack had stayed here, and made a success of himself.

"Does work keep you busy?"

"Yes, and also the children. I have them every other weekend. They come on Friday and leave on Tuesday. It's taken a while for them to get used to it. But yes, work is busy. We have offices in York and Leeds now, which are busy. I'm the main partner for Scarborough and surrounding areas. But I travel to York frequently, because we're opening an office in Harrogate."

"Posh place," Rita said, arching her eyebrows. Harrogate was one of the nicest parts of North Yorkshire. A Victorian Spa town that enclosed the medieval walled city of Ripon. Only the wealthy now could afford living there. Jack glanced at her and grinned.

"Better clients for us."

"Sure."

"How's things down in London?" Jack asked.

"Same old. Cost of living way too high. In some ways it's good to be here. Less cars and crowd. The air's cleaner. And there's the sea."

He nodded. "I like it. For many years, the ex wife and I thought of moving to Leeds. She had better job prospects there. I'm glad I didn't."

"You went to law school in Leeds, didn't you? After University in Edinburgh."

"Yes, I did my law conversion course there. It's alright, but this place is in my system, I think. If I don't see the sea, I get a little restless." He laughed. "I can't explain it."

He didn't have to, she thought. When she left Scarborough, she missed the sea as well. That wide open light in the sky, above the endless waters. It was like the land dissolved to open up a space inside her heart, drawing her eyes to beyond the horizon. She loved how space and time melted in the blue expanse.

She knew what he meant, but she felt uncomfortable sharing it with him. She didn't feel close to Jack, and something told her she shouldn't try to, either. But neither did she have to be rude.

"I get it," she said softly. He smiled without speaking, his eyes on the road.

They got to the hospital, and he parked up. Rita got out, thanking him. He also came out of the car. He was taller than her five feet seven, easily north of six feet. His expressive eyes searched her face.

"Would you like to meet for dinner one night? Just to catch up, like old mates." He held up his hand and grinned. “Nothing else. Or Sunday lunch, maybe. I could show you around. Some things have changed around here.”

Rita felt conflicted. The impulsive part of her heart said yes, but her common sense told her to be careful.

“Thank you. I’ll be very busy with the case over the next few days. I can’t make any time now, sorry.”

His smile faltered a little, but it still remained. And it still touched his eyes.

“No worries. Call me if you need anything.”

They exchanged numbers, and Rita's phone rang.

“Sorry I have to take this,” she said. “Thanks for the lift.”

“See you,” He waved, getting back in his car. She watched him drive away as she spoke on the phone.

“DI Gupta.”

It was Richard. "I've got something interesting. Susan Harrington, Clara Winters' neighbour, rang. She said you spoke to her and told her to call back if she remembered anything."

Emily’s mother, Rita thought. The old woman who had almost recognised her.

"Yes, that's right," Rita said.

"Susan remembers seeing Clara Winter at the church. It the week before she vanished. She was having a heated discussion with the vicar. The vicar had to take her to a corner where no one could see them. Susan followed and saw them from a distance, having an argument. She didn't get close enough to hear what they were saying, unfortunately."

Rita frowned. It was true that her mother went to church on Sundays, but not very often. She didn't recall her going to church that week. She thought hard, wondering if she was mistaken. She could have been at a friend's house or doing sports. She used to play hockey on Sundays for her school club.

Rita couldn't remember the name of the church. "Did she say which church it was? And by any chance, can we find out the name of the vicar?"

"It was the local church, St. Matthew's. It's a Catholic church. I looked it up and then asked Mrs. Harrington, and she confirmed it was the one. Right now, I'm looking through the Catholic Church of England database to see if I can find a name for the vicar in 1994. I'll keep you posted."

"Good work, Richard. Please let me know. By the way, I'm going to the morgue." She told him about the piece of necklace and the metal fragments on the bones.

"OK," he said. “You wanted to see Robert McFarlane today. The lads got hold of him. He’s in his builder’s yard today, on the North Side.”

“Oh yes,” Rita sighed, recalling. She looked at her watch. “I’ll go after seeing Dr Das. Send me his address please.”

CHAPTER 30

Rita walked inside the hospital and followed the signs to the morgue, down in the basement. Her shoes made a squeaky sound on the cement floor as she walked down the wide, empty corridor.

When she first started as a detective, she found morgues spooky. Now she had grown more used to them. And yet, the silence of the whitewashed walls, the closeness to all the dead bodies, played on her mind today.

She got to the green doors that had "Mortuary" written on them in bold letters. Further down, another set of doors said "Pathology." She rang the buzzer on the mortuary door and held her face close to the camera. There was a slight delay, then the door clicked open.

A young man stood on the other side, wearing surgical blues and Crocs on his feet. Wisps of brown hair stuck out from his surgical cap.

Rita showed her warrant card. "DI Gupta," she said. "I'm here to see Dr Das."

“Hello, we’ve been expecting you. I’m Stephen, Dr Das's assistant.”

He stood to one side to let her in. Rita was shown into the changing room by Stephen.

"We'll see you outside on the floor," he said. "Turn right, and you'll see us." Rita thanked him and went inside the female changing rooms.

She found a set of Crocs that fit her. She took her jacket off, then put a mask on. She tied a white plastic apron around her waist and then went outside.

Dr Das was standing by a gurney. He wore surgical blues and sterile gloves on his hands. His black-framed glasses had slipped down his nose, and he used his wrist to put them back in place.

He was older than Rita had initially thought. His hair was still plentiful but mostly white. His brown skin had withstood the sun well, and the lines on his face were light, the wrinkles soft. His cheeks had sagged with age, but he was still in good shape. He wasn't a tall man, coming up to about her chest height. She guessed he was in his mid-sixties.

"Hello, Doc," Rita said. "What have you got for me?"

He pointed to a table next to the gurney. The table was slim and had four wheels at the base. A torn piece of the necklace chain was laid out on the table. It lay next to a microscope. Dr Das carefully put the necklace under the microscope's eyepiece.

"Have a look," he said, moving to one side. "Please don't touch any of the dials."

Rita nodded and put her eyes to the microscope. The yellow gold of the chain was bright, undimmed despite the destruction it had suffered. There was a clasp, with tiny hooks on either end. She could just make out the word "Reilly's" engraved in block capital letters.

She straightened. Dr Das said, "Reilly's used to be a jewellery brand in the 1990s. They went out of business just before the lockdown. They had several jewellery shops all over the country." He grimaced. "I don't think there's any way of knowing which shop this particular piece was purchased from or when. That would have been useful for you."

Rita agreed. "Yes. In 1994, jewellery stores would have had CCTV. The film might not be digital, and we would have had a hard time getting hold of the film. Still a chance. But as you said, there's nothing in the chain that gives us any further clues."

"Yes. However, I remember visiting a Reilly's store many years ago in York. I bought a pair of earrings for my wife."

He smiled, but it was sad, and she saw a dullness in his eyes that spoke of pain. Dr Das blinked a couple of times, as if he suddenly didn't know what to say. Then he cleared his throat.

"There's never been a Reilly's store in Scarborough, as far as I know. I've lived here for three years. If there was one before that," he shrugged, "I don't know." He pointed to the chain.

“That’s 24 carats gold, by the way. Isn’t that right, Stephen?” He turned to his assistant.

“Yes,” the younger man replied. He was behind a desk, staring a screen. He walked around it, and up to them. “I sent a sample to the metals lab. Definitely high grade 24 carats.”

“Reilly’s did sell expensive stuff,” Dr Das said.

"We'll have a look for the old stores," Rita said. She wracked her brains but couldn't remember a jewellery store with that name in Scarborough. In her teenage years, she used to buy cheap imitation jewellery from the smaller shops. She couldn't afford anything from the high street. She thought the bigger brand names, but Reilly’s didn’t jump out at her.

"Thanks, Doc. This chain might well have come from the shop in York. We will make some inquiries. I grew up here, and you're right, I can't remember a Reilly's in Scarborough."

Dr Das tilted his head to one side, and his eyebrows rose. "Oh, I see. I thought I detected some northern in your voice." He smiled. He had a kind face, and his gentle eyes crinkled at the corners.

"Yes, the accent still exists, despite all my years down south." Rita grinned. "How about you?"

The pathologist shrugged. "Been a northerner all my life. I worked in Darlington Hospital, then I was in Doncaster for a while. And now here."

Rita didn't want to pry into his personal life, but she wondered why he had moved around. Dr Das moved to the skeleton and indicated the hand to Rita. It wasn't easy looking at her mother's remains, but being in this cold, clinical room made it slightly more bearable. Her initial shock now rumbled softly in the background.

Dr Das was showing her the long bones which extended from the elbow to the wrist.

"The bone on the left is called the ulna, and the thicker one on the right is the radius. They join at two ends of the wrist." His finger moved to the wrist. There are nine smaller bones clustered on the wrist. They've all been shattered, and most of the fragments are lost. But can you see the pigment on the broken ends of the bone?"

"Yes," Rita said. Red spots of colour had appeared on the bones, and they were bright. She hadn't seen them before.

"The red marks are due to uptake of the chemical reagent that I applied. The chemical analysis shows iron, steel, and a couple of other precious metals like tungsten and molybdenum that are used to make an alloy. That alloy is widely used in machetes and axes all over the UK."

"What does that mean?"

Dr Das stood straight and raised both hands above his shoulder, like he was wielding a sword. He brought it down swiftly like he was striking a blow on the wrist. Rita winced and couldn't stop herself from leaning back.

Dr Das smiled. "Sorry, I didn't mean to alarm you. When the weapon came down and hit this poor woman on the wrists, it was with savage force. Metallic fragments from the knife lodged in the bone. The fragments were microscopic and hence invisible to the naked eye. But the chemical reaction is positive, as you can see. I've applied it to other parts of the body as well."

He pointed to the collarbones and then to the right humerus, the bone that extended from the shoulder to the elbow. Rita saw the same red spots of colour on the edges of the broken bones.

"So this gives us a clue as to the murder weapon?" she asked.

"Exactly. That particular alloy is not used in kitchen knives. It's used in machetes to make them tougher and sharper. They have to slice through vegetation and are used to clear paths in jungles, and so on."

"Do you think it might point us towards the manufacturer?"

Dr Das down turned his lips. He didn't look very hopeful, Rita thought.

"You can try, I suppose. Look around for companies that make long knives and the sort around here. But it might be from somewhere else. And the alloy itself is not exclusive to one particular manufacturer. It's an industrial alloy, which means many manufacturers use it."

"Understood. I think we can still look."

The machete, or axe, was the murder weapon. She shuddered when she thought of the violence Clara had endured. Her nostrils flared as she looked down at the skeleton, and then her eyes closed. She turned away, and went to the microscope, as casually as she could. She looked through the eyepiece again, and the yellow gold glowed in the light. She needed to get a grip on herself.

When she looked up, Dr Das was gazing at her curiously. He averted his gaze, smiling as if he didn't want to pry.

"Anything else, doc?" Rita asked.

"Not for now. As you know, there's only so much we can do with bare bones. I can send her to CAHID in Glasgow, or the centre in UCL, in London. They will have more specialist input."

Rita looked down at the bones, and a thought occurred to her. The words seemed to meander and die in her brain, like an animal lost in the desert, waiting to die. She shook her head. She had to ask.

"What about the pregnancy? You said the signs were present in the pelvic bones. How many weeks was the pregnancy?"

"Yes," Dr Das said gravely. "It certainly seems the pregnancy did exist. Otherwise the ligaments wouldn't leave the indentations they did. But not very advanced. Maybe ten to twelve weeks?" He shrugged. "There's no way to be sure. It's the first trimester, that's for sure. The indentations are not that deep."

"First trimester means the first thirteen weeks?"

"Approximately, yes."

Rita pondered. Clara was pregnant for three months, roughly. She would've known of the fact for eight weeks, at least. She kept it a secret from everyone. Clara would've felt so lonely and vulnerable. Rita knew her grandmother died when Rita was little, about nine years old. She had some vague memories of going to the funeral, her mother crying, the coffin lowering into the grave. Snapshots of a grim day that came and went in flashes.

"Rita?" Dr Das said. She blinked and recovered.

"Sorry, just thinking."

"No problem," he smiled. "I can see there's a lot on your mind. Cold cases aren't easy."

"Tell me about it," Rita sighed.

The pathologist nodded, and then indicated his office. "I can give you the paper copies of all the reports, if you want."

"That would be good."

She followed the elderly pathologist into his office. She noted he had a shuffling gait, and he dragged his left foot a touch. Maybe he had a stroke in the past, or a foot injury.

The office door bore a sign: *Dr Samir Das MBBS MD FRCPath*

Inside, it had wooden walls, lined with bookshelves. Framed photos of medical degree and diploma certificates hung on the wall. The desk was neatly arranged with papers on one side, and a laptop in the middle. A faint smell of coffee hung in the air, and Rita spotted the coffee machine on a side board.

"Have a seat," Dr Das indicated the sofa. Rita did so, and the dark fabric sofa was comfortable. She looked around the cramped space. It was clear that the pathologist worked alone here. She saw photos of two young women on his desk, one of Dr Das next to a woman in a white wedding dress. She assumed they were his daughters. There was another photo on the shelf above the desk. An attractive blonde woman in her forties, she thought. It was an old photo.

He caught her looking.

"Amelia and Ariana, my daughters," he said. "The wedding photo is from the eldest, Amelia's wedding last year."

"Lovely," Rita smiled. "Sorry, I didn't mean to pry."

"You're not, don't worry. They're both busy with their lives, down south. My wife died three years ago. That's when I moved from Doncaster to here. I like the quietness. It's normally not very busy."

Rita pointed to the woman's photo. "That was your wife?"

“Yes, Elaine.” He smiled, and Rita saw that sadness in him again. He had grown used to it, she could tell, and he had learnt to bear the weight. She knew it never went away.

“I’m sorry,” she said.

“That’s life,” he spread his hands. “We can only deal with what we’re given.”

“And make the best of it,” Rita said. Dr Das nodded. He turned back to his desk and sorted out some papers.

He turned from his swivelling leather chair, and gave Rita a folder. She took it with thanks. Then the pathologist stared at Rita for a few seconds.

“Just before you go, I hope you don’t mind if I ask you a question.”

She wondered what this was about. She shrugged. “Go ahead.”

“Are you ok with this case?”

A faint uneasiness crept into Rita’s limbs, like the first touch of cold in the winter. “What do you mean?”

“You seemed, shall we say, a little affected, at the crime scene. Like it was bothering you. I know you’re a seasoned, senior detective. Most Inspectors, in my experience, regard this as a job, and deal with the crime scene without any emotion.” He spread his hands, and looked apologetic. “I’m sorry. I just wanted to make sure that you’re ok, that’s all.”

Rita’s heart thudded against her ribs slowly, each motion painful, like her breathing. “Yes, I’m fine,” she said, standing slowly. “Thanks for these,” she indicated the folder.

“You’re welcome. Take care.”

Dr Das opened the door for her. He had that kind look in his eyes, but they also suggested he didn’t fully believe her.

CHAPTER 31

The Toyota Prius left Scarborough General Hospital and drove slowly down the hill. The slope was gentle, with houses on either side. The sea sparkled in the distance, and before that, the long stretches of North Scarborough's sandy beaches. Rita patted the driver's shoulder. "Stop here." She paid the man, thanked him, and got out.

The residential street was a collection of detached and semi-detached houses. Next to number 34, there was a garage and an empty plot of land where a large shed had been built. It had a triangular roof made of corrugated sheets of iron, and the double doors were made of wooden slats, pinned to blocks of timber.

The door was open, and Rita could see a man inside. He was hammering on some metallic object on a tabletop. He was a broad-shouldered, thickset man with salt-and-pepper hair. Rita didn't recognise Robert. She had last seen him when she was a little girl, and her memories of him were scant. Her heart beat faster. Would he recognise her? It was impossible, she thought. She was nine or ten when she had last seen him. Thirty one years ago. No, there was no chance. She stepped inside the workshop, calming her rapid heart.

Robert had his back to her and didn't hear her come inside. Rita glanced around the makeshift toolshed. Three bicycles were placed on stands, and one hung from the ceiling. In the middle, there was a car that had seen better days. It rested on raised bricks, its wheels missing. The windscreen was also gone, and the seats had holes in them. Rita walked around the wreckage, and the man turned suddenly, startled.

"You scared me," he said. His cheeks were ruddy with the glow of a lifetime spent in the sun and wind. His blue eyes twinkled, and he had the weather-worn but sparkling face of a Yorkshire farmer. He had a salt-and-pepper beard that matched the sparse hair on his scalp. His blue eyes twinkled beneath black eyebrows.

Rita remembered him now, of course. He used to have a loud, booming laughter. Flashes of memory scattered in her mind, like light winking from ships in the sea. She could tell that he didn't recognise her at all.

He put down the hammer and wiped his hands on the apron.

"Robert MacFarlane?" Rita asked. He nodded. His inquisitive eyes looked Rita up and down. Rita held up her warrant card.

"Detective Inspector Rita Gupta from North Yorkshire Police. I'm here to talk about Clara Winters. She was your girlfriend many years ago."

The corners of Mr. MacFarlane's mouth tightened, and his forehead contracted. His eyes lost their sparkle. A rueful expression appeared on his face. "Oh, yes. A detective from the Scarborough station called me. Yes, I used to know Clara, like you said, a while back. What's this about, like?"

Rita thought about it, then decided to be upfront with him. The finding would be common knowledge soon, she knew. People talked. And if word leaked out, she knew some journalist would soon be harassing Robert, like a fox scurrying around the bins at night.

"The remains of a body were found in the North Yorkshire Moors. Evidence has confirmed it belonged to Clara Winters."

Mr. MacFarlane's jaw relaxed. He blinked several times, and his face seemed hollowed out suddenly, as if Rita had slapped him across the face. He leaned against the tool desk. For a while, he was unable to speak. His eyes flickered down to the floor, and he frowned.

"They found her? How? I mean, it's been a long time so…" His words trailed off as he raised his shocked eyes to Rita's.

She nodded. "Yes, it was a skeleton." She refrained from providing further details.

The frown remained on Mr. MacFarlane's face. Then understanding dawned, and he stood up straighter.

"I see. You suspect there was foul play. The police did think that, to be fair. They dragged me over hot coals at the time. Now you're here to do the same." A hard gleam appeared in his eyes, and his jaw ground together.

His voice rose. "Haven't I told you enough? I was with my girlfriend that night. She still remembers. She is my wife now, by the way. She is in the house. Do you want to go and speak to her?"

Rita didn't want a confrontation. There was something reassuring about his spontaneous reaction. He was shocked, but also upset, and not hiding that. She raised a hand to placate him.

"There's no need to speak to your wife. I just wanted you to cast your mind back to when you were with Clara. This isn't about you, to be honest. We wanted you to shed light on her personal life, as you knew her well. Who she met with, which pub she drank in, that sort of thing."

Robert stared at her for a while, then the fire died down, like a bucket of water had been flung over it. He rested a heavy elbow on the tool desk, and his spine sagged.

He rubbed his forehead, then ran a hand down his face. "It was a long time ago," he whispered, his voice dragged up from some deep chasm inside him. "Clara was beautiful. I was young then, only 25. She was a couple of years older than me."

A sad smile haunted his face. "I thought we were going to be together for a long time, if not forever. When you're young, two years can be a long time. But it went by so quickly."

Rita watched him. The expression on his face was heavy, weighed down with the memory. He looked up and met her eyes.

"She was a good woman. She worked hard and loved her daughter. I became friends with the little girl as well." He smiled again, and Rita felt a tingling sensation all over her skin, prickling her. Her breathing was faster, and she opened her mouth to gently exhale.

Robert didn't appear to notice. "When she broke up with me, I was heartbroken." He shook his head. "I wanted to have children with her," he whispered, his eyes on the floor, as if they held a map of his memories. "At first, I thought she was interested. But then she wasn't."

“Did she become pregnant when she was with you?”

Robert seemed surprised. “No. I would’ve known. No,” he repeated. “She didn’t.”

Rita considered his response, then decided to let it go, for now.

She asked, "You said she worked hard. How many jobs did she do?"

Robert glanced up at her. His forehead muscles crinkled together. "She worked in the supermarket, that I know. And she worked somewhere else as well, I'm not sure where. I think she cleaned houses. When she worked, she dropped her daughter at a friend's house. Angela, or Gloria, I think she was called." He waved a hand in the air. "Sorry, I can't be sure."

"Carry on," Rita said.

Robert shrugged. "She didn't tell me a great deal about where she worked. She was mostly free in the evenings. I used to come round after she put the little one to sleep. We went out on the sea a couple of times. I used to have a boat. I sold it a few years ago."

Little strands of memory floated like seaweed across Rita's mind. She remembered being on a boat, the blue sparkle of the water, the wind tugging at her. Arms raised, giggling and excitement, her mother's happy, smiling face. And the man with the broad shoulders and strong back, holding the wheel of the boat.

That man was Robert. She had always known, and she had wanted to confront him before, ask him what he remembered of Clara. There was never a right time. Now fate had dragged her here, and while she couldn't bring herself to reveal her true identity, she had to know what Robert truly recalled.

A shadow passed over Robert's face. He leaned forward. "I'm sorry, where's my manners? Here, please take a seat." From under the desk, he pulled out two folding chairs. He gave her one, and then sat down himself.

Rita sat down and took out her black leather notebook. "Did you ever go on holiday with her?" She didn't remember that to be the case, but she could be mistaken. Robert shook his head.

"We went on drives down the coast. If you live around here, there's always nice places to visit by the sea. We used to have long weekends in caravan parks by the sea. Me, her, and her daughter."

"Did any other friends come with you? Or did you know them?"

"I remember Angela, if that was her name. She had a couple of other girlfriends. I can't remember them, sorry."

"You were with her for two years. Was she ever in any trouble or danger?"

Robert lowered his eyebrows. "I'm not sure what you mean. She didn't have any dodgy mates, and she wasn't involved in anything criminal." He shrugged. "I mean, we didn't have much money, but we did okay. I was a mechanic back then, and then I got my own garage later on. We had broken up by then, and I met my new girlfriend."

Rita nodded. "After you broke up, did she ever call you?"

Robert shook his head. "Clara was a strong woman. When she wanted something, she did it with all her heart. But when the tide turned, she just said no. After we separated, she didn't stay in touch. I tried to, but I realized she wasn't interested. It was for the best, I thought."

"How did you feel when you heard the news of her disappearance?"

Robert stared at her for a while, as if he hadn't heard properly. Then a grimace appeared on his face.

"These were the questions the cops asked me all those years ago. Trying to get something out of me. I wish I had some news to give you. Something that would help. Of course, I felt sorry for her. I was concerned, and I even helped the police look for her."

That much was true, Rita knew from the crime record notes. Robert and Angela had been the two witnesses who had helped the most, along with Susan Harrington, the neighbour who lived opposite. Their statements had been the bulk of the investigators' evidence.

"So she was happy and lived a simple life. Is that correct?" Rita asked.

"As far as I could tell, yes. You might want to ask her friends, see if they know more. Angela still lives in Scarborough, doesn't she?"

Rita didn't confirm or deny. She moved on. "Is there anything else you can recall from around the time she disappeared? Did anything happen around Scarborough?"

Robert put his elbows on his thighs, and his thick forearms flexed. His chin rested on his clasped hands. He stared into the mid-distance, thinking. Then he shook his head.

"No. Not much happens around here. It was just sad. I was concerned about the little girl. She was 11 by then, and the poor lass got her life turned inside out. God knows what happened to her." He sighed, and a cloak of despondency seemed to wrap around his shoulders.

Rita flexed her jaws, and her nostrils flared. She shut her small black leather notebook slowly and put it inside her jacket. She got to her feet.

"If you remember anything, Mr. MacFarlane, please get in touch with Scarborough station. Just ask for me." Her hands shook as they dived inside her pocket, and she managed to retrieve her card. She handed it to MacFarlane, who accepted it with thanks.

He stood and looked at her. "I hope you find what happened to her. God rest her soul."

The black weight in Rita's throat was heavier, dragging her soul down. She nodded, trying in vain to keep her face neutral. "We will do our best. We shall keep you informed."

She turned and walked away.

CHAPTER 32

Thirty Years Ago

Clara Winters stopped by the open door, leading out into the hallway of Blue Rise Care Home. She could hear one of the men speaking. The door was only open a sliver, and she put her eye in the crack.

The children had come back from school. They were milling around in the corridor, going up the stairs to their rooms, some were filtering into the dining room and kitchen on the left before the staircase.

The man had grabbed one boy, and held him against the wall, hand on both his shoulders. The other boys went away, and silence descended on the hallway. Clara strained her ears to hear what the man was saying.

"Now, Mark, we don't tell anyone about what happens. Okay?"

Clara knew the boy was called Mark Strong. He was ten years old. The man crouched in front of the boy.

"Do you understand?"

The boy had his head down, and nodded. The man said, "If you do, then you can't live here anymore."

Again, head down, the boy nodded in silence. The man stood, and pushed the boy towards the stairs. Clara opened the door wider to watch them go up the stairs, and disappear on the landing. She felt sick inside. Her guts were twisted, acid rising in her throat. She looked around the kitchen, where another carer was preparing the boys's dinner. There was no one else here.

Clara slipped into the small room where the carers kept their coats and bags. She had suspected what the men were doing for a while now. She had seen them go into the boys room. While cleaning the boys rooms, she had seen flecks of blood on the sheets. And to her horror, she had seen one of the men undress a boy in his room.

Clara had thought of going to the police. She knew the whispers about this place. She had taken the job because of her lover. But he was one of them. Rich, powerful….and sick to the core.

Clara put a hand on her head, and sank to the floor. She couldn't accept this. She had to do something. If she couldn't speak to anyone, she could try something else. She got up and reached inside her bag. She pulled out the camcorder, and checked it was on. The battery was fully charged, and there was a video tape inside. She hid the camcorder in her jacket.

Clara came out of the small room, and saw the other carer still busy with the food. She went out into the wide hallway, and crept up the stairs.

She went into the staff toilet and locked the door. There was a window here, that looked out across the courtyard. She opened the window. She saw the man in the room with Mark. She felt like vomiting as she watched. With trembling hands, she picked up the camcorder. She started taking the video. She had a good view of inside the room, and she zoomed in. Nausea pooled in her stomach, and her body shook with disgust. But she kept taking the video.

CHAPTER 33

As Rita sat in the taxi, she thought about Robert. Now that she had met him, she had him low on the suspect list. He didn’t have any reason to lie. If he killed her, he wouldn’t live here for so many years after the crime.

But she hoped he might still remember something about Clara, and she wanted to stay in touch with him. In time, she would reveal her identity to Robert. After all, he had known Clara well, and had also been a part of Rita’s own life, albite for a brief time.

Her mind returned to Dr Das’s parting comments at the morgue. Was she that transparent? The thought made her cringe. She couldn't have avoided a visit to the morgue, and she was glad that she went. She found valuable evidence, but what she was slowly unearthing was a dark and grim picture.

How did Clara buy that 24 carat gold necklace?

She couldn't remember her mother having much jewellery. That gold chain was 24 carats; it couldn't have been cheap. Clara couldn't have afforded that. It must have been a gift.

A gift from Edward Salt? Or Lord Northallerton?

Or was Clara a part of Blue Rise Holdings, hence she had their bank account details? If Clara had that sort of money, why did she live in a council house?

She rang Maggie, who picked up on the first ring. "I've got an appointment to see Mr Salt tomorrow. Can you tell him it's urgent, and I need to see him today?"

"I'll try, guv. Calling his secretary now."

Rita hung up. Like the black caves in the massive raw mountains that faced the North Sea, questioned loomed in her mind. Her mind lashed against the rocks like restless sea, but the answers remained hidden. She needed to speak to Mr Salt, quickly.

They were going through a residential street, semi-detached houses on either side. Green front lawns, nice cars. Children playing hopscotch outside. The sort of nice, middle-class suburban life that she had missed out on. Her childhood had been in that dingy, cramped terraced, council house on a street owned by the council.

She looked away and inspected her nails. Clara had tried her best to give her a good life. In the 11 short years that she had shared with her mother, Rita had always felt loved. Clara did everything she could to protect her.

Rita couldn't dwell on the past. Somehow, she had to let it go and move on. The car rolled down a hill, and the glittering blue sea appeared, winking in the sunlight. She saw the distant cliffs and the lighthouse on top. For her, this was the final frontier. The last barrier before she could finally lay the past to rest. Then she would be free, like the wind and water over that blue sky.

***

Back at the station, she found the team busy at work. All three were on the phone. The whiteboard now had more information on it. There was a timeline of when Clara was last seen and of her daily routine.

She sat down at the table and pulled up her laptop. Maggie put her phone down and got her attention.

“The drones are up. There's nothing to report as yet, but they’re searching. They're also using infrared heat wave maps to see if anyone is hiding in the woods. They found a couple of walkers so far, but not much else. Ideally, I'd like them to search for the murder weapon. I know that might not be possible,” Maggie said, spreading her hands.

Rita nodded. “But even if we never find the murder weapon, Dr Das has given us some valuable clues.”

She explained her discussion with the pathologist. Richard had also put his phone down and listened carefully.

“Only specialty stores would make knives like that. We can make a list of them and see which ones were active in 1994.”

“Good,” Rita nodded. “While you're at it, also look for a jewellery shop called Reilly's. Now, I can't remember any shops like that in Scarborough, back in the 90s. But Dr Das said there was one in York.”

Rizwan and Maggie looked at each other, and there was a short silence. Maggie said, “Guv, so you're from around here? You do have a slight northern accent, to be fair.”

“Yes,” Rita grinned. “I grew up in Scarborough.” She changed the topic quickly, not wanting any more questions about her past.

"From what I can see, Reilly's doesn't exist anymore. Find out what happened to them and get a record of jewellery sales from their shops in Leeds and York."

"OK, guv," Maggie said.

Richard was looking intently at his laptop screen. He glanced at Rita.

"Blue Rise Holdings ran a children's care home. It was called Blue Rise Care Home. Imaginative, isn't it?" He grinned.

Rita frowned. "I didn't see that last time. Must've missed it. Is that the only care home the company ran?"

"Yes."

"So this company ran a children's care home? Isn't that a specialised field? I mean – a property developer wouldn't just buy a children's home, would they? Then they have to deal with social services, medical issues and so on."

"Yes, but they might have bought them as going concerns."

Rita rubbed her chin. Something about this didn't sit right with her.

Rita called Scarborough Council, and asked to speak to the Social Service and Children's Department. After going through three people, she finally spoke to a senior care worker for children. The woman's name was Natalie.

"Blue Rise? That doesn't ring a bell," Natalie said. "I've been in this job for twenty-two years, and I haven't heard of them."

"It was closed down in 2000, and the building was demolished. But you must have records from it?"

"Let me check. Can I call you back?"

Rita hung up and got busy with her emails. The phone rang again and Rita answered swiftly. "DI Gupta."

It was Natalie. "Hello. I can see the care home existed. We have a list of residents, the carers, and…"

"And?"

Natalie sounded hesitant now, like she didn't know what to say. "Well, there should be annual inspection reports. The council has social workers like me who act as Inspectors. We go out and speak to the children and staff, and compile a report. If there are concerns, we take them up with the care home management."

"Where are the inspection reports?" Rita narrowed her eyes.

Natalie sighed. "Yes. The reports aren't present. I can't see them online. They might have not been filed. We might have physical copies. I need to check."

An uneasiness nudged against Rita's spine like a spined nettle. "And it's usual practice to find these reports online. Correct?"

"Yes. But I do have the names of the resident children and the carers, if that helps."

"That does, thank you. But I do need the inspection reports as well."

"May I ask what this is about? I mean, you are a police detective, correct?"

"Yes, and this relates to a murder case from many years ago. So this is urgent."

Natalie's voice dropped several octaves. "A murder at the care home?"

Rita thought for a while. "I don't know," she answered truthfully. "But we have evidence to suggest the care home was related, somehow."

Even as she said the words, she wondered about the connection. Both Mark and her mother had the photo. True, the largest building on the street had belonged to the care home. And it was now demolished. Rita nodded to herself, the conviction firm in her mind. Yes, there was a connection, there was no doubt.

If her mother had been at the care home, could she have been murdered there, and then taken to her final resting place?

Did Clara work there? Is this the job she hid from everyone?

“Please send us a list of the staff and carers at Blue Rise Care Home.”

Rita out the phone down, and sat in silence, but her mind buzzed louder.

Was her mother linked to this care home? It was owned by Mr. Salt and Lord Northallerton Something didn't add up here, and it kept gnawing at the back of Rita's mind, like an army of termites feasting on wood.

"I'll be back in a minute." She went outside to the rear car park. The sunlight was still playing hide and seek with the clouds. At least it wasn't raining. A stiff breeze blew in from the side of the castle, carrying the scent of salty brine with it. She called Angela, who answered.

After the pleasantries were over, Rita asked Angela if her mother had known Edward Salt. Angela was silent for a while.

"Not that I know of. Who is he, anyway?"

"He's a big businessman around here. He owns nightclubs, properties, and fisheries."

There was silence again, and then Angela spoke. "I don't know, love," she sighed. "Your mother did have friends, yes. She was a beautiful woman, and men liked her. If she was involved with another man, I wouldn't be surprised. But I don't know why she'd keep it a secret."

Rita paused to think. “Alright. Do you know if mum worked in a care home called Blue Rise Children’s Home?”

“No, love I don’t.”

“Think carefully,” Rita urged. “Are you sure she didn’t tell you anything about it? This could be the job that she was stressed about.”

The line was silent, only the faint hiss of static audible. Angela said, “No, she didn’t tell me about this. How did you find out she worked there?”

“I don’t know for sure. It’s just a guess, to be honest. But she had the bank account details of the company that owned the ccare home.”

“I see. That’s odd.”

“Yes.” Rita was quiet, wondering if Angela was being completely honest with her. She decided to change the topic, for now.

"This might come as a surprise. But did Mum have anything to do with Alfred Northallerton?"

"You mean the Northallerton family? That man's a lord, isn't he?"

"Yes," Rita said. She heard Angela smile. "Next you'll be asking me if your mother knew the Queen. I doubt she knew Lord Northallerton, love. These people move in different circles, don't they?"

Rita thought for a while. "Can you ask around?"

"Yes, I will do. If I find anything, I'll let you know."

“Who will you ask?”

Angela was silent again. “Your mum’s friends have mostly moved away, or died. I’ll have to make a few phone calls, to see if I can find their friends. So friends of friends, if you know what I mean. I need to have a think.”

“What about her ex-boyfriend? Actually, I can ask him.” She slapped her forehead mentally. She should've thought of that before. "Speak to you soon."

"I'll ask around and see what I can find out." There was a note of hesitancy in Angela's voice now. "Love, you know these people are powerful, don't you?"

"What do you mean?"

"I mean…well, just be careful. I don't know what you're dealing with here. But these rich people have connections."

Was Angela trying to warn her? Rita decided to have it out in the open. "Are you worried about something?"

"No, love. I just don't want you to get into trouble, that's all."

Rita waited, listening to the breeze in the trees, and trying to gauge Angela's words. "I'll be alright, don't worry. I'll call you soon."

She hung up on the phone, and called Robert McFarlane. He answered.

Rita introduced herself. "Mr McFarlane, do you remember Clara Winters working in a care home called Blue Rise?"

There was silence, punctuated by the sound of heavy breathing. Then Robert's voice drawled again. "No, sorry. Nothing like that springs to mind. I mean, she worked in the supermarket, but that's all I know."

Rita thought for a while. “That’s okay. Thank you, and please get in touch if you remember anything.”

She went back into the office. Richard and Rizwan were sitting close, looking at Richard’s laptop. Maggie was on the phone.

Rita asked Richard, “Did you follow up on the vicar at St Mathew’s Church?”

“The church records indicate the same problem we had with the bank. There are no digital records before 2005. So they have to pull out a paper copy. I’m waiting for them to get back to me.”

“Okay.” Rita’s mind returned to the church. She remembered being there. It was an imposing grey stone edifice, a cemetery behind it.

She suddenly stopped, her body going rigid. That photo near Clara’s body. It had a church spire on it. She pulled out her phone and thumbed to the image on her phone. She zoomed in on the church spire. It didn’t look familiar. She opened her laptop and searched for St Mathews Church. She recognised it as soon as it appeared on the screen.

She had been there several times. She even recalled going up the nave, the white frocked vicar standing at the pulpit, holding his hand out in blessing to the congregation. But the vicar was faceless, a shadow in the mist of her memory.

Was that the same vicar Clara had an argument with?

Rita's memories focused on the time around her mother's disappearance. She went to the church with Clara a few weeks before the event. Clara helped out with the homeless people who attended the church. She made bread and soup for them, and with a few other women, helped to stock the kitchen for the homeless.

The more Rita thought about it, the more she realised the vicar had to be the same person she remembered, and whom Susan Harrington recalled. There was no other vicar in the church at the time.

"What is it, guv?" Rizwan asked.

"Just wondering how we can find the vicar." She looked at Richard. "Find out how many Catholic vicars were in Scarborough at the time. I want to make sure they didn't take turns to visit St Mathew's Church."

"That's unlikely, guv. My mum's Irish, and she's Catholic. The vicar belongs to the parish. He won't change quickly, unless…" He stopped and held Rita's eyes.

"Unless there was some sort of scandal," Rita said softly.

"I didn't find anything scandalous," Richard said. "But of course, these things can be swept under the carpet."

They were quiet for a while. Questions floated around in Rita's mind like snowflakes descending from a cloudy sky. She needed to get some answers, soon.

She glanced at her watch. It was getting close to 1 PM. "Let's get in touch with the Church again today. Why don't you guys get some lunch?" she suggested. "I'll catch up with Shola to see if she has anything."

Maggie hung up on her phone and waved at Rita. "I did it, guv. Scared Mr Salt enough by saying his name had turned up in connection with a murder investigation. Didn't give any

names out. I said you would disclose more info when you see him later today. He will see you in an hour's time."

Rita grinned at Maggie. "Well done."

Rita checked her emails, and happily enough, Natalie from the council had sent her the list of staff and children at the Blue Rise Care Home.

She sat down with Maggie to go through the list. Maggie did the list of children, and Rita took the staff and carers list. They were divided up into years. The care home existed for ten years, from 1990 to its closure in 2000.

Rita started with the year of closure. She ran her thumb down the list. She didn't find any familiar names. She got to 1993, and she was getting tired. Her eyes hurt and she yawned. She needed a coffee.

She squeezed her forehead with her fingertips and closed her eyes for a few seconds. Stifling another yawn, she stood. Maggie was still engrossed in the list, her younger eyes able to withstand the strain of the small print. Small for Rita, that was. She needed glasses. Sighing, she focused on the year 1994.

Then she saw it.

The name was like a punch to her guts, bending her over. She couldn't believe it, and then peered closer. There was no mistake in that carer's name.

Clara Winters.

CHAPTER 34

It was two in the afternoon, and Rita was sitting in the reception area of Mr. Edward Salt's office. The redbrick Victorian building was in Scarborough's High Street, and she imagined it was one of the many offices Mr. Salt had dotted around North Yorkshire. It was a large, detached house that occupied a prominent corner on the High Street, next to a national bank. Rita scrolled through the emails on her phone as she waited.

Rita glanced at the receptionist's empty desk. The middle-aged lady had just disappeared through a side door. Rita was thinking of going up to the desk when the lady reappeared. She looked a little flustered. She smoothed down her hair and attempted a nervous smile.

"Mr. Salt will see you now." She came out from behind the desk and walked Rita to a set of double doors. She pressed a fob key on the wall, and the doors slid open.

"First door on the right," the woman said. Rita thanked her and stepped inside the well-decorated, modern corridor. The floor continued with the same deep blue carpet, and the white painted walls had large framed Impressionist paintings that, to her untrained eye, looked original. If they were, they would cost a fortune, she knew.

She knocked on the door, and a voice asked her to enter. The office was large and airy. Windows occupied the entire length of the far wall, and sunlight streamed in. Mr. Salt stood from the desk and came forward. He was a tall, lean man dressed in a blue shirt and dark grey trousers. His hair was receding at his temples, and he had a light, salt-and-pepper goatee beard. His blue eyes were attentive, and they crinkled at the corners when he smiled. He smelled of a nice aftershave.

Rita showed him her warrant card, but he brushed it away.

"There's no need. I know who you are. Your colleague spoke to my secretary." He smiled without a trace of the rancour Rita knew he must be feeling. He offered his hand, which Rita shook. He pulled up a chair for Rita, and she took a seat, thanking him, and declined his offer of tea or coffee.

He sat down opposite and stared attentively at Rita. A light smile remained on his lips, and his manner was relaxed, as if he had plenty of time on his hands.

"I must say, I'm surprised you wanted to speak to me. As much a pleasure as it is to see you, a visit from a detective inspector is a little alarming, as you can imagine." The smile faded. “Your colleague mentioned my name came up in a murder investigation. What is this about, please?"

Rita didn't waste time on preamble.

"The remains of a woman's body were found in Raptor's Viewpoint, near Sawdon village, recently. Her name was Clara Winters. Our investigation leads us to believe Miss Winters worked as a carer in a children's care home that you owned. It was called Blue Rise Holdings."

Mr. Salt had a frozen expression on his face, and he was barely breathing. Then his lips moved, and he inhaled. He became aware of Rita's eyes and tried to act nonchalant. But the tension on his features was unmistakable. Rita continued.

"Clara Winters was killed. Her body was left in a shallow grave at Raptors Viewpoint, where she wouldn't be found." She paused. "Did you know Miss Winters?"

Mr Salt's looked confused, as if Rita was speaking in a foreign language. "How would I know an employee from so many years ago? Surely you don't expect me to remember all the carers who worked in that care home?" He frowned. "What did you say the name was?"

"Blue Rise Care Home."

Mr Salt blinked, and then narrowed his eyes. He stared at the table top, as if that held an answer. Then he nodded, and the relaxed expression was back on his features. He adjusted himself in his seat.

"Yes, I do remember that care home. It was being sold, and the council approached me. I didn’t have any experience in that field, but the staff were already in place. I bought it as a business, and then sold it. I;m afraid I don’t recall the carers who worked there, as you can imagine.”

Rita stared back at him, trying to gauge the sincerity of his words. He was far too relaxed, almost as if he had expected her questions. She couldn't help that feeling. His answer had been glib and precise, like he had practiced it beforehand. As if he knew what she'd ask. Or was she being paranoid?

She felt a touch deflated. She cleared her throat. "If I describe her to you, it might ring a bell. Clara Winters was a brunette, about 5'6". Slim build, green eyes. She lived on Oak Road near Falsgrave Park in Scarborough. Not far from the bay. She had a daughter as well. She was a single mother who worked in a supermarket."

Mr. Salt downturned his lips and shook his head slowly. "No, I’m sorry. I don’t recall her."

Rita decided to level with him. “Miss Winters had the bank account details of Blue Rise Holdings. Do you know why that might be?”

The lines on Mr Salt’s forehead crinkled together. “No, I don’t.”

"She would not have those details if she didn't have a financial relationship with the company. Do you agree?"

The man blinked a few times. He licked his lower lip. "I don't really know, Inspector. Actually, if she did, is it not your job to find out why."

"That's what we are trying to do," Rita said casually. "Your company must've paid her, correct?" Mr Salt nodded cautiously.

"Then why is there no salaries on her bank account from Blue Rise Holdings?"

"I don't know. Maybe she had another account?"

"We checked the two accounts she had. No salaries were received from your company. And yet, she worked there."

Mr Salt spread his hands. "I have no idea, Inspector. Really, I'm not sure what you want me to say. The company was closed down 21 years ago. That's almost a quarter of a century. Look, I'm sorry that Miss Winters died, but it had nothing to do with me."

"Why did Miss Winters not get any money, and yet have the company's bank account details? Can you explain? It's highly unusual for an employee to have those details."

Rita's persistence was having an effect. Mr. Salt's nostrils flared once, and then he attempted a smile again, but it was forced, like invisible fingers were stretching his lips.

He spread his hands, "I'm sure there's an explanation. Maybe Miss Winters specified a different account for the money to go to. That account might not have been in her name. It could be her mother's, for instance, I don't know."

"Her parents had died by then. No money was transferred to her relatives' accounts," Rita said flatly.

Mr Salt shrugged. “Sorry. I really can’t help you in that regard.”

He glanced at his watch. "Now if you'll excuse me, Inspector, I have to get on with my day. I trust you have things to do as well, and I don't wish to keep you any longer."

Rita made no effort to move. She sat still, her notebook open, her eyes unblinking as she stared back at Mr. Salt.

“Did you present Miss Winter with a gold chain necklace?”

Mr Salt’s eyeborws rose as his jaws relaxed. “What? I jus told you I don’t remember the woman. Why on earth would I buy her a necklace?”

“So, no then?”

“Yes, of course. Now if you’ll excuse-

“I’m not done yet,” Rita ground the words out, glaring at Mr Salt. He sighed, then sat down on his chair with a little shake of the head.

“You owned the company with Lord Northallerton, is that correct?”

Mr Salt blinked. “I believe so, yes. He was my business partner.”

“How many companies did you form with him?”

“That was the only one.”

That much Rita knew was true. “You were a property developer, and yet you owned that care home with Lord Northallerton. Why is that, Mr Salt? Not your usual line of business is it?”

“I told you, the council offered it to me.”

“But you sold it very quickly, back to a company owned by Alfred Northallerton. For a very cheap price, as if you wanted to get rid of it. In fact you made a loss on that deal. Is there a reason?”

Darkness fell across Mr. Salt's face, thunder rumbling in his eyes. "This meeting is over, Inspector Gupta. I don't have time for your questions anymore. Now, if you'll excuse me." He stood slowly, indicating he was done with answering questions.

Rita had pushed the boat far enough for one day. She also stood. "My staff will be contacting your secretary for the details of all your companies."

Mr Salt's jaws tightened. "As you wish."

Rita smiled. "I will be in touch again. If you remember anything, please give us a call." She pointed to the desk. "I've left my card there."

*****

Mr Salt paced his office after Rita left. He went to the window. They faced the rear of the building, and the rectangular garden space. With unseeing eyes, he watched the sunlight fade as clouds scudded overhead. Drops of rain appeared on the window pane. He strode over to his desk and called the front desk. The receptionist answered.

“Has the Inspector gone?”

“Yes, sir, she has.”

“OK. Do not let her in if she comes again, and even if I'm in, say I'm busy. The same goes for any other police officer.”

“No problem, sir.”

Mr Salt pulled a desk drawer, and took out a digital keypad. He took it to the wall, and unhooked a painting, and rested it on the floor. There was a safe behind it. He lifted the keypad, and inserted a code. The safe door swung open. There was a phone inside, and a few stacks of cash. He got the phone, locked the safe, and put the painting back in place. He would need this phone over the next few days. He called a number he used rarely. Alfred Northallerton answered.

"A Detective Inspector was here today. Rita Gupta, her name was. She knows about Clara, and the company. This is getting ridiculous."

"What did she ask you?"

"All sorts of things. I fobbed her off the best I could. I think she knows."

Alfred was silent for a while. "It's time we met up."

CHAPTER 35

Rita walked to the canteen with the team. As they joined the queue, Maggie turned to her.

"Why don't you have a bite to eat, guv?"

The offer was a tempting one. Rita had lost her appetite after her meeting with Mr Salt. But the smell of the chicken roast in the canteen was making her tummy rumble. She ignored it with the thought of the task she had set herself.

"Get me a chicken wrap, please, and a bottle of still water. And get something for yourself as well. All of you." Rita pulled out two twenty-pound notes, and waved away the protests from Maggie, Rizwan and Rich. The team was working hard, and they deserved a treat from her.

"How did it go with Mr Salt?" Maggie asked.

Rita had spoken to Maggie already, asking her to liaise with Mr Salt's secretary about the rest of the company documents.

"He's dodgy, that's for sure. He's not telling us the truth about the victim."

"You think he knew her?" Rizwan asked.

"Yes. He was defensive when talking about her. Probably gave her that necklace as well."

Richard asked, "Did you tell him how the victim died?"

"No. I'm saving that for later, because I want to see him again. Do we have all the info we need on Northallerton and his family?"

"Chasing that up now," Richard said.

"Good. See you soon."

Rita went back to the office. The lack of clarity with the care home was still bothering her deeply. She picked up the phone and called Natalie at the council, who answered.

"Hello, this is DI Gupta again. Did you find the paper records for Blue Rise Care Home's inspection reports?"

Silence met her ears. "Hello?"

Natalie cleared hr throat. "Yes. I went down to the records office in the basement where we keep the paper records." She stopped again, seemingly lost for words. For some reason, a chill crawled over Rita's skin, giving her goose bumps.

“I’m not sure why,” Natalie continued, “But there are no Inspection reports for the last ten years. From 1993-2003.”

“So where are they? You said the Inspection reports are compulsory, correct?”

“Yes, they are. I can’t think of any reason. I would have to ask my boss…but even she wasn’t around then. I’m sorry, but I need to make more enquiries.”

The uneasiness was now sprouting thorns inside Rita’s mind. “Do you think they might have been removed from the paper records? Can we find out if the Inspections actually happened?”

“Maybe. If we find the senior social care workers at the time, and then narrow it down to who did the inspection visits, but that’s like looking for needles in a haystack. It’s all historic, and it will be a lot of work.”

“And it won’t tell us what happened to the inspection reports.” Rita frowned. “We need to escalate this. Can you please speak to your boss?”

“I will.”

There was something in the woman’s voice which made Rita think she wasn’t being sincere.

“I will make my own enquiries,” Rita said. “Please call me when you find something.”

She hung up, then stared at the phone, wondering what was going on. She opened up her laptop and checked the social services website, and the children's care homes section. As she had expected, Inspection Reports were an annual, and compulsory event. Rita frowned, a knot of concern tightening in her mind.

Then her thoughts turned to what happened on the way to the morgue. That man who was following her around.

Who was he?

She went out of the office, and walked to the staircase. She took the steps up to the third floor, where Traffic Control was based. Compared to her previous station in Cricklewood, North London, the traffic department here was tiny. Through the glass door, she watched about ten officers, all sat around a bank of screens, watching the CCTV's in operation around Scarborough.

Not much happened in Scarborough in the winter season. It was a peaceful town, and here the miscreants were more concerned with getting the time right for surfing, rather than picking pockets or planning robberies.

Rita pressed her fob key against the door, and walked into the open plan office. She introduced herself at the nearest desk, manned by a female sergeant whose name badge said Madeleine.

"DI Gupta," Rita showed her warrant card.

Madeleine was in her forties, rosy cheeked and plump, with a smiley face. "Hello guv. Heard the crime squad is getting a new boss. That must be you."

"For my sins, yes," Rita smiled back. "Nice to meet you. I had a favour to ask, if you don't mind."

"Sure."

"A man's been following me around. I saw him in Hedley last night, and today just outside the nick. He was hiding behind a tree outside the front entrance. Do you think you can see him on CCTV? I chased him, but he got away. This happened about an hour and a half ago."

Madeleine nodded vigorously, and tapped on the keyboard. Two screens on either side of her desk flickered to life.

"Was he armed?" Madeline shot her a concerned look. "You need to be careful, guv. Even Scarborough has nutters these days."

"I don't know. He was in his thirties or forties, I'd say. He ran well. He wore a dark jacket and jeans, with white trainers. Caucasian, slim build, average height. No other distinguishing features."

"Let's have a look."

The camera feeds popped up on the screens. Rita saw herself, walking outside the front gates, engrossed in her phone. Then she looked up and crossed the road.

The man became visible, in the upper right corner of the screen.

“Let me try the opposite angle,” Madeleine said.

Her fingers flew over the keyboard, and a new camera feed appeared, this time on the central screen on the middle of the desk. It showed the black and white image of a man running, facing the camera. Madeleine zoomed in, and then stopped.

Now Rita could see the man’s face. He had dark, floppy hair that fell over his face. He wore a white vest under the jacket. He was slim, and not tall. She was right about his age, he was in his forties, no more. Was he the same man she had seen outside Angela’s house? Last night it was too dark to notice much. But the slim outline of his shape was the same.

How had he known she was going to be there? How long had he been following her around? Disturbing questions rose to the surface of her mind like a slick of oil in water.

“Can you please print out his images? And please keep this to yourself for now.”

“No problem, guv”

Once the photo was printed out, Rita looked carefully at the man's face. He had a light beard, but he didn't wear glasses. She noticed again his white vest and white trainers.

"I lost him when he took the first left at the end of the road, opposite the station," Rita explained. "Can you see if he appears on the street later on?"

"Sure," Madeleine said. She typed the name of the street into the CCTV camera feeds, and the black-and-white images came to life on the screen. The time was midday.

Rita said, "Scroll through to 1 PM, and then have a look."

At the timestamp of 2 PM, Rita, who was watching the two screens intently with Madeleine, raised a hand. "Stop, I think that's him there."

Madeleine zoomed in on the image of a slim, bearded man in a dark jacket and white shirt who had just come out of a corner shop. They tracked him as he looked around, clearly to make sure he wasn't being followed. Then he walked rapidly to the bus stop and boarded a bus number 56.

"That goes to the town centre, and then to Stainforth in the south."

Rita remembered the place vaguely. It was a residential area and reasonably respectable. A small town in its own right.

Madeleine fast-forwarded the images, following the bus.

"This will take some time, guv," she said. "Do you want me to track him all the way and then get back to you?"

Rita stared at the screen, feeling pensive. If this man was trying to hide himself, he wasn't doing a very good job. He didn't have a hoodie on or sunglasses to cover his eyes. He also wore a white shirt and white trainers. Most criminals would be head-to-toe in black and would cover their eyes with dark glasses.

"No," she said, "I want to see how far he gets. Carry on."

Madeleine did as she was told. Outside Linden Road Park, a green area in the east of Scarborough, they saw the man get off. He went inside the park and then vanished from view. The park was close to Scalby, an area Rita knew of, but had never visited.

The screen showed a blank grey front. Madeleine turned to Rita apologetically.

"CCTV dark spot, guv. We only have them around the main areas of Scarborough. But we can see if we can pick him up after he emerges from the park and goes into one of the main streets."

Rita stood, scratching the back of her scalp. She knew now that it would take time. "Yes, please search for him. You can use image recognition, yes? We have facial recognition software. We'll find him, don't worry. If he's a resident of Scarborough, he'll go inside a house sooner or later. If there's CCTV on his street, we can get his ID within seconds."

"Thank you," Rita said. "Keep me posted."

Madeleine gave her three photos, with varying degrees of close-up. Rita said, "Can you please distribute these to the teams out on duty? We will put his images through HOLMES and see what we find." HOLMES, or Home Office Large Major Enquiry System, was the British government supercomputer that stored the details of virtually every known criminal on Earth.

Madeleine gave her a thumbs up. "No problem, guv."

Rita went downstairs and showed the team the man's photos.

"This guy's been following me around. I want to know why. He even took the risk of coming outside the police station and then ran away when I chased him." She explained what she had found on CCTV with Madeleine. She pointed at the constables.

"Can one of you please liaise with Madeleine? It might take her some time to find this guy, but we need to bring him in when we find him."

Richard said, "Do you think he's connected to the cold case?"

Rita turned slowly towards him. "That's a good question. It's been bothering me, to be honest. He knew I'd be at my friend's house yesterday night. Now he was outside. Clearly, he knows who I am."

"We'll find him," Richard said firmly, and the constables nodded.

CHAPTER 36

Rita needed to sort her accommodation out and had just received a text from the department. She went outside, crossed the car park, and entered the rear courtyard. The low, squat building that housed the Administration was made of red bricks and had a triangular roof that slanted on both sides. It was decidedly old, not having received a makeover like the main building less than a hundred meters away.

An elderly woman with her black hair tied up in a bun and wearing a bright pink floral dress looked at her suspiciously as she entered. Rita showed her warrant card, and the woman's manner didn’t change. She took her time examining the card, which annoyed Rita.

"DI Gupta. I've recently joined. Accommodation just sent me a text saying they managed to find me quarters. I need to go upstairs."

"Oh yes," the woman said slowly. "I can see that." She handed the warrant card back to Rita, staring at her like she was a visitor from another planet who needed special permission to enter this private sanctuary. Rita raised her eyebrows. "Can you let me in?"

There was a sliding door she had to be buzzed through. Beyond that, through the glass partition, she could see signs on the wall. She had to follow directions to get to the accommodation office.

"Yes," the woman said. She didn't have a name badge, and Rita could tell she was a receptionist and not a very friendly one. The woman grimaced at Rita, as if she had trouble swallowing that morning's breakfast. Then she pressed something under her desk, and the sliding doors opened with a buzzing sound. Shaking her head, Rita went upstairs. At the accommodation office, a thin, balding man called Jim Swales handed her a folder and keys.

"We rent apartments for the force all throughout Scarborough. We managed to find you something a stone's throw from the general hospital. It's not that close to the station, unfortunately. But if you take taxis, you can claim back the travel costs."

Rita thanked him and looked at the property photos in the folder. It was a ground-floor, one-bedroom flat. She would have to pay rent, but it would be at a reduced rate. She thanked Jim and went outside. There was a spring in her step. Sunlight found some respite from the clouds, lighting up her face. She enjoyed the warmth briefly. It was nice to have her own place. It might be a shoebox, and it wouldn't be home, but it would be a damn sight better than a hotel room.

She went up to the forensic department on the third floor and pressed the buzzer. A man's face appeared on the door's glass panel. Rita recognized him as Henry, Shola's colleague and assistant. He opened the door and let Rita in. He blinked behind his glasses. "How can I help you, Inspector?" he asked.

"Is Shola here?"

"No, she's just popped out to her daughter's school. Can I help?"

"Yes, I came to ask about the evidence we had collected. The camcorder and the photo."

Henry's eyes brightened. "Yes, I've searched up on the camcorder." His face became animated, and he moved towards his desk, asking Rita to follow. He had shaved his stubble and wasn't wearing his white coat. He looked smarter in a shirt and tie. He pulled up a chair for Rita to sit.

"I looked into the retail outlets that sold Panasonic video recorders in 1998. I found three stores in Scarborough that stocked it. All three stores have now closed, unfortunately."

"Do you have the name and address of the stores?"

"Yes," he said slowly, looking confused. "But it's not much good, as those businesses don't exist anymore."

Rita thought back to her mother's bank and credit card statements. She hadn't seen a purchase of a camcorder. She could have bought it with cash, of course. Or someone gave it to her.

"I want to visit those locations and also see if we can find anything about them online."

Henry nodded. "Yes, of course." He printed out the data and gave Rita the papers. "You wanted to know about the photo as well?" he asked.

"Yes, did you find anything?"

Henry had a smile on his face. "We haven't dealt with evidence like this in a long time. Personally, I must say I am enjoying it. I've taken various photos myself and looked at them under the microscope. Unfortunately, I can't say we have a location for you as yet. It could be any small town or village along the coast. The sea is the only real landmark." He shrugged. "It might not even be in England. We have to consider that possibility."

Rita stared at him, and the smile on Henry's face faltered. She didn't think the photo showed a town by the sea outside England. In fact, she felt it deep in her bones: that church spire by the sea was somewhere in Scarborough, or very close by.

"When does the electron microscopy come back?"

"In a couple of days. I rang this morning, but the University has a lot of demands for their electron microscopes. They're doing the best they can."

Rita thanked him and went downstairs, and back into the office.

As Rita stepped slowly down the stairs, her thoughts changed gears. She couldn't help thinking why her mother would keep the videotapes and camcorder separate. There was no valid reason.

If Clara went to the trouble of hiding the camcorder, she would have done the same with the tapes. Why would they not be in the same place, behind the bricks? She made up her mind.

She strode back into the office and stood in front of Richard's desk, her thumbs hooked on her waist. Richard looked up at her expectantly, a slightly alarmed look on his face.

"We found the camcorder behind the chimney stack in the loft of the victim's house, but we didn't find the tapes," she said. "I want the chimney stack to be taken down, without destroying the property, obviously. Expose the brickwork, and have a look in all the gaps to make sure we've not missed the tapes hidden somewhere else. Lift up the floor in the loft, if necessary, and have a look. We need to find those tapes."

Rizwan had returned with a stack of printed photos of the man Rita had chased. He said, "That's going to be a big job. We need to get the builders in, and the uniforms will have to supervise it."

Rita turned to him. "I'll speak to the uniforms' duty inspector. We need to get the ball rolling." Her eyes swivelled back to Richard. "Property developers have an ultrasound device they use to look for pipes behind walls or damp. They can be used in police work as well. Do we have any of those machines?"

Richard shook his head. "Not heard of them being used in Scarborough, but I could ring up the scene of crime departments in Leeds and Sheffield and see if they have anything."

"Please do that. I know we're looking for videotapes, which are small objects. But we need to find them. They should be visible with the ultrasound machines."

CHAPTER 37

On her way back to the office, Rita spoke to Dr Das. She had to be careful in her dealings with him. He had seen through her armour, and Rita suspected so had Maggie, although the constable was keeping her silence. Dr Das, on the other hand, had made his feelings known, but she didn't suspect anything malicious in his attitude. She had only seen genuine concern.

"Hello, Doc. It's me, Rita," she said.

"It's my lucky day," Dr Das said, his voice warm and sonorous. She didn't detect any irony. "I'm speaking to you twice in the space of three hours."

"You won't be saying that when I keep calling you," Rita smiled.

Dr Das gave a short laugh. "You wouldn't be the only detective who did that."

"Okay, Doc. I need your help to release the remains for burial. The victim's family has been in touch."

Dr Das paused. "There's nobody to identify, so the next of kin doesn't have to visit the morgue. Do you want us to deliver the remains to the undertaker, or will they collect them from the morgue?"

Rita's mind was busy searching out the options. If the undertaker came to the morgue, she didn't know what questions Dr Das would ask them.

"I'll ask the family to send you the undertaker's address. Is that okay? As long as you think you're all done with the remains, that is. There's no rush."

"Give me till tomorrow," Dr Das said. "I think the majority of the work is done, but I should hear back from the lab by the end of tomorrow."

"Thanks, Doc." Rita hung up and rang the undertaker she had already looked up online. They were Wilson and Sons and had a chain across North Yorkshire. A man answered, introducing himself as Mr. Cuthbert.

He listened to what Rita had to say and then was quiet for a few seconds. "You are the next of kin?"

"Yes."

"Your surname is different from your mother's. Is Gupta your married name?"

"No, it's my father's last name."

She could hear a pen scratching against paper. Mr. Cuthbert said, "I will need a legal document, like an LPA, to show that you are the next of kin."

Rita's eyebrows furrowed in irritation. "What is that?"

"Lasting power of attorney. That proves you have control over your mother's estate and that you are indeed her daughter."

"I've got my mother's birth certificate. It's got her name on it. Won't that do?"

"Yes," Mr. Cuthbert said slowly. "But we need an LPA as well, I'm afraid. We need proof that you will pay for her burial."

Frustration mounted in Rita's veins, but she knew better than to argue. This grim task had to be completed sooner rather than later. She didn't even know what to expect. Apart from Angela and herself, and the possible outlier of Robert Macfarlane, who would even attend the burial? But she owed it to her mother, and to her memories. Clara deserved a proper resting place, where Rita could visit and pay her respects.

"Okay, I'll see what I can do. I'll be in touch."

At times like these, she wished she hadn't given up her cigarettes. That had been five years ago, and it was strange how even the smell of cigarette fumes now annoyed her. But when she was stressed, a hit of nicotine was just what she needed—or so she thought. She went out into the rear car park and leaned against the wall. She searched for the names of solicitor firms in Scarborough, then slammed the phone back into her pocket.

Which lawyer could she trust? She didn't know any of them in Scarborough. Or anywhere up north. In fact, she couldn't remember the last time she had used a solicitor for any purpose. Then a lightbulb went off in her mind, but its light dimmed as she considered her options. Jack Branford. She got the impression he wouldn't mind helping out, but she would have to let him into her secret, and was she ready for that?

Jack knew people who could be her colleagues. Rita's fingers dug into the sides of her skull. How long could she keep this a secret?

It seemed like Dr Das suspected something already. But if people did know, was it so bad? The real issue was her own shame. Her own sense of guilt that she hadn't been able to find her mother, and now that she had, she didn't have a clue as to who her killer was.

Rita started walking. She felt restless suddenly and needed to get it out of her system. She thought about those lonely, heartbreaking days when she felt so desperately sad. Her teenage years were defined by the sorrow of that loss. Her broken heart became mired in guilt, and she had become a police officer to find a way out of that quicksand. But the more she searched for her mother, even as a detective, the deeper she sank into the pits of her own despair.

Until now.

Fate had thrown her a lifeline. But it seemed less a beacon of hope than a noose around her neck, slowly dragging her into its dark depths. She didn't know what she was letting herself into. What she did know, without any doubt, is that she had to see this to the end. Perhaps, a part of that would be sharing her secret with someone she could trust.

She leaned against a tree and rang Jack. He didn't answer. She was walking back into the station, when he called back.

"Hi," she said hesitantly. "It's me."

"Oh, hi, Rita," he sounded surprised, but in a pleasant way. "Is everything okay?" His voice dipped in concern.

"Yes, fine. Look, I need to tell you something." She took a deep breath and poised herself. "I came back because my mother's remains were found. Her skeleton, to be precise. They were in a shallow grave, at Raptor's Viewpoint. It seems she was murdered. I don't want to go into it right now. But I want you to keep this to yourself. It's a very confidential matter."

Jack was silent for a while. His tone was slow and heavy when he replied.

"I'm so sorry. I know how much this affected you."

He was quiet again, and she felt a faint emotion gather around the corners of her heart like water lapping against a barrier. The pressure grew, as did the wetness in her eyes. She blinked them away and sniffed. She was surprised by her spontaneous reaction. It's true that Jack had been there when she was a teenager, trying to find her mother. He helped her, when no one else had. It was a long time ago, but the memories came flooding back. Maybe she should've told Jack sooner.

"I need your help with something. I need a lasting power of attorney drawn up. Without that, I might not be able to bury her. Is that okay?"

"Of course. Come to the office with your passport, birth certificate, and any documents you have that belonged to your mother. Something like her ID, or bank account details. I'll sort it out myself."

Rita looked at her watch. "Is 5 PM today okay?"

"Absolutely fine. I will text you my office address to this number."

Rita thanked him and hung up.

When she got back to the office, everyone stopped talking and stared at her. Rita knew something had happened.

"What?" she asked.

Richard said, "We found the name of the vicar. Duncan Sheldrake. He’s retired now, obviously, and lives just outside Scarborough." He glanced down at the notes he had made. "A village called Wessington. I spoke to his wife. She doesn't mind us dropping by to have a chat."

Rita knew this was an important breakthrough. In the weeks before her death, Clara had argued with the vicar. Rita needed to know why. Her sixth sense was ringing loudly, telling her the vicar knew something he had suppressed all these years. He had never been questioned by the police in connection with Clara. And yet, he had been involved with her; otherwise, they wouldn't have had a heated argument.

"Let's go," she said.

CHAPTER 38

Wessington was a charming little village of yellow and white stone cottages. It was set on the slopes of rolling green hills that went gently down to the seaside.

Rizwan drove, and Rita saw the long stretch of beach as they drove down the hills and the pretty collection of houses before it. They drove through the quiet high street and came to a stop outside a bungalow. The house had a white picket fence and a large front lawn that was well-tended. There was a little pond in the middle, with a miniature Japanese rock garden.

The curtains twitched as Rita walked down the brick path and rang the bell. An elderly woman, with white hair up to her shoulders, opened the door. Her cheeks had sagged with age, and she had deep wrinkles around her jaws and forehead. She peered at Rita through her glasses.

"Are you the police?" she asked.

"Yes," Rita said, and held up her warrant card for the woman to see. The woman peered at it closely, then nodded, satisfied.

"I'm Mrs. Elizabeth Sheldrake. Everyone calls me Liz. Please come in." The woman opened the door and stood to one side. Rita and Rizwan got in, and Liz shut the door.

"I know this is a safe place," Rita said, "but please ask for a stranger's name and identity before you open the door."

Liz said, "My husband is in the living room, and he saw you getting out of the car. He knew who you were."

Rita smiled. "Do we look that obvious? We are in plain clothes, after all. Unless your husband has had some dealings with the police."

"Oh no," Liz shook her head. "He just knew, that's all." Liz looked away, and something in the woman's expression told Rita she wasn't happy. She had agreed to the detectives coming around, but what about her husband?

Rita cleared her throat, and Liz sighed. "This way, please," she said in a resigned tone.

The living room was pleasantly decorated. It was larger than Rita had imagined. The bungalow had a wide footprint, and it was spacious. The living room's walls were painted lavender, and bookshelves stretched across them.

There was a TV in one corner and two sets of fabric sofas facing the TV. Photos of grandchildren rested on the bookshelves. There were also two armchairs, the type where one could recline and put their feet up. The paisley carpet on the floor was deep, and the bay windows let in shafts of sunlight.

An elderly gentleman sat in one of the armchairs, and he straightened as they walked in. Stiffly, he got to his feet. He was tall and thin, but age had bent his spine. His cheeks were sallow and clean-shaven. He still had some white hair left on the sides of his scalp. His dark grey eyes were alert and attentive. He shuffled forward to greet them. Rita shook the gnarled but warm hand.

"Duncan Sheldrake," the man said in a raspy voice. "I used to be a reverend, but that's a long time ago." He smiled, and it touched his eyes. "Please have a seat," he offered. They sat down on the sofa, facing Duncan.

Liz asked if they wanted tea or coffee, which they both politely declined.

Duncan said, "I understand you wanted to speak to me about one of my parishioners."

"Yes." Rita took out her black notebook. "Clara Winters. She used to live on Oak Road near Falsgrave Park. She disappeared on November 22, 1994. Do you remember her?"

Duncan remained impassive, and he blinked a few times. Despite his blank features, Rita saw a jolt in his eyes. His hands moved on his lap, and his right foot twitched.

Rita held his gaze. Duncan grimaced, aware he had to answer. "That was a long time ago, Inspector. I had a lot of parishioners in that area. It was a large congregation."

"Clara's disappearance was a big event. The police questioned many people in that area. They would have been your parishioners. Surely you remember people talking about it?"

"Yes, I do remember. Gosh, that was a terrible thing to happen, wasn't it?" He shook his head, sadness passing like a shadow over his face. "I do remember people talking about it. Everyone was upset." His head lowered as if he was deep in thought.

Rita's gaze would have penetrated a stone wall, and Duncan seemed to shrink under it, like he was being radiated with x-rays. He kept himself erect, his spine supported by the armchair. His hand rose up to his face, and he patted his chin.

Rita asked, "Now that you recall, can you tell me more about Clara Winters? Did you meet her in person?"

Slowly, the old reverend raised his head. He locked eyes with Rita, and his remorseful expression remained unchanged. "Can't say I did, to be honest. Mind you, I met a lot of people in those days. It was part of my job, of course, to listen to people's troubles."

Rita persisted. "But did you talk to Clara Winters, specifically?"

A flicker of emotion passed over Duncan's face, like ripples in a pond. He squared his shoulders, and his eyebrows lowered a fraction. "May I ask what this is about?"

"We have discovered new evidence which sheds light on Clara Winters' disappearance. We believe she may have been murdered." Rita spoke slowly and clearly. The words had their desired effect on Liz, who gasped audibly from behind them. Rizwan turned to the elderly lady, but Rita kept her gaze fixed on Duncan. A rictus of tension now stiffened his neck, and his jaws were taut.

"That's awful," Duncan said.

Rita inclined her head a fraction, still staring at Duncan. "If you could please answer my question. Did you know Clara Winters?"

Duncan spread his hands. "No, I didn't. I remember her disappearance, and it was a tragedy. She had a little daughter, I remember. Everyone felt sorry for that little child. I don't know what happened to her."

A new light danced across his eyes, and he frowned, staring at Rita. He glanced at her black hair, and then looked at her face closely. Rita's heart thumped against her ribs. She could tell Duncan was trying to make a connection between Clara’s child, and what he saw before him.

"I'm sorry to ask this again," she spoke quickly. "But did you speak to Clara Winters before she died?"

Duncan’s eyebrows raised, and a puzzled expression appeared on his face. Rita felt he was being insincere, masking his true feelings behind his expressions.

"Not that I recall. Inspector, I'm not sure why you're asking me these questions. I understand you have a job to do, but believe me, I don't know anything about it. The police didn't question me at the time. I heard of the unfortunate news from my parishioners."

Rita went for the jugular. She had enough of treading softly.

"About two weeks before Clara's death, one of your parishioners saw you arguing with Clara. It was so heated, in fact, that you had to take Clara to one side, where the rest of the congregation wouldn't hear your conversation."

Rita paused. Duncan's chest seemed to fall inwards, and his shoulders were bravely trying to hold him upright. His spine was folding, collapsing him deeper into the armchair.

"What did you argue about?"

Duncan blinked several times, and his right hand rose again, touching his forehead. He seemed lost in the rivers of time, his mind drawn far back. "I… I don't know, inspector. I don't remember, I'm sorry."

"To have an argument, you must have been closely involved with Clara Winters. What was the nature of your relationship?"

Duncan tried to shrug, but his body was so stiff his shoulders barely moved. A tightness had claimed his face, and his lips barely moved when he spoke.

"I didn't have any sort of relationship with her. Some of the parishioners helped out with the soup kitchen for homeless people at St. Matthew's Church. They also helped to organize events, and the church fair. They raised money, which was looked after by the church secretary. That was Sister Philomena, who has now passed away, God rest her soul. Maybe this woman was one of those parishioners who helped out?"

"And if Clara did so," Rita carried on like a bloodhound running after meat, "she must have had an important position in the church. If so, you would remember her, wouldn't you?"

"Inspector, I really don't know what this is about. You're talking about a long time ago, and I'm afraid my memory isn't what it used to be. I'm getting tired now, can we please stop this?"

He raised both hands, as if he was trying to push away the past.

Rita looked behind, where Liz was sitting very quietly, observing them. "What about you, Mrs. Sheldrake?" Rita asked. "Do you remember Clara Winters and her disappearance?"

Liz's lips moved, but no sound emerged. Then she cleared her throat. "Yes, I remember. It was awful, like Duncan said. I never went to St. Matthew's Church, and I don't know what happened." She stared back directly at her husband. Rita followed her gaze. Duncan wasn't looking at his wife. His large hand cradled his head, and he was looking at the carpet like he was exhausted.

Rita stood. She stepped forward, and Duncan seemed to flinch as she approached. She took out her card and gave it to Duncan. He accepted it with a shaking hand.

"Please call me if you remember anything. We are going to find out what happened to Clara Winters."

She glanced at Rizwan, who was diligently taking notes in his notebook. She nodded at him, and they walked out of the living room. Liz sat there staring at her husband, who looked as if he was in a dream, with his eyes open.

“By the way,” Rita asked, addressing Duncan. “Do you know a man called Edward Salt?”

A vacant expression appeared on Duncan’s face. Rita felt again he was deliberately trying to look lost, and not really succeeding.

“Can’t say I do. Why?”

“Mr Salt had business dealings with Clara Winters. He might have been your parishioner as well.”

Duncan shook his head slowly. “No, Inspector. I don’t know anyone of that name.”

“He’s a prominent businessman in this area, actually,” Rita said airily, as if her comment didn’t matter. “Owns fisheries, nightclubs and properties. I wonder what a man like him would want with a supermarket worker like Clara.”

Behind the blank look on Duncan’s face, Rita could see his jaws moving, and chest moving a little faster. His Adam’s apple bobbed up and down as he swallowed hard. He shrugged, the vacant look in his eyes now gone. He shrugged, feigning nonchalance.

“I’m not sure what you want me to say.”

“So you didn’t know Mr Salt?”

“I just told you, Inspector. No, I didn’t.”

“How about Lord Alfred Northallerton?”

Duncan shook his head. “No, sorry, I don’t.”

Rita stared at him for a while, till it became uncomfortable. Duncan stared back at her, then coughed into a fist. Rita nodded at him, and then at Liz.

"We'll see ourselves out," Rita said.

*****

Duncan waited until the front door was shut. He got up slowly, his back and hips hurt most of the day, and the pains were worse when he was sitting for a while. He shuffled to the window, and watched the female detective and her younger assistant. The young man got into the driver's seat, but the woman stood there, watching his house. Her black hair flew in the wind, and she dragged a hand across her face. Something about her seemed familiar.

Could she be Clara's child?

He trembled suddenly, like the wind outside had found its way in the living room. He watched the woman get into the car, and drive away.

Duncan brushed past Liz, who was walking back into the living room. He didn't look at her, but felt her eyes on his back. He went into his room, and shut the door. He took down a thick Bible from the shelf. Behind it, there was a small safe.

He opened it, and took out a phone. It still had some charge left. He turned the phone on, and then walked through the kitchen, into the garden. He made sure the patio door was firmly shut. The garden was big, and he walked down the stone path that led to the tall trees at the rear. When he turned, he didn't see Liz standing by the patio door.

He dialled a number he hadn't used for so long, he's almost forgotten it existed. But it was there. Indelible, like the torture now unfolding like a fire in his soul. The phone rang for almost ten rings before the man answered.

“Hello. Long time.” The heavy voice was still unmistakably familiar.

“We need to talk,” Duncan said.

CHAPTER 39

Rizwan said, "I don't trust that man as far as I can throw him.”

Riz was driving up into the hills, the landscape gently cascading into undulating patterns of green and blue all around them.

"I got that impression too," Rita said. "He knew who Clara Winters was."

She paused, thinking about the moment when the vicar had stared at her like he recognized her. Her heart had stopped, and even now, she wondered if he had made the connection. She sighed and looked out the window.

This case was opening up into a dark and dangerous space, and she could see the yawning chasm appear, pulling her deeper into it. Voices whispered in her head, dangerous murmurs from a distant past.

"Why is he lying," Rizwan remarked. It was a statement, not a question. "If he had an argument with the victim 27 years ago, who cares? There might be a simple explanation. Perhaps she had messed up one of the church affairs. Or she lost some money the church collected." Rizwan shrugged. "I don't know."

Rita glanced at him. “Very good. You’re right. There was no need to be defensive about what could’ve been a small matter many years ago.”

“Ergo,” Rizwan said, sounding very posh all of a sudden, making Rita smile. “It wasn’t a small matter.”

“That’s right, Detective.”

They were silent for a while. The car raced along the picturesque road, the sea now appearing on their right. Shafts of sunlight lit up patches on the restless, grey waters. Pools of light were starting to illuminate the dark corners of Rita's mind. And she didn't like the picture that was emerging.

"He's lying because he has something to lose if he speaks the truth," Rita murmured. She glanced at Rizwan, then her vision flickered back to the road. The black asphalt was bisected by a white line that curved to the left. The road disappeared between the green folds of the hills.

"Has to be something important if he is still hiding it after all these years," Rizwan said.

"Yes," Rita whispered. She realized now she knew very little of her mother's life. Clara had led a double existence, and her second life had been a secret from everyone.

The phone rang, and it was Richard. Rizwan pressed a dial on the dashboard, and the voice appeared on the loudspeaker. "Two things," Richard said. "We found the shop where the Panasonic camcorder was purchased from. Remarkably, the shop still exists, on the high street. It's still an electronic shop, owned by the same family."

"Fancy that," Rizwan said. "They didn't sell out to a big chain."

"No, they didn't. And the old owner is still alive, his son now runs the business. They have archives over the last 30 years, stored in disk drives. Mr. Whittington, the business owner, still has the files in his attic. Floppy drives, remember those?"

Rizwan looked perplexed, and Rita had to smile. "You were probably still in nappies then," she said to Rizwan. She asked Richard, "Do we have the data from the floppy disks?"

"That's what Maggie and I have been working on," Richard said. "Clara Winters bought the camcorder in 1993, and she also purchased four videotapes. We have the serial numbers of the videotapes."

"Does that help us in locating them?"

"Not really. The victim bought them, but what she did with them is anyone's business. All we know is that it's not in the property. The builders are in the house now, and they have removed most of the chimney stack. There's nothing in there, I'm sorry to say, guv."

Rita pressed her lips together. "What about the ultrasound machines to look behind the walls?"

"They're doing that as we speak. So far, apart from the usual pipes, they have not found anything of interest. They have done the loft and first floor, and are now doing the ground floor, and outside. Something might be buried in the garden, you never know."

"Thanks, keep looking. Anything else?"

"I saved the best till last," Richard said, and there was a note of excitement in his voice.

"Go on then," Rizwan urged. "Spit it out."

"The drones have found a burnt-out car about 2 miles from Raptor's Viewpoint and the crime scene. It's a wreck, and it looks decades old. Uniforms have cordoned off the area. Shola and Henry are on their way to inspect it."

Adrenaline pulsed through Rita's veins, and she sat up straighter. Her eyes widened, and a heady concoction of hope and fear surged in her heart. That could be her mother's car. The killer had destroyed it and managed to hide it all these years.

"Do you have any news of the model or the make?"

"Not yet, guv. We are still waiting to hear back."

"Send us the coordinates," Rita said. "I want to see it."

*****

It took them almost an hour to get to Raptor's Viewpoint. En route, they stopped at a café to pick up coffee and biscuits. Doughnuts for Rizwan, which the young man ate with relish as Rita drove. She eyed him enviously, declining his offer of trying one.

As they got closer to the looming, dense forest of the Yorkshire moors, Rita felt the tension thicken in her blood. They parked, and she wasted no time in trudging up the trail through the dense patchwork of pine trees and undergrowth. Rizwan followed a few paces behind. From his strenuous breathing, she could tell he was making an effort to keep up with her.

Although the car wreckage was found 2 miles away, cutting through the forest in a straight line didn't take that long. They went down the slope and had to cross a shallow river. Wooden logs had been placed over it, creating a makeshift bridge. They were in a valley, with steep hills rising on either side. Paths snaked in through the dense undergrowth, and Rita assumed some of them must be wide enough to let a car through. The killer had driven the car down from wherever Clara had parked. If, of course, this car had belonged to Clara.

Soon, they saw the blue and white tape and the two uniformed constables standing guard. A scene of crime van had appeared on the right edge of the clearing. In the middle, the undergrowth had been hacked away to reveal the remains of the wreck.

Weeds and plants had grown between the rusting hulk.

The charred remains had turned black, and wind and rain had done their best to corrode what remained of the metal. Rita signed her name on the clipboard, then accepted the mask, apron, and shoe covers with a murmur of thanks. Richard was already there, kneeling to the left of the wreck, observing it closely. Next to him, Shola was inspecting a piece of the bodywork with a tablet device. She held it with both hands and scanned it slowly across the rim of the wheel space.

They both turned when they saw Rita behind them.

"This is a digital image enhancer app," Shola said, holding up the tablet device. "You can buy it as an app and put it on the tablet. Much better than a microscope or magnifying glass."

Rita surveyed the wreckage, a strange, hollow sensation in the pit of her stomach. "Have you found anything? What make is the car?"

Richard said, "We found the brand logo, didn't we?"

Shola nodded, and they walked to the rear of the car. The vehicle had tilted to the left, the wheels sinking into the earth. The entire car had slid, and the lid of the boot had detached, lying on top of the wreck.

Rita wasted no time in crouching by the rear bumper, trying to read the logo. Rust covered it, and when she wiped it with her hand, more crumbling, black metal came off in her hands. She scratched at it until she saw the red and brown logo appear. What remained of it anyway, it was hard to see with the naked eye.

"Here, I took some photos with the image enhancer," Shola said. She gave Rita the tablet device. She flicked through it, and the logo of the Volkswagen Polo was now clearly visible. Blood lurched in Rita's limbs. Her vision swayed, blurring, and she blinked to sharpen her focus.

Clara used to drive a Volkswagen Polo. She remembered the small car, and judging from the wreckage in front of her… it was either the same car or the same model. But had it belonged to Clara? Or was it just an accident, a cruel twist of fate that another random car just happened to be here?

Her sixth sense told her this wasn't a mere coincidence. After all these years, she still recognized the rusting wreckage. Emotion trembled in the corners of her heart, clutching at her throat. She felt it deep in her bones. This was her mother's car. No, she didn't have the proof as yet. That would be in the chassis number and in the confirmation from the manufacturer.

She turned to Richard and asked him. "Yes," he said sombrely. "We managed to find the chassis number on the underside. It wasn't easy, but we got it. As soon as we get back to the station, I'll email the manufacturer."

CHAPTER 40

Lord Alfred Northallerton was a stout, portly man. He didn't like the weight he had put on in the last decade, but he had reached that age where he didn't care anymore. He finished speaking to Duncan Sheldrake, then slowly put the phone down. His right hand rested on his ample belly, and he stared at the black mahogany table top.

The long office stretched ahead of him. He was on the first floor of the Northallerton Manor home. The home had twenty bedrooms, and the living quarters were at the rear. The office faced the front of the house, and the long gravel drive that led to the broad wrought iron gates, which were invisible from the window.

Alfred got up and walked to the French windows that extended from floor to ceiling. The sky was cloudy, and the gloom descended upon the vast fields in front of him, across the gravel drive. He could see the fountain in the distance, built by his great grandfather in the late 1800's.

The family had made its money from the sugar business, in India and the West Indies. The good old day of the colonies. No one asked questions those days. It was harder to make money now. He could only do business in England, and that meant being accountable. And being honest. Two qualities he doubted his ancestors had maintained when they built their empire.

But Alfred had no choice. He had to be accountable, especially when problems like this reared their ugly head. Accountable to his family fortune, which he couldn't allow going to waste. Neither could Edward Salt, for that matter.

Alfred called the butler, and asked the driver to get his car ready. The Porsche, not the Bentley. Alfred would be driving himself today. True, the Porsche 911 Carrera wasn't exactly inconspicuous, but he wanted to be alone for his meeting.

His phone chimed, and it was his wife, Melanie. "Are you going to be here for lunch, dear?"

"No," he sighed. "I've got a meeting in York. I'll be back for dinner though."

"Everything okay?" Melanie said. She was clearly used to the changes in his mood. Perhaps he should've sounded more upbeat.

"All good sweetheart. I'll see you soon."

He sensed her scepticism, but hung up quickly. The family business was in trouble. They had moved from sugar to property, and that market was down now. His father, Robert, had a gambling habit, and his two failed marriages to women far younger than him had drained the family coffers. Alfred had learnt from that, and stuck to his wife and two boys. The boys were now starting to take charge of various property portfolios. One was in Edinburgh now, and the other in London.

He thought of the shit storm that would unfold if this news hit the fans. The boys, and their legacy, would be affected, no doubt. He couldn't allow that to happen. Alfred went down the sweeping curve of the stairs, and into the large reception hall. His driver was waiting by the Porsche, just outside the main doors. Alfred's boots crunched on the gravel. He took the keys from the driver, thanked him, and started the engine.

The deep throttle of the Porsche's powerful engine always pleased him. He drove out slowly, through the wide iron gates, then picked up speed as he drove along the single lane that led to the main road.

In forty-five minutes, he had reached the disused warehouse in the outskirts of Scarborough. Graffiti adorned the walls of the rusting hulk. It was large, this had been a brewery that strangely enough, his family had owned, almost fifty years ago. Alfred parked under the shade of trees, where the car was hidden. Up ahead, he could see Duncan's little Fiat Punto.

He went inside the warehouse. The corrugated iron roof had caved in, and the doors were now missing. He looked up as he heard the tap of falling water.

Tepid sunlight slanted in through the cracks in the iron sheets, and water dripped from one corner.

A voice cleared its throat, and moments later, Duncan Sheldrake appeared from behind a disused fork lift truck. He stood there motionless, watching Alfred as he came forward.

"Thanks for coming," Alfred said. Duncan nodded in silence. The old man was looking pale, Alfred thought. His sagging cheeks were bereft of colour, and behind the square frame glasses, his eyes had a haunted look on them, as if he'd just seen a ghost.

"So, the body belonged to Clara Winters? The skeleton, I mean."

Duncan nodded in silence again. Then he spoke. "And the police have proof it was her. They also know she was murdered."

Alfred's face twisted. "How do they know that? All they found was a skeleton."

"I don't know. This detective won't leave it alone. She's got an axe to grind, I think."

"What do you mean?"

Duncan had a glimmer in his eyes now, and a tension in his jaws. He swallowed once. "Clara had a little girl. I think her name was Rita."

Alfred felt a stab of uneasiness. "So?"

"This detective is also called Rita. Gupta is her surname, but that could be her father's last name."

"What does she look like?"

"Tall and slim. Long black hair. She looks mixed race. Half Indian, I think, given that last name. She reminds me of Clara. Same green eye colour."

The twist in Alfred's face was now descending into his guts, coiling up like a serpent.

"I spoke to Ed. Damn it. Clara's daughters come back as a bloody detective? And she's investigating her mother's death as a murder?"

Duncan nodded, the light dying in his eyes, but the hardness in his jaws remaining. "Sounds strange but I think so. And that's not all. She knows about Edward, too. I daresay she's found out about you as well."

Alfred breathed faster, the coil in his stomach now turning into nausea. "I know. Ed told me." Then he stopped. "Ed told mem about the land lease contracts. But has she found out about…"

Duncan spoke quickly. "I don't know. The fact that she asked me about Ed, and then you, is weird."

Alfred closed his eyes, and shook his head in frustration. "Call Ed and let him know. We need to deal with this before it gets any worse."

"You need to call your man. Make sure he's aware."

Alfred held eyes with Duncan, and he understood perfectly. "I'll tell him," Alfred said quietly.

CHAPTER 41

Light was fading from the sky as Rita drove back. Richard was the driver this time, Rizwan having returned early to help Maggie with the paperwork. Rita's tired mind was busy passing through the details of the day. She pulled out her black notebook and went through the list of evidence.

"The necklace," she murmured, then glanced at Richard. "Any news from Reilly's, the jewellers?"

Richard shook his head. "Maggie has reached out to them. They have a shop in York, the nearest city to ours, but they haven't gotten back to us with any details yet."

The blue velvet shroud of evening was deepening over the hills, and the sea in the distance was a dark, seething mass, more felt than visible. As they got closer to Scarborough, Rita saw the outline of the castle against the evening sky. It was past 5 o'clock, and she was late to meet Jack. They parked, and she called him. He was still at the office, and she promised him she would be there in half an hour.

The two constables were still busy at work. "Maggie said Dr Das tried to call you. He said it's about the knife manufacturer."

"He probably didn't get a signal on my phone as I was at the crime scene," Rita said. She called Dr Das, and the pathologist answered.

"Hi Rita. The results of the metal alloy have come back from the lab. It's a little different from what I expected. This is actually an old composition, used in the last century. There's more brass and tin in it, metals we don't use anymore. The chances of it being a modern machete are slim to none."

Rita frowned. "What does that mean?"

"It means the murder weapon was probably a sword or an axe used more than a hundred years ago. Such instruments are rare these days. It also helps us to narrow down our search. We can now look for antique dealers who still sell these weapons. There are a number of them across the North East. Your team should be able to find them."

"Still a needle in a haystack," Rita said. "Do you have anything more specific?"

"That's all I have, unfortunately," Dr Das said. "Did you get hold of Reilly's?"

"We're still waiting. Thanks for this, Doc. We'll start looking." Rita hung up. She rested her butt against a desk and folded her hands across her chest. She bowed her head in thought. When she looked up, three pairs of eyes were focused on her. She repeated what Dr Das had said.

"An antique weapon," Maggie echoed. "There can't be that many shops that sell them."

"Or sold them thirty years ago," Richard said. "We might have to look for shops that have closed down now."

"Let's start searching early tomorrow. For now, go home. All of you. It's been a long day."

Richard said, "The builders have finished their search in the victim's former home. Ultrasound scans of the ground floor and the front and rear gardens haven't revealed anything." He raised both hands, then flopped them down on the table softly. "I'm sorry, guv. No sign of the videotapes."

"It was worth a look," Rita said. "Well done. Now we need to ask our suspects." She strode to the whiteboard. Under Edward Salt's name, she wrote down Duncan Sheldrake. "These two men know a lot more about Clara than they're letting on."

Maggie said, "I have also found out where Mr Salt lives. It's in Briggs, a posh village about 30 miles from Scarborough. It's close to good schools, and lots of rich people live there."

"Good," Rita said. "Send me the address, just in case." Rita massaged the weariness in her forehead. She realized she hadn't seen her new apartment yet. She'd be visiting it for the first time in the evening, and she would have preferred to have seen it in the daytime. But at least she had somewhere to live. She now had to return to the hotel, pack her stuff, and then head out to her new quarters.

"See you tomorrow," she said. She pointed at all three of them. "No staying back. Go home, now." She smiled at them. They were a diligent, hard-working trio. She had only known them a couple of days, but she was beginning to like them. They were working in sync, and the early signs were positive.

They left together, Richard locking the door behind them. "Would you like a lift?" Maggie asked.

"No, it's okay. I'll just take a cab."

"It's no bother, honestly. Where do you need to go?"

"At the Mayfield and Weathers law firm, on the high street."

"That's on my way home," Maggie said. "Jump in."

They said goodbye to Richard and Rizwan, and walked to the car park. Rita strapped herself into the passenger seat of Maggie's black Astra.

"How are things at the media liaison office? Any approach from journalists?" Rita asked, as Maggie came out of the car park and took a left. She stopped at the traffic lights before turning left at the junction where the man who had followed Rita was last seen.

"Pretty good. No sign of reporters yet," Maggie said. She started to drive as the lights turned green.

Rita looked at both sides of the street, at the brightly lit cafés and restaurants. She thought of the man she had chased down. This wasn't a professional stalker, she knew that much. Only an amateur would wear those white clothes and make it obvious that he was on her tail. She wondered if it could be a reporter.

"Anything on the news? Or social media?" Rita asked.

Maggie shook her head. "I did look on my phone. Nothing on social media, as yet. Only a matter of time, though."

Rita nodded, and they drove in silence for a while. Rita felt Maggie's eyes on her, and the constable quickly looked away when she returned her gaze.

"Anything the matter?" Rita asked gently.

"No, I was just wondering if you're okay. You didn't seem very well after we saw the skeleton at the crime scene."

"Oh yes, I'm fine." She smiled, but it was forced. "Just brought back some old memories, that's all." The words slipped out before she could stop them. She cursed in silence and looked out the window.

Maggie nodded in sympathy. "I hope you find out who did that to the poor woman. I can't believe she was pregnant."

Rita sighed. "Neither can I."

They battled through the traffic, and finally got to the High Street. Rita waved at Maggie after the constable dropped her off outside the lawyer's office.

It was a Victorian building, three stories high, and made of red bricks. It looked like an old bank building. The logo of Mayfield and Weathers was displayed in white letters across the front.

A secretary was still inside as Rita walked in through the glass door, which chimed as she entered. The young woman looked up as Rita got closer. Rita showed her warrant card, and the woman nodded.

"Mr. Banford is waiting for you," the woman said, rising. "This way, please." She led Rita down a narrow corridor with wood-paneled walls and modern art hanging from the panels. She knocked on a door that said "Jack Bamford, Partner."

It was a pleasant office, in keeping with the brown wood panels of the corridor outside. Jack rose from behind a large mahogany desk. Behind it, the windows were dark in the evening, with yellow streetlights visible beyond. The corners of his eyes crinkled as his lean, square-jawed face broke into a smile. He shut the door behind the secretary and pulled up a chair for Rita.

"How are you?" he asked. "Would you like a drink?"

"No," Rita said, waving her hands. Jack wore a blue checked shirt that hugged his wide shoulders and narrowed at the waist. His light grey eyes rested on hers.

"Long day?" He smiled.

"You could say that," Rita sighed. "I keep uncovering things that I can't make sense of." She lapsed into silence, not wishing to give away too many details about the case.

Jack nodded, observing her. "I'm sorry. I know how much this must be affecting you. You looked for your mother after she disappeared, and I remember those days. You didn’t stop when you were doing your A-levels."

The memories came back like patches of sunlight piercing the clouds. Jack had helped her distribute leaflets in the neighbour’s houses. She had done so on the advice of the detectives who had searched for her mother. They got nothing out of it, and that only sharpened Rita's hunger to find out the truth.

Back then, Jack had been her confidant, her real friend. Yes, she had her three girlfriends as well, but she was closest to Jack. It seemed like a lifetime ago. And it was. Their lives had moved on, but the memories lingered.

Jack picked up a folder and gave her the last page from a stack of papers. "I've created the lasting power of attorney document from what you sent me. The undertakers like to make a fuss about these things, and so do the banks. But don't worry. You've got enough evidence that you are your mother's daughter. Just sign on the line over here and date it."

He rested a finger on the dotted line. Rita signed it and then sat back in her chair.

"If you give me the undertaker's address, I'll send it directly to them." He shrugged. "That makes it look more official, that's all."

"Thank you. How much do I owe you?"

They both smiled, holding each other's eyes. "It's okay," Jack said lightly. "I'm not going to charge you."

Rita shook her head vigorously. "No way." She didn't want any favours from Jack or anyone else. More importantly, she didn't want Jack to think she needed any favours. She could have gone to another lawyer and gotten the same service, after all.

She gave him her card, sliding it across the desk. "My email is on there. Send me an invoice. Please."

Jack glanced at it, a brief spasm of disappointment moving across his handsome face. He looked different now. His eyes had a harder glint, the high cheekbones sharper. He seemed thinner, and fitter than he had been in his youth, his wide shouldered form now more masculine.

"If you insist," he said.

Rita smiled at him to make sure there was no hard feelings. “Yes, I do.” Then she rubbed her hands on her trousers, and stood. "I best get going." She patted her pockets. "I've got my own apartment now, thankfully."

"That's great," Jack said. A little mischief danced in his eyes, or did she imagine it? "I guess we'll see more of you then," he said.

She grinned. "It's only a two-bedroom flat that I'm renting. Hardly setting down roots."

"Well, that's how it starts," Jack said easily. "Before you know it, you'll be buying a car."

She had been thinking exactly that on her way here. Without a car in Scarborough, moving around was difficult.

Jack said, "I can drop you off at your apartment. Where is it?"

"Oh, don't worry. I need to get to the hotel first and pack my stuff. Won't take me long. Then I'll head down to the apartment."

Jack looked at his watch. "It's 6:30 already. I'm on my way home, anyway." He opened his desk drawer and pulled out car keys. Then he picked up his jacket draped across the back of his chair.

"Come on, I'm giving you a lift back to the hotel, and then I'll wait while you pack your stuff." Rita started to protest, but he raised a hand. "I won't hear of it." He stared at her, and Rita could see that he was serious. In her own mind, she was relieved. Her forehead throbbed with a headache, and her limbs were weary from the day's activities.

She stood and grinned at him. "If you insist," she said, echoing his earlier words. He held the door open for her.

"Yes, I do," he said.

They came out of the offices, and then walked to the car park at the side. Rita put her hand on the sleeks BMW’s door handle and stopped.

“I don’t want you to think I’m making a habit of getting lifts from you,” she said. “Twice in one day.”

“Twice in like, twenty years?” His grin was visible in the half glow from the streetlights.

“Well, I’ll be sure to call you next time I’m in Scarborough. Who needs an Uber?”

They got into the car. Rita smiled at him. “You do have the best taxi in town, I daresay.”

“That I do.”

Jack reversed the car, and then joined the traffic on the road. As he sped up, Rita caught a flicker of movement on her right. A man had run out from the side alley opposite. She caught a flash of his white shirt, and the white trainers. Clean shaven, and he didn’t wear glasses. He ran after the car, then slowed down as the car slowed in traffic. It was the man who was following her around.

"Stop!" Rita shouted. Her hand went on the door handle, but the car was still moving.

"What's the matter?" Jack pressed on the brakes, diverting his eyes from the car in front, to glance at her. His head swivelled to his right to follow his line of sight.

"That man, he's following me."

Her eyes were focused on the street behind her, but the man seemed to have realised he had been spotted. He had slowed down. The car moved forward; Jack couldn't stop as the cars behind him were getting closer. Then Rita couldn't see the man anymore. Either he was hiding, or…her head whipped around as she looked in every direction. The man had disappeared.

Jack's face was taut with tension. "What do you want to do?"

"Nothing," Rita said, settling back into her chair. The man was still following her, and that wasn't good news. He would definitely be caught on CCTV, she realised. And he was still wearing white trainers. She frowned. Why was this guy such an amateur? No vigilante, or criminal, would wear a white shirt and shoes at night. It made her wonder if he wanted to be found out. In that case – why didn't he just walk into the station and speak to her?

"Why is he following you?"

She looked at Jack. A bead of sweat trickled down the side of his forehead, and he was still tense. She felt bad.

“I’m sorry. I should’ve taken a taxi. This is not your problem.”

“Are you bloody joking?” His jaws hardened. His eyes were like flints as he glanced at her. “You’re a guest in our town, eh? No one messes with my mates.”

She had to smile at the typical Yorkshire attitude. That’s one thing she missed down south. People up north were a different sort. Tougher, in many ways, and friendlier.

The traffic moved on, and soon they were from the knot of cars, and the BMW’s powerful 3 litre engine smooth picked up speed on the A road. The hotel wasn’t far from the high street. Jack pulled up in the front yard.

“I’ll wait for you here,” he said. Rita felt relieved. She had no intention of inviting Jack up to her room. She went up swiftly and packed her bags. She just stuffed everything, dirty laundry included, into the sole suitcase she had. She hurried down to see Jack standing at the door. He took the suitcase from her, despite her protests.

“Boy, am I glad I don’t have to live there anymore,” she sighed as Jack drove out.

"Not good?"

She grimaced. "Just impersonal, you know? Another hotel room. Not like having my own space. Looking forward to my flat."

"I hear that. During the divorce, and after, I lived in one of my rental flats. It was small and cramped, and bloody hard with the children in it. I slept on the lounge floor so they could have a room each. Then I had to rent a house, and with the lawyer costs, I became bankrupt."

She glanced at him. "Three years ago, right?"

"Yes. Things are better now, thank god."

"Glad to hear it."

Jack navigated to the residential street near the hospital. The houses were semi-detached and large, with well kept front lawns. One of the larger detached townhouses had been separated into flats, and that's where Rita had her apartment.

"Number 54," Jack said, peering into the dark. "Is that right? My eyes aren't what they used to be."

"I can see fine." She said, and grinned when she caught his eyes.

"You're six months younger," he grumbled. Rita laughed at that. She was surprised he remembered.

They got out, and she went to the front door, fishing out her keys. A front door light came on, making her task easier. Jack got her suitcase to the door. She went inside, but Jack remained where he was. She turned. It was rude not to invite him in for a cup of tea, but she didn't want him to stay. He was being nice, but she had no time for anything more than friendship. She hoped her attitude had made that clear.

"Come in," she said. The lights on the landing came on with the motion sensors. There was a door to her left, which made the landing smaller. Straight ahead, another door led into the ground floor flat which was hers. The key turned into the lock and Rita stepped inside.

Wooden floors continued from the landing. A small corridor led to two doors on the right, and a kitchen and living area at the rear. The open plan kitchen was large, with a TV and sofa set opposite the kitchen counter.

She checked the main bedroom. It had space to walk around in after a king-sized bed, double wardrobe and desk chair. She parted the curtains and looked at the darkness outside. The sash windows were long, and the wood was well maintained. It was nice to have a spacious bedroom, after the cramped living spaces of London. She was glad.

Jack was in the kitchen, sitting at one of the counter bar stools. He stood when she came back. "Good?"

"Yes," she sighed. "Better than I hoped, really."

"Sure you're going to be okay? I mean, there's some weirdo following you around." His eyebrows knotted together.

"I'll be fine, don't worry."

"I would say call the police, but I guess there's no point." He shrugged, and she smiled.

"Thanks for everything," she said, and meant it.

"All I did was give you a lift. Anytime." He held her eyes for a few seconds, then looked away. "I best get going."

She nodded, and walked him to the door. He waved at the entrance, and she did the same. Then she shut the door and locked it. She went into the bedroom and collapsed on the bed, shutting her eyes for the first time that day.

CHAPTER 42

The Guardian stood motionless in the shadows, hidden behind a rubbish dump. He was watching the entrance of the Mayfield and Weathers solicitors' offices. The High Street was still busy with evening traffic, and no one noticed him slip down the side alley. He had followed the inspector and the constable as they left the police station.

His car was a black Ford Fiesta, more than a decade old. Millions of cars like his existed on England's roads, and he knew he wasn't noticeable. Just an average man, minding his own business. He smiled to himself. If only the world knew what he was capable of—the rivers of blood he would unleash to remain true to himself. He was the Guardian, after all, the protector. As long as he was alive, the secrets of the brotherhood would remain intact.

He watched the constable drive away. She was a pretty little thing. If it hadn't been for the black-haired inspector and her exotic looks, he would have considered going for the female constable. He smiled wolfishly in the darkness. It was good to have options.

More than half an hour passed, and he wondered what the inspector was doing inside the solicitors' office. He hoped she wasn't digging deeper into the brotherhood's secrets. Only time would tell, but he was getting a bad feeling. Alarm bells had sounded in the distant corridors of power. Old ghosts were being rudely awakened. The balance was shifting, creaky doors full of dust forcibly opened. The Guardian breathed faster, and his lips curled into a snarl. It was his job to make sure the secrets remained buried. He wouldn't tolerate an upstart like this new inspector disrupting the symmetry of history.

Time passed slowly, and he occupied himself with thoughts of what he would do to the inspector when he finally got his hands on her. Right now, he was enjoying playing cat and mouse. The thrill passed through him, becoming a shudder of delight. How fresh her skin would feel when his hands closed around her throat. How soft her limbs would be when she had stopped struggling. That was the moment he liked best—their body suddenly going dead and limp, and then he could do as he pleased. Patience was the key virtue now, and he knew how to wait. Patience brought its own rewards.

Ahead of him, a shadow shifted past the bus station and turned into the alley. He crouched instinctively and then peered down the side. A man stood there, but he too had crept into the shadows, as if he didn't want to be seen. He wore a white shirt and white trainers. He turned around and leaned against the wall, watching the solicitors' office as well. There was something familiar about his posture. The Guardian racked his brains, and a distant memory ignited. Tension spasmed in his belly, and his eyes widened. Could it be...? Then he shook his head. With it, came a new found worry. If this man was here, what did he know?

The front door of the solicitors' office opened, and the Inspector stepped out, followed by a man dressed smartly in a dark suit. He was tall, with a square-jawed, sharp-nosed face. He said something to the inspector, and the Guardian could see she didn't mind his proximity.

Jealousy stabbed him like a knife. She was his now, a deranged voice screamed inside his head. How dare she! Bloody harlot! The Guardian wanted her just for himself. He wouldn't let another man lay a finger on her.

He watched as the couple disappeared down the side of the building, and moments later, a sleek BMW trundled slowly down the car park, its headlights glowing like a pair of eyes in the darkness. The Guardian saw Rita and her male friend in the car.

The man in front of him detached himself from the wall. He got closer to the road but still remained hidden. As the car swept past them, he saw the man move quickly, running down the road. Well, that was stupid, the Guardian thought. He picked up pace as well, but he didn't run like the other guy. That just attracted attention.

He increased his pace and saw that the man had now come to a stop, realizing he couldn't chase the car. He turned around, and the Guardian hid himself swiftly, stepping inside the bus stand. From the corner of his eye, he saw the man walk towards him but not notice him. An electric jolt of ignited in his spine.

Of course, he knew that man.

His initial suspicion had been correct. He was a lot older now, but the Guardian never forgot his preys. Especially the ones that got away.

He gave the man a head start, then followed him leisurely. Mark, that's what his name was. Mark Strong, unless the Guardian was mistaken.

He smiled thinly to himself. It would be nice catching up with Mark. Then his smile faded. What the hell was Mark doing up here? There must be a reason. There was no need for him to be in Scarborough. Unless he had heard about the skeleton, and somehow, he knew it belonged to Clara.

Was that why Mark was following the Inspector? Did he want to confront her and tell her what he knew? The Guardian's jaw set tightly. His hands became fists. He could never allow that to happen.

Mark went inside a pub, and the Guardian stopped outside. He knew the cameras inside would pick him out. It was bad enough watching out for CCTV.

Mark however didn't seem to care if he was caught on the cameras. That worried the Guardian.

Anxiety condensed into anger in his mind. He was prone to fits of pure rage. His hands became fists, and he slammed them against his legs. Mark would pay like the others had. Like Clara had.

Another thought struck him. Was Mark alone? He knew about the others. He needed to make sure they weren't acting together.

He waited for Mark. Patience was a virtue. Eventually, Mark emerged.

He followed Mark again, and this time, the man did some food shopping, then went into a fast food restaurant. Again, the Guardian stayed out of sight, and away from the cameras he knew were present inside the restaurant.

Doggedly, he kept track of Mark for the rest of the evening, not letting him out of sight. He wanted to catch up with him when he was alone.

Around nine pm, his time came. A cold wind blew leaves from the nearby park, their spines making a sound like bones being dragged across the road. Mark walked towards the park, and the Guardian felt a stab of excitement. He followed carefully, a good distance behind, so Mark didn’t spot him, and he wasn’t obvious on the CCTV cameras. Even if the cameras saw him, his head was covered in a hoody, and he walked with a limp, just to fool people.

The park had high black iron railings alongside it. There was a gate made of the same black ironwork. Mark looked around him once but didn't notice the Guardian behind him. He went inside the park and quickened his pace. The Guardian ran forward, adrenaline pulsing through his bloodstream.

The park was in darkness. It was big, and he guessed the man was taking a shortcut. Mark's footsteps echoed in the darkness. The thick oak trees raised silent, menacing heads, watching the scene unfold beneath them.

The Guardian got closer to Mark. The man felt his presence and looked behind him. The Guardian knew he was nothing but a shadow, a clot of blackness. Mark started walking again, faster this time. The

Guardian now walked faster and narrowed the gap between them. Mark stopped and whirled around. Their eyes were used to the darkness, and the Guardian could see the palpable fear in Mark's big eyes.

"Who are you?" Mark asked.

The Guardian grinned, an evil, lopsided, smile. He took out a flashlight and flicked it on, turning it to his face. He kept it there, aware he was lit up from underneath, giving his face a ghastly glow. Mark gasped and stepped backward.

"Recognize me now?" the Guardian said.

Mark was rigid with fear, then he pointed a finger, which shook like a leaf in a storm. "Stay… Stay away from me."

"And what will you do if I don't?" the Guardian said, stepping forward.

Inside his coat pocket, he kept his weapon. His hand tightened around the handle, and he drew it out. Mark saw it, and his jaw dropped. Fear ran across his face, and with a stifled scream, he turned to run. But the Guardian was too quick.

In a flash, the axe was out, and he brought it down in a chopping motion, catching Mark across the shoulders. The weapon was light, but the blade was strong and sharp. It sliced through Mark's clothes, and with a scream, he stumbled to the floor.

He got up, but the Guardian slid a foot under him, tripping him over. Mark sprawled on the floor, and before he knew it, the Guardian had brought the axe down with savage force, smashing into his neck. Mark screamed, but his anguish was lost in the hush of the lonely trees.

CHAPTER 43

Rita woke up feeling tired, with an aching in her temples that wouldn't go away. Like the previous night, she hadn't slept well. The flat was new to her, and she woke up several times, imagining she heard voices. Sleep had been in fits and spurts, and when she did wake up, she had slept through her alarm.

It was 7.30am, late for her. She got ready quickly, and called a cab to take her to the station.

While she had her breakfast of coffee and porridge in the station, she scrolled through her phone. Social media was alive with images of the crime scene and uniformed inspectors standing by the tape fluttering in the wind at Raptors Viewpoint. Well, it was expected.

Luckily, no photos of the skeleton had emerged as yet. Rita was grateful for the small mercies. She would've felt terrible seeing her mother's remains all over social media.

She imagined one of the ramblers had sold some photos to a journalist. Or they had sent it to a friend. News leaked out easily, and something like this would go viral in an instant. That killed her appetite. Now she had to deal with the media frenzy as well.

Rita knew that she would have to release a press statement, and sooner or later, arrange a media conference. All of which would detract valuable time and resources from the investigation.

Her phone rang, and she answered. "DI Gupta."

"Guv, it's me," Richard said. "Bad news, I'm afraid. IC1 male found in Valley Park, not far from the high street. He was hacked to death, and the body left there. Uniforms have set up a perimeter, and we're on our way."

“When did you hear?”

“Just now. A jogger found the body in the park half an hour ago.”

"Do we have a description of the victim?" Rita asked, clutching the phone tightly to her ear.

"Yes. He wore a dark jacket and trousers, and a white shirt and trainers. He had a light brown beard and short brown hair.”

Rita frowned. “White shirt and trainers? How old was he?

“Uniforms said in his thirites to forties. No more than that.”

“That matches the description of the man who followed me. But let’s not jump to conclusions.”

Richard cleared his throat. “Madeleine from traffic also got in touch. She saw the man last night, appear briefly outside Mayfield and Weathers' law office. Isn't that where you went after work?"

A coldness was seeping into Rita's limbs, turning her fingers into ice. She breathed rapidly, her pulse surging against her ears.

"Yes, I did. Did Madeleine find the CCTV footage after I left the office?"

"Yes. The man went after a car and then walked away in the opposite direction. He went inside the park. Unfortunately, the park where the man was killed is in a CCTV blackspot. But he was seen going inside the park, where this man’s body was found." Richard paused.

“Guv, its possible the victim is the man who was following you.”

Rita could her own rapid breathing. “I’ll meet you at the crime scene. Send me the location please.”

Rita drained her coffee, and rang Madeline, the traffic officer.

"Hello, Guv," Madeline said, her cheerful voice more subdued today. "Your constable Rizwan Ahmed is with me. We are going through the CCTV footage currently."

“Ok, I’m coming up.”

Rita raced up the stairs. Rizwan was sat next to Madeleine and waved at Rita when she walked into the open plan office. She joined them, pulling up a chair to sit next to Madeleine, and the bank of CCTV screens.

"Does the victim resemble the man who was following me?"

"Yes, it looks like the same person," Madeline said quietly. "We have done a facial recognition match. Our matching software has picked him up at several spots around Scarborough. Yesterday, after you chased him down, we found him changing buses a few times. He went down to Eastfield, a small town about 30 miles south of here. CCTV coverage in Eastfield isn't great. But the train station and the main streets are covered. The shops have cameras, but they're private, obviously, and we need to ask for their footage."

"Was he living in Eastfield?"

"Looks like it," Madeline said. “Here loo.” She clicked on the keyboard and pulled up the relevant films.

"After he gets off the bus in Eastfield, he walks to a nearby street with terraced houses. We're trying to get the door number, so we should be able to track him."

"That's good news," Rita said. She felt cold and shaky inside. Who was this man, and who killed him?

Rizwan said, "I've already asked one of the researchers' downstairs to look up who moved there recently. We can check with the council tax department."

"Good. When do we pick him up again?"

Madeline said, "We don't actually see him until he appears opposite the Mayfield and Weathers law offices. That's where Gemma dropped you off. But we don't know how he followed Gemma."

"Have you looked at the CCTV outside the station? He could have followed us in a car."

"Good point," Madeline exclaimed. She browed through the files on her screen, and clicked on the right one.

"There's a blue Honda that follows Gemma's car from the station at 5:30 PM yesterday. The car stops in an alley about a hundred meters opposite the point where Maggie dropped you off. That alley doesn't have

CCTV, but we pick him up on the main road, coming out of the alley. He must've been driving that car."

"Get the registration of that car, and check with the DVLA. If he owns it, that's great, but we should be able to find out who he is if he was renting the car. Rizwan, did you get that?"

The constable nodded. "On it right now, Guv. We should be able to get an ID soon."

Rita frowned. “I wonder why he wasn’t using the car before. He took the bus back to Eastfield yesterday. Is that correct?”

Rizwan’s spoke up. “Yes. He might’ve been hiding the car. Easier to spot, I guess.”

"Maybe. Keep me posted." She stood. “I’m going to the crime scene. Richard’s there. Where’s Maggie?”

“On her way in. Do you want me to give you a lift?”

Rita nodded. She thanked Madeleine, who promised to keep working on tracking the man. Rita followed Rizwan outside, and out into the car park. As he drove, thoughts swirled in her mind.

Why was this man following her around? What did he know about her?

More importantly, what did he want from her?

The man didn't threaten her. He simply followed her around, almost as if he was afraid to approach directly. If he had been a criminal and wanted to harm her, Rita suspected he would have done so at the first opportunity.

No, this man was an amateur.

Hence, he was so easy to spot on CCTV. Criminals wore black clothes, hats, and covered their eyes with glasses.

No one had followed Rita up from London. Apart from her boss in the London Metropolitan force, no one down south knew she was coming up here. She felt a strange tingle in her spine.

Was it a coincidence that his man was here when Rita came to investigate Clara's death?

There was considerable traffic nearby, as the road leading up to Valley Park had been cordoned off. Two squad cars with blue and white flashing lights blocked the main road, and uniformed sergeants were diverting traffic. Motorists were frustrated, and several cars honked as they slowed down to see what the commotion was about.

Rizwan pulled the car up on the kerb, and they got out. Rita ducked under the crime scene tape, and crossed the road. At the entrance of the park, a uniformed constable held out a clipboard for her to sign. She put on the usual mask and shoe coverings, then stepped on the sterile boards placed on the ground.

A row of mature oak and birches lined the grass verge, shielding the park from the street. A tarmac path ran along the perimeter, and she stood on the path now. The path also went straight through, and up ahead, she could see the white forensic tent, and the knot of uniformed officers.

She looked behind, at the blockade on the street. Across the road, she could see a knot of onlookers had gathered already, and the uniforms on duty were trying their best to disperse them. She knew news about this would spread rapidly.

Richard appeared next to her. "Dr Das is on his way." Rita nodded, and they walked up the path together. A woman in a white forensic suit appeared, a specimen bag in her hand. Behind the mask, Rita recognised Shola.

"Looks bad, does it?" Rita asked.

Shola lowered her mask with a gloved hand. "You could say that. His head and neck is a mess. I just hope he died quickly."

"How many of you in the tent?"

"I can ask Henry to come out, if you want."

"That's ok," Rita said. "I'll have a walk around first."

Shola went back inside the tent, and Rita caught a glimpse of Henry, in his white space suit, crouching by the feet of the body. Rita looked at the black tarmac, where the dark patches of blood had been circled in fluorescent yellow paint. A line of them led up to the tent. The uniform officers were keeping their distance, not wanting to disturb evidence. Two of them stood under a tree, and another two outside the perimeter marked by the tape.

Rita kept her eyes on the ground, and walked carefully. Behind her, Richard was repeating the process on the other side of the path.

"Look on the grass verge as well," Rita called out to him. "I'll do the same here."

Richard gave her a thumbs up. They both looked painstakingly. Rita examined the grass, which was mown, and the grounds well looked after. Trees stood in rows, the next one about fifty yards away, running by the side of another path that bisected the park. That path ended in a children's soft playing ground.

Rita finally saw what she was looking for. A boot print. She saw a cluster of them, as if the person had stepped off the path, then got back on swiftly. She knelt by it, and called Richard. She took photos with her phone.

"Judging by the size, and the depth of the impression, this is a man-sized shoe, size ten or eleven, I'd say,"

Rita remarked. “Not that I’m an expert of men’s show sizes, but I’ve seen my fair share of boot prints.”

“I’d agree, guv,” Richard said. “That’s a size eleven. I’m size ten and that’s bigger.” Richard put his foot by the print, holding it in the air.

“Do we have a forensic gait analyst?”

Richard seemed to have difficulty in understanding her words. Then his mouth snapped shut, and he shook his head vigorously.

“No, guv. That’s only in Leeds or Sheffield. But I can send them the photos and see what their analyst says.”

“Take a video of the entire area. His prints are on the tarmac as well. I just hope we haven’t stepped on them. And also put the prints on the database, see what they show up.”

Rita was referring to the forensic boot print database, which held a record of criminal’s shoes.

“That I can do,” Richard grinned. He walked away, and Rita went to the tent. Henry was outside now, brushing a spot on the tarmac. Rita lifted the flap and went inside.

CHAPTER 44

The halogen tripods were blazing inside, which was good as the sunlight was obscured by clouds. The lights also created heat, and the tent had windows built in to release heat that might otherwise aid the body's decomposition.

The man lay on his back, eyes staring upward, forever frozen in shock. Deep lacerations covered his neck and upper chest. He had been struck repeatedly there, as if in a frenzy. Blood had congealed over the wounds, turning black, forming pools under the head and shoulders. The abdomen was relatively spared, but Rita saw the wounds in the forearms and hands as well. The legs were free of injury, but the dark jeans were damp from laying on the ground.

Rita moved towards the head, her practised eyes starting with the hair, then methodically moving to the forehead, eyes, nose and rest of face. Specks of blood were visible on the cheeks. The head lay twisted to the left, the body turned at a slight angle. The white shirt was turning black and red, soaked in blood.

From the CCTV images, she now recognised the man as the same person who had followed her. He looked younger than he had seemed before. Maybe in his early forties, she thought.

She looked at the lacerations. They were deep, then trailed to a thinner edge. Knife stab wounds looked different – they were not as deep or thick. She wondered if a machete had been used…a strange thought reared up inside her head, and a shock slapped against her spine.

Could this have been an axe? Or, the same weapon that was used against Clara, twenty-seven years ago?

Her mind in turmoil, Rita looked at the hands. They had several small cuts, with deeper gashes above the wrists in both arms. She crouched and inspected the hands closer. She noted the gashes on the knuckles, as if they were made by glancing blows from a sharp weapon. Again, the dark rumblings of a strange suspicion gathered at the back of her mind. She recalled Dr Das's words. Clara had indentations on her knuckles in keeping with sharp blows. As if she had fought to protect herself with her hands, like this man had.

The man didn't have any rings on his fingers. She had checked the neck already – no chains. His fingers were thin, this was not a working man's hands. His shoes had mud on them, and they were not size eleven. She thought he was less than six feet certainly, only slightly taller than her five feet eight.

There was a sound behind her, and Dr Das entered. He adjusted the glasses on his eyes with a gloved hand. Then he blinked at Rita.

"I hope we're not making a habit of meeting like this."

"Me neither," Rita said with a grim smile that faded swiftly. "I'm worried about the injuries. They seem similar to the cold case victim. Of course, it's hard to draw a comparison, given that we have such different samples."

"Let's have a look," Dr Das said. He laid his briefcase on the floor, and took out his instruments. He took the rectal temperature, helped by Rita and Shola. Rita waited while he examined the body.

"I can see what you mean," Dr Das said. "The collar bone is definitely broken, and several of the ribs as well, I suspect. That would be due to heavy blows, and not from a knife. I suspect something like…" Dr Das's eyes went back to the victim, and stayed there. Rita knew what was on his mind. He was mulling over what she had mentioned earlier about the wounds being similar.

She spoke softly. "Could it be the same weapon, doc?"

He turned his head slowly, and his eyes were troubled. "There is a chance, yes. Something heavy, yet sharp, means either a machete, or an axe. A sword would cause thinner wounds than these."

He nodded to himself. “I will do the same chemical reagent tests at the wounds, and see if I can get the metal residues.”

Shola was crouching by the head, taking hair samples. She looked up. “Oh, you must tell me about that. I love my reagents.”

Dr Das smiled. “No problem. If a weapon leaves any metallic residue, I find these tests very useful.”

“Did you find a clue about the murder weapon in another case?” Shola asked.

“For the cold case victim, yes.”

Rita said, “And it’s possible the two weapons are similar. Of course, the chances of it being the same weapon thirty years apart is slim to none.” She raised both hands and shrugged. “But stranger things have happened.”

At the back of her mind, the whisperings were starting again, malevolent, sharp voices that ripped through her mental peace like a scythe. Her heart thudded painfully against her ribs as she fought for composure.

What was she unearthing here?

In the fractured contours of her mind, she was reliving the nightmare again.

Had her mother’s killer surfaced again?

Her eyes closed, and she heard the screams, the cries of anguish from her eleven-year-old self. The sleepless nights, knowing she would never see her mother again.

Then she became aware of someone speaking to her. Dr Das was on his feet, and he was peering at her with a concerned face. Shola stood as well.

“Rita,” Dr Das used her first name. “Are you okay?”

She exhaled, and the stuffy air inside the tent was suddenly unbearable. “Yes,” she smiled weakly, aware it fooled no one. “Yes, I’m fine.”

“You look rather pale,” Dr Das said. “You should get some fresh air.”

Shola remained inside, and she stepped out with Dr Das. She avoided his eyes. She saw Richard, speaking to one of the uniformed sergeants near the park gates. He was taking notes.

“Maybe you should sit down,” the elderly pathologist said.

“Honestly, doc, I’m ok.” She tried to look brighter. Whatever that meant. Blowing out her cheeks, trying to get some blood flowing again. She had to do something.

“What did you think about the time of death?”

Dr Das gazed at her meditatively, as if he was trying to decide if it was a genuine question or a distraction method. In reality, Rita thought, it was a bit of both.

"I'd say around ten pm last night. A rough window would be nine to eleven pm. It rained a little last night, but not enough for the moisture to affect the body temperature. I will have a more precise time when I put all the numbers in my spreadsheet."

Rita nodded. "We have him on CCTV. Believe it or not, this man was following me around. I think we will have an ID soon."

Dr Das's lined forehead lowered, and his eyes constricted. "Following you around? But you've only just arrived in Scarborough. Is that correct? Unless I'm mistaken."

"No, you're not. I've only been here two days. I mean I know this place as I grew up here."

She stopped, racking her brains once again. For the life of her, she couldn't think of someone she knew who resembled this man. Her mind went back to her three friends - Julia, Vicky, and Nina. She had looked last night before going to bed and found Vicky's number. She should call her once today.

"Either this man knew who I was, or he was a random weirdo. I guess I'll never know. Either way, I do find it strange."

Dr Das's face remained meditative. "The chances of him being a random weirdo is very little, I'd say. This was someone who needed to get in touch with you. Why, is the more important question."

"And like you said, we might never know. That's my job, I suppose. What bothers me is that he was silenced like this. I can't help the feeling he knew something important."

The pathologist nodded. "You need to find that out soon. I will say this however. The MO is similar to the cold case victim." Dr Das raised his hand above his head, moving his shoulder to the right. He made a scything movement, bringing his arm down slowly.

"The blows slashed down like this. From right to left. That means the killer was right handed. It was the same action with the cold case victim. The fractures in her collar bones, ribs and wrist point to the same direction of attack. And potentially, a similar weapon."

Rita's jaws ground together. "Thanks Doc. If you find anything else, let me know asap. When can you do the PM?"

"The Post Mortem will take place tomorrow. I can expedite it for you. Is the afternoon okay?"

"Should be, yes.

CHAPTER 45

Rita was visible through the binocular lens, and her long legs, and lithe body made the Guardian smile.

He was on the other side of the park, hidden safely behind the thick branch of a tree. His eyes feasted on Rita, and he longed to touch her hair. She had watched how she tied it up into a ponytail before putting the mask on. Then she ducked inside the tent. She had no doubt seen his masterful handiwork.

The Guardian was proud of the way he had killed Mark.

Just like he'd killed Clara.

Sweeping, sharp curves of his axe, like a lethal artist's scalpel. He had sliced through Mark's defences. Marks should never have come back. Even worse, he was looking to meet up with Rita.

The Guardian knew why. Mark couldn't just walk into the police station and ask for an interview. There was too much risk in that. He knew how high the stakes were.

That's why he was searching for an opportunity to corner Rita, and tell her…but he was an idiot. The Guardian felt a tingle of joy, and the hairs stood up on his arms. It was all falling into place now. His role as the Guardian was almost complete.

His phone rang, disturbing his grandiose visions. He cursed. He was enjoying watching Rita, undressing her with his eyes. The things he would do to her when she was finally in his grasp. He pulled out his phone and relented when he saw the number. He had to answer.

"Where are you?" Alfred Northallerton's voice was harsh.

"I'm just making sure everything's ok. Don't worry."

"Shut up you fool," Alfred shouted. "Did you have have anything to do with what's happened in Valley Park? Everyone's talking about it."

The Guardian frowned, his earlier confidence now suddenly fractured. "Yes," he said slowly. "So what? No one knows what happened."

Alfred swore loudly. "You idiot. News has spread already. What have you done?"

"I got rid of him. He was chasing after that detective. We couldn't let him talk to her, could we? I did what was necessary."

"Oh my god," Alfred exhaled. "I told you to just watch, and not do anything."

"But Mark's now gone. It's better for all of us. So what if I had to get rid of him?"

"So what? Do I need to spell it out for you? Now the police will know who he is, and they will hunt you down as well."

"He was going to speak to the detective Inspector. What would happen then?"

"Who would believe him?" Alfred raged. "No one cares. And even if that detective followed up on his story, she wouldn't find anything. But now they think something's afoot."

"It's going to be alright, don't worry."

"Shut up, you fool," Alfred raged. "If you had just let this be, it would've blown over. Now, it's out of control." He seethed in silence.

"Come to the meeting place. Now." The phone went dead.

The Guardian sighed and got to his feet. He took one last longing look at Rita through his binoculars. Then he stashed them away in his backpack, and slunk back through the bushes.

He came out through one of the gates, where he had locked his bike. He cycled to his place, then stashed the bike and got changed. He walked to the garage where he kept his car, and drove to Lord Northallerton's meeting place.

He could never visit the grand mansion, but there were plenty of farms around, several of them derelict. As he drove up the long drive, he saw the other three cars. Everyone had arrived today.

The derelict barn, where they usually met, had its door open. He stepped inside. Cold, grey sunlight lit up the place with shafts of light. The stone slabbed floor had a slick of water on it, from the rain that poured in through the cracks in the roof. At first, he didn't see anyone. Then Alfred Northallerton emerged from behind the shadow of a post.

To his right, a tall, slim man appeared, and he recognised Edward Salt. The two men stood silent for a while, then Alfred came forward.

"What have you done?" Alfred hissed.

"I was protecting you. Just like I have done, all these years."

"You call this protection, you idiot?" Alfred raged. "The cops would've treated Mark with suspicion, and not believed him. But now, you've created a situation that we can't back out of."

"No one saw me," the Guardian said, unmoved. "There's no CCTV there. I went in and out, that was it."

"But when the police investigate, and they find out more about him, then they might connect him to us." Edward said softly.

"How?"

"I don't know. Mark was obviously around here for a reason. He could've had something he wanted to either show or tell the detective about. She might still find out what that was."

"She? You mean Inspector Rita Gupta?" the Guardian smiled like a wolf.

"Yes."

He glared at Edward, then at Alfred. "Leave her to me," he growled.

"What will you do?" Alfred asked.

"If she's gone, then problem solved, correct?" The Guardian looked at both men. Edward and Alfred looked at each other. Then Edward shrugged.

"Correct," he said calmly. "As long as no one can trace it back to us. It has to be as neat as Clara."

"It will be. No one will find her." The Guardian smiled. "Like mother, like daughter."

CHAPTER 46

"His name was Mark Strong," Rita said. She faced the assembled group of detective and uniformed policemen.

Nicola Perkins was sat in the front row, stone-faced as usual. Rita wondered if the woman ever smiled.

Behind Rita, Mark's face was displayed in the projector screen. He looked younger than his forty-five years. His cheeks were shaven, and in the blown-up passport sized photo, he was a handsome man – dark, sensitive eyes, prominent cheekbones, and full lips. His cheeks were sallow, a lean, desolate look in his eyes that had worried Rita when she first saw it. It was as if Mark was searching for something he had lost, even while posing for the simple task of taking a passport photo.

"Born in Leeds to parents who were both drug addicts. He lived in social care, and we don't know where exactly, due to missing council records." Rita glanced at Richard, Rizwan and Maggie who were also in the front row. "But we are awaiting an update for them. Records weren't digitised till 2005, and it seems some photocopies are missing."

"That's right," Richard confirmed. "We still have data from the rest of his life, but his early life is a little hazy. We will visit Leeds County Council offices tomorrow."

"Thanks," Rita said. "Mark left school at the age of sixteen, and lived in Swillington, a small suburb in the south of Leeds. He worked a variety of odd jobs, then set up a business as a painter decorator, from what we can find. His medical records show a battle with alcohol and cocaine addiction. He visited rehabilitation centres, and was an inpatient in a substance misuse psychiatric hospital ward."

Rita cleared her throat. The gathered policemen were listening to her intently. Only the sound of breathing punctuated the silence of the room.

"Lately, Mark wasn't doing well. He was on the dole, getting benefit payments every week. If he was working on the side, getting cash for jobs like most builders do, we don't know. In any case, he never owned a house, and always rented. I can only assume that's because he never made enough to buy. About a week ago, he rented a one bedroom flat in Eastfield. We don't know why. Eastfield isn't exactly a holiday resort." Rita shrugged. "Maybe he was doing a job here."

“Whatever the reason, Mark left his home in Leeds, where he also rented a flat. He started to live in Eastleigh, it seems. It was a short term let, hence not cheap.” Rita looked inquiringly at her team. Maggie spoke up. She half turned in her seat so people at the back could hear her.

“The victim drove a blue Honda. The car’s not been spotted on ANPR data as going back to Leeds in the last week. He’s been spotted on CCTV at Eastleigh and Scarborough station several times. He also drove around in Scarborough, again spotted on ANPR. Traffic will have more information.”

Inspector Botley, sitting the third row, raised his voice. “He visited Raptor’s Viewpoint, the cold case crime scene. Well, at least he headed in that direction, according to Traffic.”

“That’s right,” Maggie nodded. “His blue Honda was seen going down the A56 and taking the exit for Wykeham Hills.”

“He could’ve gone anywhere,” Inspector Botley said. “But one of my constables remembers a blue Honda in the car park when he arrived at the scene early one morning. The car was empty, and by the time he notified us and came back, the car had gone. He had noted the reg number, good lad that he is.”

“Indeed a clever lad,” Rita said. “Got his head screwed on.” She was noticing that the Yorkshire accent was creeping back in her tongue. “Because of your constable, we know Mark visited the crime scene.”

She stopped, disturbing thoughts clouding her mind. Why did Mark want to see her mother’s shallow grave?

“He’s out on duty,” Botley said, “But I’ll pass the message on, like.”

“Since then, he’s followed me around,” Rita said. “Which is rather strange. I’m not sure why he was trying to hide. He doesn’t have a police record, unless he’s flown under the radar. Last night, he was seen close to the High Street, and then he followed a car I happened to be in.”

Rita had instructed her team, and Traffic, to keep the law office name out of the case files. She didn’t want to drag Jack into this.

Rita turned to the screen, and aimed her remote at the projector. Maggie got up from her seat, and adjusted the laptop to bring the CCTV on screen – and a black and white image of Mark Strong, seen from both front and behind, on a dark street, appeared. The park railings were visible to his left. Rita pressed play, and the screen now showed Mark walking through the gates, and then the darkness in the park swallowed him up. The film kept running, but no one else appeared on the street.

"We've asked Traffic to monitor all the streets around the park to see who else walked in there before or after. Unless the killer was inside for several hours, we will see them on CCTV. Logic dictates he either followed Mark, or they had set up a meeting."

Rita flicked screens again, and now the gruesome photos of Mark lying on his back appeared.

These were the forensic photos taken by Shola and Henry. "The MO is the same as the cold case victim," Rita said softly. "According to Dr Das, anyway. The lacerations in the arms and neck were made by the same type of weapon – which he thinks was an axe, sword, or machete."

"Any sign of the murder weapon?" One of the uniformed surgeons asked.

"Nope," Rita said. "But we know from Dr Das that the metal alloy used in the weapon is old, like a hundred years old. That leads us to believe it was an antique weapon."

Rita indicated to Maggie, and she rose. She switched the lights on. Everyone blinked in the sudden glare. The Incident Room was small compared to what Rita was used to. But it was packed, about forty odd officers, both detective and uniforms, had turned up. It was pretty much the entirety of Scarbrough's police force.

"If there is a link to the cold case, then it means someone was trying to stop Mark from speaking to the police," Rita said. "Our job, apart from getting justice for Mark, is to find out why he was silence."

"And what his relation was to Clara Winters," Richard said, from his seat in the front row. "Mark went to see her remains, but he knew the police would be present. He didn't care. Maybe he had a close relationship with her, from years ago."

Rizwan spoke up. "Clara Winters would be 65 now, if she was alive. Mark is more than twenty years younger. I doubt it was a romantic relationship. He would be 18 years old when she died."

A soft murmur swept across the room. Rita observed the various faces whispering to each other. She had thought of the same problem. How did her mother know Mark? She had to ask Angela.

"We have identified Mark Strong's address in Leeds. West Yorkshire Police will lend us a hand. His flat is now a crime scene, and West Yorkshire Police has agreed to us taking a lead role. Hence, our Scene of Crime team will be involved." Rita glanced at Shola in the second row, who waved at her.

"That's correct. Once you give us the go ahead we can start."

Rita smiled. "That would be now. I'm on my way after the meeting, and you can follow us. For the rest of you," Rita looked at her team, and then everyone else.

"I want a door to door in Eastleigh, where the victim was living. Another door to door where Clara Winters used to live, to see if anyone remembers Mark, or anyone like him." She looked at Richard. "Did the boot print analyst come back with anything?"

He shook his head. "Not yet, guv. Early days yet, I will chase them again."

"OK, enough to get cracking for now. Let's go."

CHAPTER 47

Leeds was a good hour and a half away on the motorway, but Rizwan made short work of it with his police siren, and the BMW's powerful engine. Swillington was a small suburb to the south of Leeds. The gridwork of narrow streets with small, terraced, redbrick houses were familiar to Rita, she had grown up in a street like this in Scarborough. But there was no sea here, only the endless sprawl of closely knit houses over a leaden grey industrial sky. Smoke belched from a factory chimney nearby.

They parked outside a house where two West Yorkshire Police cars stood. A uniformed constable stood guard outside it. Rita got out and introduced herself, and both Rizwan and herself showed their warrant cards.

"Good morning marm," the man nodded. "We were expecting you."

Rita and Rizwan entered the house. The corridor was narrow, with not enough space for two people to squeeze past each other. The house was divided into a ground floor, and an upstairs flat. The carpet under their feet was threadbare, and the walls were once white but now a vague yellowish colour, stained with cigarette smoke.

The place smelt of it – a musty, suffocating smell of nicotine and unwashed clothes. It seemed windows had not been opened her for a while. Pinching her nose, Rita went rapidly up the similarly narrow stairs, Rizwan jogging up behind her. At the top, another small landing led to an open door.

The flat was larger than it seemed possible, judging from the size of the building outside. But Rita knew many narrow terraces were bigger than they looked. They stretched back, and some even widened out at the rear. The entrance hall had a cheap lino floor, and there was a mirror and table. Two bedrooms opened out on either side of the mirror, with a bathroom opposite. Rizwan tackled one bedroom, and Rita stepped into the other. This seemed like the main bedroom. The double bed in one corner looked slept in. A wardrobe in the corner had a mirror, which reflected the meagre sunlight from the windows.

It was a man's room, that much she could tell. The walls were bare, a dead potted plant stood morosely on the mantelpiece. There was a desk and table, with a mess of magazines and papers. With gloved hands, Rita rifled through the papers.

They were invoices and bills for different clients and builders. Many of them were receipts for paint and materials. Why Mark had left them lying around she couldn't understand. She looked at the clothes and underwear strewn on the bed. Had he left in a rush?

Another thought raised its uneasy head. Had this flat been searched already?

She opened the wardrobe. A couple of suits hung inside, with black shoes in the racks below. The shelves had regular clothes, some folded, others not. But most of the shelves were empty. Rita went down on her haunches, and looked through the shoe rack at the bottom. She found nothing inside two shoeboxes.

She was glad she was wearing a mask when she took off the duvet and bed cover. There was a faint whiff of stale sweat and body odour, and the bed sheets were stained. Dust particles swirled in the air, and she waved her hand. She lifted the pillows, and stilled. There was a photo under the pillow. It was an old photo, and the colours were faded. Rita picked it up, and moved to the light.

It was a street scene, taken from a height, as if the photographer stood on a hill. The street had large detached houses, all handsome white brick Victorian mansions. There was a small park opposite. Behind the houses, the land sloped down, with small terraces houses built on them. A tremor began in Rita's fingers, and her lungs were suddenly made of iron, and she couldn't breathe. The photo, and the room, started to shake.

She recognised the street vaguely. But what she remembered with crystal clear clarity was the the long church steeple on the extreme right, and the undulating sea in the background, stretching to the blue sky.

Rita felt two hands grip her chest and squeeze till all air was expelled from it. She opened her mouth to breathe, but it was impossible.

This was the same photo she found in her mother's shallow grave.

This photo was intact, while her mothers was destroyed.

More importantly, she now knew why she had found the even the destroyed photo familiar.

Lights clashed and blinded her eyes, and her tortured past whined into her heart with the force of a tornado, ripping her to shreds.

She had seen this street recently. Yesterday, when Jack Banford gave her a lift to the hospital morgue. This same street, the same houses, the same blue sea beyond, and the church spire. But yesterday, there was a house missing in the street, like the gaping hole in the middle of a fence.

With frozen fingers, Rita pulled out her phone. She called Jack. He answered on the first ring.

"Jack Banford."

“It’s me, Rita. Jack, do you remember that road I asked you about yesterday? Where we stopped in traffic. Sawyer’s Hill, I think the place is called.”

Jack was silent for a while, then he exclaimed. “Oh yes. That row of big houses. The middle one was demolished a good ten years ago.”

Rita was staring at the demolished house now, when it had stood, decades back. An imposing structure, with double doors, and four windows on either side.

“Why was it demolished?”

She heard a voice speaking to Jack, and he asked them to hold on, and came back on the line.

“I don’t know why. Because it was derelict for too long, I guess. I can’t think of any other reason.”

Rita’s eyes were bulging as she pinched the photo tightly, her finger turning white. Her synapses were igniting, lighting up the dark spaces, connecting dots. Like a steam train in a tunnel, the past was screaming back to her.

“Rita. Are you okay?”

She gulped and forced herself to stop breathing hard. “Yes. I’m fine. Look, I’ve got to go. But I’ll call you.”

“I don’t know what this is about, but I can ask our property division to look up the history of that demolished house, if you want. If anyone living there had a criminal record, that will also come up in our search."

Rita hesitated. She didn't want to drag Jack into this. He sensed it. "Look, it's no skin off my back. I just need to ask them to do it, and then forward you the email. That's all."

"Okay," she sighed. "If that's alright with you."

"No problem." He was silent for a couple of beats. "Are you okay?"

She sighed. "Kind of. Can't talk about it now."

"Call me later."

He hung up. Rita stared at the photo, then closed her eyes. She snapped them open when she heard Rizwan shout for her.

CHAPTER 48

The second bedroom was smaller. It had a window that looked out to the side, like the main bedroom. The bed was single, and didn't look slept in. The room was crammed with two ladders, assorted paint brushes, drills and hammers. It seemed like Mark used this as his storage space. Rizwan had opened up a red and white gymbag on the bed. He was holding up a phone in his gloved hand.

"It's got battery. I turned it on, and tried a couple of passwords, but the phone's locked."

Rita took the phone from Rizwan. The lock screen was showing, and she entered Mark's date of birth as the password. She tried a few combinations, but nothing worked. She knew these phones could be hacked into, but she needed to send it to the lab.

"Won't take that long to get the data from the phone," Rizwan said. "We just need a call log, and the network provider can give us that. I've taken down the phone's IMEI number."

"Get cracking with that, please," Rita said. "We need to know who Mark called from this number."

Rizwan went outside. Rita searched the room, but found little of interest. The living room was next to the kitchen. An old black leather sofa faced a flat screen TV on the wall. Posters of Leeds United Football club were stuck on the wall.

There was an empty pizza box on the floor, and a couple of beer cans. She looked out the rear window, which showed a garden at the back, and its fence. Opposite she could see the rear lots of terraced houses of the next street.

Rita raised the sash window, and lowered her mask to breath in the air. It helped to relieve the stuffy air inside. She continued her search, picking up a cigarette stub from the ashtray, a beer can for fingerprints and skin samples, and in the bathroom, an old toothbrush. She had a collection of specimen bags soon. In the bathroom, she also found a vial of medicine called Quetiapine. She looked it up on her phone – it was an antipsychotic medication. The vial was empty. She couldn't find any shaving kit, or other toiletries.

She rang Richard, who was in the victim's flat in Eastfield, with Maggie.

"Yes," Richard said. "We've got all his toiletries here. Electric toothbrush, razor the whole lot. He was definitely living here. Found a credit card and an old driving licence photocard with his name on it."

"Anything else?"

"Yes. A couple of invoices, to a company that sounded familiar, so I looked it up. It's a property maintenance company run by Edward Salt's empire. Mr Salt has twenty-four companies under his belt, all controlled by one big parent company that he oversees."

"I'll call you back," Rita said.

She went back to the main living room, and looked through the invoices scattered on the table. She had taken a few in a specimen bag already. She held them close to her eyes, and memorised some of the company names. After a while, she realised one name appeared more often. The invoiced amounts varied – from a few hundred to a couple of thousand.

She called Richard back. "I see the name Magnum Properties appearing several times."

"That's the one. Mr Salt's company owns it. The houses are scattered all over the region, but mainly in Scarborough. One of the neighbour's said she's seen Mark before. He came here frequently to work, it seems."

A distant buzzing in Rita's mind was getting louder, till it crashed against her eardrums. "Is there anything there to suggest Mark knew Ed Salt personally?"

"Not that I can see, guv. We did find a laptop, but it's locked. We also got a phone. We're taking it back to the lab now, see what they can do for us."

“Did Mark live there alone?”

“Looks like it. It’s a tiny one bed flat, and looks like only person slept in the bed. What did you find?”

“The bed looks slept in by more than one person. A couple, I’d say. If he had a girlfriend, I don’t think she lived here. If his partner was a woman, that is.”

“We’re almost done here, guv. Shall we see you back at the nick?”

“Yes. Please tell Shola to come around here when she’s done there.”

“I will.”

Rita hung up. Rizwan was waiting for her downstairs. “Are we all done?” Rita asked. “Is there any access to the loft?”

“Not that I could see. I think the loft space is sealed off.”

Rita thought for a while, looking back at the house.

Mark Strong wanted to speak to her about her mother, she knew that now. He followed her around for that purpose.

But why did he run? Was he afraid of Rita? That didn’t make any sense, if he was trying to tell her something.

Or perhaps…he was running from someone else. Someone who was watching him, as well as Rita. Mark didn't want to expose his identity to that person.

Rita kicked the wall in frustration. Too many questions, hardly any answers.

CHAPTER 49

"Let's get some treats for everyone," Rita suggested, when they arrived back at the station office. Rizwan and Maggie looked up expectantly.

"What do you want?" Rita asked, rising. The team had worked hard this morning, and she had to keep their spirits up.

"I could get used to this," Rizwan said. "Will you pay for us all the time, guv?"

Rita pointed a finger at him. "Only when you work hard. Now, what do you want?"

"Doughnuts?" Maggie suggested.

"Coffee?" Richard said.

"One of you come with me then," Rita said. Maggie offered to help, and they walked down the corridor.

"Shocking to see a murder here," Maggie said. "Not seen one in ages."

"When was the last time?" Rita asked. She knew Scarborough was a small town, and crime was pretty much confined to bar brawls and car thefts.

"A good five or six years ago. I was in uniform then. A woman was found dead in a farm. Old lady, in her sixties. It was in one of the villages out in the Moors."

"Who killed her?"

Maggie shook her head, down turning her lips. "We didn't find out. She lived alone, out there. Probably a vagabond who broke in and they got into a fight."

There was no queue in the canteen. Maggie got a tray, and Rita loaded it with doughnuts, biscuits and four cups of coffee. Only coffee for her, although her stomach was rumbling.

They walked back to the office. Richard had a gleam in his eyes. "The DNA samples from the car's come back. We found a torn piece of clothing. It had dried blood on it. The DNA matches with Clara Winters, but there's another sample for which there's no match."

Rita felt excitement spike in her veins. "If there was blood, it could be the killers. After all, he must've driven the car away and put it in that valley before he set fire to it."

"No matches on the DNA database. So it's from someone who doesn't have a police record. And no match with Mark Strong, before you ask."

"That was going to be my next question," Rita smiled. "Anything else?"

"The chassis number of the car is the same as the DVLA records for Clara Winter's vehicle. So there's no doubt it belonged to her."

Rita sat down at her desk, and sipped her coffee.

"When Clara vanished, her car was last seen on CCTV the night of her disappearance?"

"Yes," Richard said. "Hang on, let me check." He clicked on his keyboard and got the files up. "The car was seen leaving her house at 23.00 on 22th November. It was picked up on the A170, and it took a left from a village called Pickering." Richard got a local map up on his screen, then turned his laptop so the other could see. Rita got up from her chair and walked over.

"That left is called Sawdon Lane, and you go up into the hills of North Yorks Moors. No CCTV there. Clara was last seen taking that left at 23.24 that night. That was her last sighting."

Maggie said, "And that's the road we went up, guv," speaking to Rita.

"Was Clara alone in the car?" Rita asked.

Richard nodded. "Yes, she was, according to CCTV images from the time. We don't have the video footage, but there's a close up of her in the car."

He scrolled to the image and showed it to them. Rita felt that familiar emptiness as she looked at the grainy black and white close up, her mother's face pixellated and distorted – like the fractured past in Rita's memories. But still, it was Clara, there was no doubt. Her familiar brown hair, and facial features were instantly identifiable to Rita.

Rita straightened. "The car was burnt, and I guess anything else inside the car was destroyed?"

"That's right. The ripped piece of clothing survived as it was under the car. Uniforms are still searching the surrounding area, but nothing's been found as yet."

"That second DNA from the torn clothing is now vital evidence," Rita tapped her unpainted fingernail against her lower lip. A sudden thought seized her. "Have we taken swabs from Edward Salt? He is our prime suspect at the moment."

"Not yet, guv," Rizwan said. "But we can arrange it for today."

"Please do. And also from the others." Rita knew DNA swabs had been taken thirty years ago, even from herself. The neighbours, Clara's ex-boyfriend, Robert McFarlane, had all been checked. But they did not have this new piece of evidence. And people like Ed Salt, Duncan Sheldrake, and Alfred Northallerton had definitely not been checked.

"Do we have new swabs from Mr McFarlane, the ex-partner? It's my fault if not. I should've taken swabs when I went to see him. In fact, I should visit him again. I need to ask him about Mark Strong."

"Speaking of whom," Rizwan said, "the lab from Sheffield just got back to me. They've managed to get the call lists of the two phones Mark had." He stared at his screen, and took a bite of his doughnut. He closed his eyes as he chewed.

"Oh, that's so nice. Nowt like a proper donut, eh?"

"Watch the waistline," Maggie piped up. "Getting a little fond of donuts, ain't yer?"

Rizwan frowned at her. "My body is a temple. I hardly touch sweet stuff, apart from these, occasionally." Maggie made a face to show she didn't believe a word of what Rizwan said. He looked back at his screen with a grimace.

"Right, I'm now running a search for a match on the numbers on Mark's phone. Guv, any suggestions?" He looked at Rita.

"Ed Salt, Alfred Northallerton and Duncan Sheldrake, definitely. Look at Robert Mcfarlane. And try the numbers of Clara's friends – Angela Watson, also Susan Harrington, the neighbour." Rita frowned. "Also try. Have we spoken to him, by the way? I want to see him."

Maggie raised her hand. "I got in touch with his office. He can see us tomorrow, he said."

"Make it today," Rita said firmly. "Call the office back, and say we don't have much time. His link is with Mr Salt, but it seems their financial bonds are deep, which makes me think they might have a personal relationship as well."

"On it," Maggie said. Rita thought back to the photo she'd just found in Mark's house, and a shiver ran down her spine. She pulled out her phone, and checked for messages. Then she saw the missed call from Jack.

"I was just about to ring again," Jack's warm voice came down the line. "I found a few interesting facts about that demolished building. It used to be a care home for children. The funding was provided by the council, but the contract was won by a private company that ran the service. The building was bought, and then sold, by the private company. It was sold back to Scarborough Council."

"Did the children's care home have a name?"

"Yes. It was called Blue Rise Care Home."

Rita couldn't breathe. The shockwave was like a hammer blow to her head. She felt dizzy and held on to the table for support. Her vision swam.

"And what was the name of the company that ran the service?" She closed her eyes, aware of the answer already.

"Blue Rise Holding Limited. The company has shut down since, but I looked up their records, and was just about to email them to you."

Rita crashed down on the chair, and held her head. A soft moan escaped her lips. That building had been right in front of her all this time and she had ignored her.

"Are you okay?" Jack sounded concerned.

Rita couldn't speak for a while. "Yes." She explained to him, and he was silent as well.

"My god. There's something else you should know about that care home." Jack's voice was quiet and Rita had an awful premonition she knew what was coming her way.

"I spoke to Carol, one of our secretaries. She's lived here all her life. She told me about the whispers that the care home got shut down due to kiddy fiddlers. In other words, allegations of sexual abuse."

Waves of nausea were rolling in Rita's stomach. She clenched her teeth and toes, holding on to the edges of her sanity.

"I knew it," she whispered.

"That ties in with why no inspection reports were filed for ten years. I mean, that is a remarkable lapse. The Council must be held accountable for that. Someone high up there made sure the reports were never filed. I don't think any social worker would have the power to do that."

Rita exhaled. "These people have powerful friends."

“Yes. And Ed Salt pretty much owns a third of Scarborough. My solicitor friends in the property business have done thousands of deals for him. He must know senior figures in the council.”

“And Lord Northallerton.”

“Yes, him too. His family owns a lot of land in North Yorkshire. Guess who leases that land to build homes for the poor?”

“The Council,” Rita whispered. The sordid circle was now exposed in all its horror.

“Thank you, Jack.” She felt a debt of gratitude, and while he was an old friend, she didn’t want to feel indebted to anyone. “You didn’t have to do that. But thanks again.”

“No problem. And by the way, the building was demolished by a company owned by Edward Salt. Thought you might want to know.”

“I guess that makes sense.”

Rita hung up. Maggie walked over to her desk, a light shining in her eyes. “We finished the number check from Mark’s phone’s call log. Guess what? He called Alfred Northallerton several times.”

Maggie placed the call sheet on Rita’s desk, and pointed at the circled numbers.

“Some of the calls lasted a few seconds, which meant it was either engaged, or someone hung up. But there are some calls that went on for six and seven minutes."

"We need the call data. Have you rung the network provider?"

"Yes, but they will take a couple of days, at the least."

Rita frowned as she stared at the sheet. "Mark called Northallerton's office quite a few times, didn't he? Or is that his personal number?"

"His personal number's not on the directory. I think is his office. All the calls were in the last three weeks."

Rita heard a sound from Rizwan's desk. The constable was standing, clutching a piece of paper.

"My god," he whispered under her breath.

"What is it?" Rita asked.

"I was looking through the list of the children under care at the Blue Rise Care Home."

"And?"

"Mark Strong. He was a resident there."

"When?" Rita walked to Rizwan's desk and leaned over. His finger pointed to the entry he had underlined in red. The residents named, like the staff's, was arranged by year. For the children, the age was also inserted, and the DOB.

"From 1991 to 1995."

"The DOB is the same, guv," Rizwan said. "It has to be him."

"Is there any information about where the children came from?"

Rizwan shuffled through the papers, and extracted one sheet. He read from it quickly, his forefinger sliding down the page.

"Yes. He came from a foster home in Temple Newsam, in Leeds. There's no reason why he left the foster home, but he came here in 1991."

"He was there from the ages of ten to sixteen," Rita remarked. Adrenaline spiked in her blood. This couldn't be a coincidence. Her mother and Mark were in the same place, at the same time. Their paths must've crossed.

She felt the truth stirring in her veins as she stood up. There was a reason that photo was under Mark's pillow, and next to her mother's body.

And for the first time, she thought she understood why. Mark had confided in Clara. Or Clara saw something happen to Mark. A whiplash straightened Rita's spine.

"The camcorder," She whispered. She looked at the others. "Did we get anywhere with finding the tapes?"

"No," Maggie said.

Rita's mind was spinning loops. "We need to find them. They contain critical evidence, I think. I might be wrong, but we need to find them."

"Okay, focus on the list of staff and visitors to the care home again," Rita said.

"Search for the suspects in that list," she said, giving Maggie a portion in that list. Rita made a quick call to the council, to speak to Natalie, the social worker's boss. She was put on hold.

Maggie got her attention.

"Duncan Sheldrake," the constable said, a triumphant note in her voice. "He was the vicar of that parish, and he visited twice a month."

Rita's eyes burned as she thought, her mind on fire. "Sheldrake denied knowing Clara. Would he also deny knowing Mark?"

"If he did, we can't do nowt, eh?" Maggie said. "It's not like we can prove anything."

"But Susan Harrington saw Sheldrake and Clara together," Rita said. "Let's go through the list and see if we can find other names that are familiar."

They examined the lists, but did not find any other familiar names. Rita couldn't get through to the people at the council. Frustrated, she hung up.

Rita exhaled, opening up her black notebook. She needed to prioritise matters now. She called Angela, who didn't answer. Rita wasn't happy with Angela. Her gut told her Angela knew something about the care home, but hadn't told Rita.

Even worse, Rita knew, was the probability that Clara had confided in Angela, and the woman had kept silent all these years because she was scared.

It was bugging Rita now. How much did Angela really know?

She sent off a text to her, asking her to call ASAP. Angela didn't reply immediately.

"Call Duncan Sheldrake, and get his DNA. And ask him what he remembers about the care home," Rita told Maggie.

"Shall we get Sheldrake in? It can't be a coincidence that him, the two victims, and Lord Northallerton, are all involved in the care home."

"No, it's not. Let's get his DNA for now, and see if we can find a match."

Maggie nodded.

"Get the car ready," Rita said in a low voice to Maggie. "We're going to pay Lord Northallerton a visit. I don't care if we have an appointment."

CHAPTER 50

"I must say, this is most unusual. Sir Alfred doesn't allow private visitors to attend unannounced."

The man's voice from the intercom on the gate wall was stiff and formal. A well rounded, so called Home counties accent. Totally out of place in rural Yorkshire. Aristocrats popped up everywhere like cockroaches, Rita thought. Maggie looked at her and rolled her eyes.

Rita had already mentioned who she was. "This is a murder investigation, and it possibly took place in a property that he owned. We need to speak to him as a matter of urgency."

The nameless man, who had been called by the security guard, was silent for a while. "Sir Alfred doesn't own any properties," he said eventually, a trace of irony in his voice. That irritated Rita. The man was right, of course. Lord Northallerton was the director of a company that had owned Blue Rise Care Home. That was his excuse.

"In which case, I'm sure Lord Northallerton wouldn't mind if the details were released to the media in a press conference. That will happen tomorrow. Would you like to inform him?"

More silence this time, and for longer. Then a sigh of exasperation. "What was your name again?"

"DI Rita Gupta."

The man switched off, and Rita, with Maggie stood around, waiting. The huge wrought iron gates allowed sight of a long, winding gravel path, with dense conifers on either side. Somewhere inside was the mansion, but they couldn't see it from here. A bored looking security guard was inside his little hut, his face resting in his hand as he looked at them through the window.

"Good threat that," Maggie grinned at her.

"If that doesn't work, I'll bloody well arrest him," Rita said. "We'll see how he likes that."

The man came back on the intercom. His voice had a resigned tone. "Lord Northallerton will see you now. Please come to the main house."

Maggie and Rita got into the car as they huge gates slowly swung open. Rita drove the black BMW down the gravel drive. The road curled to the right, and then the mansion became visible. It was a sandstone building, with six doric columns on either side of a grand entrance, accessed by a broad flank of stairs. There was a fountain in the foreground, and Rita went around the circular drive, parking close to the dry fountain. A man in a grey suit came slowly down the stairs.

“How the other half live, eh?” Maggie remarked as she unbuckled her seat belt.

“More like the other one percent,” Rita said. “But they hold ninety nine percent of this country’s wealth.”

They got out, and approached the man, who stood stiffly at the base of the stairs, staring at them with the kind of hostility a lion reserves for a pack of hyenas. Rita walked right up to him and held up her warrant card.

“DI Gupta of North Yorkshire Police, and this is DC Long. We are here to see Alfred Northallerton.”

The man was past middle age, his dark hair thinning at the top. His thin lips quivered, like the tip of his long nose.

“Mr Rutherford,” he said stiffly. “I am Sir Alfred’s secretary. This way, please.”

He turned, and went up the stairs without further ado, his spine as erect as the pine trees on the drive. He opened a small side door to the right of the massive double doors, and they stepped inside.

They were in a large hall with dark wooden parquet flooring. Paintings of old men in horses, or just standing and staring out of the canvas, were framed at regular intervals on the similarly dark wood panelled walls. Chandeliers hung from the high ceiling.

Their footsteps echoed around the hall as they followed Mr Rutherford to another door, at the left of the large hall, which showed them into a corridor. The green carpet was patterned with what Rita thought was the family coat of arms. The same deep brown wood panelled walls continued.

Mr Rutherford opened another door, and took them inside a spacious lounge, with green coloured sofas that matched the carpet. A long stretch of concertina glass doors looked out into a side garden. The garden was so big Rita couldn't see an end to it, only the trees in the far distance. The room was freezing cold, like the hallway.

"Have a seat, please. I shall notify Sir Alfred you are here."

"We don't have much time. A murder investigation takes a lot of work, as Sir Alfred must understand."

Rita held Mr Rutherford's grey eyes. His lips stretched even thinner, and his expression seemed to suggest Rita had just slapped him across the face. Spots of colour appeared on his cheeks.

His tone was withering like the wind outside. "As I said, I shall inform Sir Alfred that you have arrived."

"Thank you," Rita smiled.

After the door shut behind Mr Rutherford, Maggie chortled. "He wasn't happy about that. Nice one, guv."

Rita scanned the corners of the ceiling, and sure enough, she saw the tiny black CCTV cameras. She didn't point, but indicated with her eyebrows. Maggie turned to look.

"Say hello to Sir Alfred," Rita said. "He's watching us as we speak. Or someone is."

Maggie rubbed her forearms. "They could put the heating on. Bloody freezin' in here."

"I heard once that all stately homes are cold in the winter. They have old plumbing and narrow pipes, and in some rooms, no pipes at all."

"Fantastic. All this money and they can't even stay warm."

"Oh they're warm alright," Rita whispered, wondering if they were being heard, as well as watched. "It's just us they keep cold. Come on, let's sit down."

The two women sat down close to each other for warmth. The door opened soon, and a short, podgy man entered. Rita had expected to recognise him from the photo on his website, but she was still surprised. Alfred Northallerton looked like he had stayed up all night. His hair was dishevelled, and the baggy woollen top he wore had stains on it. His cheeks were chubby, like the rest of him. There was a mad professor look about him, but one who didn't know how to dress himself.

He approached them, adjusting the thin frame glasses on his nose. He stood at a distance, as Maggie and Rita got up from the sofa. He stopped, not offering his hand. He stuck his hands in the side pockets of the woollen top, and watched them curiously, like a scientist inspecting a new species of life. His brown corduroy trousers had seen better days, threads emerging from near his black, rubber soled shoes. His voice was thin and high pitched.

"I'm Alfred Northallerton. How can I help?"

Rita and Maggie introduced themselves again. "Can we sit down?" Rita asked.

"Yes, of course, please do. Would you like a cup of tea or coffee?"

I'd like you to put the bloody heating on, Rita thought to herself in silence. "No, thank you."

They sat down, Lord Northallerton taking the single armchair opposite them. He wasn't wearing a jacket, but he didn't seem to mind the cold.

"We're investigating two murders," Rita started without preamble. "One is a cold case from 1994, and the other only yesterday. The cold case victim's name is Clara Winters, and the man murdered yesterday is Mark Strong." She paused and watched his reaction. His hands were folded on his lap, his body still as he watched her without any expression.

"Do the names of the victims mean anything to you?"

Alfred downturned his lips and shook his head. "I'm afraid they don't."

"Did you own a company called Sun Rise Care Limited? The company ran a number of children's care homes in Yorkshire. It closed down in 2003."

Alfred blinked, his face still blank. "That rings a bell, yes. It was closed a long time ago. I had invested in a number of social care contracts around that time. I am not active in that field any more. Why do you ask?"

His expression remained blank. Rita decided to play along, for now.

"Sunrise Limited owned a care home called Blue Rise Care Home. It was number 7, Hill Crescent Road, in Scarborough. The care home was demolished in 2003. Do you recall the building?"

Alfred's face remained expressionless, but this time it was an effort. Rita saw it immediately.

"Yes, I think so." Alfred cleared his throat. "The company was closed down, and the building was sold back to the council. We didn't demolish the building. The council did that, I assume."

"We got details of the demolition from the council. A company owned by Mr Edward Salt carried out the job. Do you know Mr Salt?"

"No."

“Mr Salt purchased a number of fisheries, which were leased on land that you own. Mr Salt and yourself used the same lawyers for the transactions. Does that ring a bell?”

Alfred spread his hands. There was a tightness around his eyes now, and his careful composure was under more strain. His feet moved as he crossed them.

“No, it doesn’t. There have been many transactions on land that my family owned, over the years. I don’t recall all of them.”

“You don’t know Mr Salt?”

“Not personally, no.”

Rita stared at him for a while. She decided to come back to this later.

“Both the victims were present at Blue Rise Home. Clara Winters worked there as a carer, and Mark Strong was a child resident there. We think they met in the care home, and they knew each other.” Rita rested her elbows on her knees as she leaned forward.

“A care home that you owned. A property whose evidence was found on both the victims. We know that Clara Winters kept her work in the care home a secret from her friends and family. Mark Strong wanted to speak to us, but he was killed before he got the opportunity.”

“I’m sorry, Inspector. I don’t understand. I never owned that care home, the company did, and it was sold back to the council. I had nothing to do with the care home. I'm not sure why you're here, to be honest."

"Did you know Duncan Sheldrake? He was the parish vicar, and he visited the care home twice a month."

"No, I didn't."

Rita stared at him for long enough for Alfred to shuffle in his seat uncomfortably. She said, "For the last ten years of its existence, the care home didn't file any inspection reports. Your company was in charge of the service. You must know this is a serious breach of the rules. All children care homes have to submit annual reports. The Inspectors visited, apparently, but there was no report."

A shadow settled over Alfred, and it remained there. His face darkened. "I don't know, Inspector. This was a long time ago. I suggest you take up your enquiries with the council."

"I have, and they directed me to you." Rita's eyes could have burned holes in Alfred's skull. "You must have records of the inspection reports. You were the director of the company, and this was a compulsory requirement of the company. How can you not know?"

"As far as I know, the reports were done and submitted to thc council. Like I said, please ask them.

“They don’t have it, even in paper copy. They’ve either vanished, or they were never written in the first place.” Rita paused for a few seconds, still staring at Alfred unblinkingly. “Are you saying the council is lying?”

Alfred’s composure was melting like ice cubes in a glass. He tried to rise above the discomfort, but like a drowning man clutching at straws, he failed.

“No, I am not. I simply don’t know. Now if you will excuse me, I have other appointments I need to attend to.”

“Sir Alfred,” Rita said softly, going in for the kill. “There were allegations of child sexual abuse at the Blue Rise Care Home. Did you know about them?”

Alfred turned bone white, and it seemed he couldn’t breathe. His Adam’s apple bobbed up and down.

“No, I do not. Now if you’ll-

“Given those allegations, do you not think the lack of the inspection reports is quite suspicious?”

“Inspector, please. I have no idea what you’re trying to insinuate. Can you please leave now?”

He rose, and so did Rita. She nudged Maggie, and the constable cleared her throat. “We need to take your DNA swab, Sir Alfred. Is that ok?”

Alfred looked like he’d swallowed an entire bee hive. His face reddened till Rita was sure there was steam emerging from his ears. His fists clenched, and a snarl appeared on his lips.

“Is this a joke? You come here and….” Words failed him, and then he swallowed, his face changing as he seemed to realise he was overstepping the mark.

“Why do you need my DNA sample?”

“It’s just routine, sir,” Maggie said. “As this is a double murder inquiry, we have to take DNA sample from all parties involved.”

“But I am not involved,” Alfred stressed. The snarl remained on his face, but he was less hostile. He glared at Rita.

“If there’s no concern on your part, then surely you have no objection to us taking the DNA sample,” Rita said with a smile. Her sardonic mirth fell on Alfred’s face like an expensive China vase chucked on bricks. His jaws ground together but he said nothing.

Maggie stepped forward and he opened his mouth as she took the swab.

“Thank you,” Rita said. “We will be in touch.”

CHAPTER 51

Maggie took the wheels, and they drove slowly down the long gravel drive, and then into the private road outside the gates. Rita rested her head against the rest and glanced at Maggie. It was getting late, light fading from the sky. It had been an eventful day, to say the least. She could feel the tiredness creeping in behind her eyes.

"Back to the nick?" Maggie answered.

"Yes. Are the lads back?" Rita glanced at her watch. It was close to five PM.

"I'll call them."

While Maggie rang Richard, Rita looked at her phone. Still no message from Angela, which bothered her. Where was she? A tingle of concern ignited in Rita's mind, and burnt slowly, like a flame consuming dry paper.

She called Angela, and it went to answerphone. She left a message to be called back. She wished she had Derek, Angela's husband's number. She tapped the phone against her chin, thinking.

"How far are we from Hedley?" She asked Maggie.

"Quite far. We're now north of Scarborough, and it's going to take us half hour to get back. Maybe less, if I put the siren on. Hedley is just south of the main town. Why?"

Angela wasn't a suspect, and Rita didn't want to involve her in the case as yet. But she needed to speak to her without delay. She had to do that this evening.

"Don't worry. I need to visit a friend there. Let's get back to the nick and catch up with the lads."

"OK."

Maggie picked up speed on the A171, and the car hurtled past the sleepy Moors villages. Dusk had claimed the sky, slowly strangling the remaining light. The sun fought valiantly, lighting the last clouds with patches of red and fading gold.

"What do you think Lord Northallerton knows?" Maggie asked.

"A lot. He wouldn't have seen us if he wasn't worried. Only the guilty are worried. He's right that we can't pin this on him – he was only the director of the company. But he was personally involved in that care home, that's for sure."

They were silent for a while, only the engine's whine keeping company as the miles slipped away. The road dipped, and the darkening, seething mass of the North Sea appeared in the distance. The waters were choppy tonight, dashing against faraway cliffs.

"What happened there was bad," Maggie said quietly. "Those poor children. Mark knew something, didn't he? Or wouldn't be killed. Right?"

Rita's jaws clamped together. "Yes. That's also why the Inspection Reports are missing. I've kicked it higher up the council, but tomorrow I need to call the council leader."

"That should rattle their cage."

"It is rattling. That's why they don't like it."

Maggie drove on as a granite darkness claimed the land, obscuring the land from vision. The lights of Scarborough twinkled in the distance, getting brighter.

They stopped at a service station to get petrol. There was a pizza parlour next to it, and Rita got four pizzas for the team. They were back in the office soon, and Rizwan was waiting for them in the car park. He took the pizza boxes from Rita with evident delight.

"Oh, that smells so nice," he patted his stomach. "I'm starving Marvin, guv, thanks for this."

"You're welcome," Rita said, as Maggie locked the car and ran up behind them.

"Make sure you go to the gym eh, our kid? Your belly's showing." Maggie poked Rizwan in the ribs.

"Shut it, you."

The canteen was still open, and Richard joined them. Rita didn't normally eat pizza due to the heavy carbs, but for once, she didn't care. She was famished. They talked between mouthfuls.

"Got the DNA swabs from Ed Salt, Duncan Sheldrake, and also Susan Harrington. Robert McFarlane wasn't at home," Richard said. He reached for his drink and sipped. "I've sent the samples to Dr Das, and we should have a result tomorrow."

"Excellent work. Has Shola picked up anything else from Mark Strong's home?"

"Nothing apart from more DNA samples, for which there are no matches. The torn piece of clothing from the car is being checked, but the DNA from the blood is the main evidence there."

Rizwan said, "And we heard back from Reilly's in Leeds. They did make necklace chains like the one we found on Clara Winters. It's an old design they stopped about twenty years ago. The manager can't confirm which store it was sold from. Probably the Leeds store, he thinks, but there was a store in York and Sheffield as well."

"What about the video cassettes?" Rita asked all of them. Richard answered.

"We didn't get a response back from the three shops that used to sell them. All three businesses have folded. But we know the store the camcorder was brought from. That store still exists, but its now been brought by a national chain." Richard shook his head. "The manufacturer's serial number confirms the camcorder was sold from that store, guv. But they don't have CCTV saved from thirty years ago. So we don't know who bought it."

Rita nodded slowly, swallowing her food. "What we do know is that it ended up hidden in Clara Winter's house. She must've had access to it. And there was a reason why she hid it."

"Did someone steal the tapes?" Rizwan asked.

"Yes, I think so," Rita sighed. Her belly was really full all of a sudden and she pushed the plate with two pizza slices away.

"I don't understand why they didn't take the camcorder as well, though," Rita said. "Surely that would be easier."

"Unless Clara kept them somewhere else," Maggie said. "Or she never had them in the first place."

"No, I think she had them alright." Rita said. "She might have separated the videos and kept them somewhere safe."

A figure approached them, and Rita looked up. Her eyes narrowed as she recognised Nicola Perkins, the D Superintendent. Nicola's petite form stopped at the table. Her hard green eyes focused on Rita. She ignored the others.

"Can I please have a word with you in private, Inspector? Now."

CHAPTER 52

"Upstairs, in my office, if you don't mind," Nicola said, when they left the canteen. Rita nodded, and followed Nicola in silence as they went up the stairs. A premonition was gathering at the pits of her stomach. She could guess what this was about.

Nicola walked into her office, and Rita shut the door behind them.

"Sit," Nicola said, and Rita did so. Nicola held her eyes, gently rocking her chair. Then she pressed her lips together, and shook her head once.

"When I agreed to let you be the SIO in this case, I knew I was making a judgement call. Your boss in the London Met spoke highly of you. And I felt sorry for the troubles you had been through after your mother's disappearance."

Rita sensed a *but* coming, but she held her tongue.

"This isn't London, Rita," Nicola used her first name, for the first time, and Rita looked up sharply. Nicola's tone wasn't friendly. It was metallic hard, and she spat out Rita's name like it was an expletive.

"We don't go around pointing fingers and making wild accusations at people. Especially people who have done a lot for our community. Do you understand?"

Rita could feel her temper rising, a heat that suffocated her throat. She exhaled. "Not sure that I do, to be honest. I assume you're speaking of the people I have interviewed so far. I have evidence that suggests they were involved with the victims."

"What evidence? A few companies from almost thirty years ago? A demolished care home? What tangible proof do you have that ties these men to the case?"

"Marm," Rita seethed, "The old folk in this town know what happened in that children's home. It was a den of kiddy fiddlers. These men are evil, and they need to answer for their crimes."

Nicola went to speak, but Rita raised a hand.

"If they were not guilty, then why do they hide their involvement? Mark Strong called Lord Northallerton several times in the weeks before he died. Is that not significant? Edward Salt and Lord Northallerton owned that care home, and the inspection reports never got filed with the council. Can you really deny that these men are not connected with the two victims?"

Rita's voice was rising and she couldn't help it. "The Council must be complicit in a cover up of what happened at Blue Rise care home. Tomorrow, I shall speak to the Council leader."

Nicola grimaced, and her lips thinned. "Don't worry. Rhodri Williams has spoken to me already. He's the CEO of the council, and an MP as well."

Light dawned in Rita's mind. There was no pressure like political pressure. She should've seen it coming. She stared at Nicola, who averted her eyes eventually.

Rita said, "I've got other evidence. DNA from a burn out car that belonged to Clara. For thirty years, that car has been there. Now, that DNA will tell us who else had been there when Clara died."

"And what if it doesn't? Is that your last roll of the dice?"

"Marm, can you not see that Mark Strong being a resident at the care home is significant? Tomorrow we are going to get in touch with the rest of the children who lived there once. We have their details. This is the start of something big. A truth that's been buried for so long. Don't you think we need to find out happened?"

Nicola's eyes bored into Rita's, and her jaws clenched. "What are you suggesting?"

"That what happened at the care home needs to be brought to light. Clara died for it, and now so has Mark. The MO of their deaths are similar. The killer is still here, in this community. And I'm going to find out who it is. I don't care if I live or die, but I will reveal him."

A blind rage was pulsing behind Rita's eyes, and a fire burning in her chest. She breathed rapidly, and felt a trickle of sweat down the back of her neck. Nicola seemed to sense she had pushed Rita far enough. A coldness replaced the irritation on her face.

"Whatever you do, please don't soil the good name of this department." Nicola raised a hand before Rita could speak. "If you have evidence, and you can prove what you're suggesting, then go ahead. But remember you're skating on thin ice. We can' build a case on what you have so far, and you know that."

"I will have a case, and the CPS will accept it. I just need a couple of more days, that's all."

Nicola's face was now a blank, as if she didn't want to show Rita any more of her emotions. Then she nodded.

"Very well. But I don't want you or your team to see Mr Salt or Lord Northallerton again. Is that clear?"

"Even if they are suspects in a double murder?"

A flare of anger rippled across Nicola's face. "Prove it first, Inspector. If you're good at your job, then do it properly."

"I am Marm. But I need others to help me," Rita said pointedly. Nicola got the drift, and she didn't like it.

Her expression darkened, and her lips pinched together.

"What do you mean?"

"I need your support, Marm. Like you said, I'm new here. I might've ruffled some feathers, but only because it was necessary. Give me a couple of days, and everything will be clearer, I promise."

Rita was controlling herself now. She hadn't come this far to give it all away. If Nicola suspended her, she couldn't carry on with the investigation.

Nicola blinked, but the hard glint in her eyes remained.

"Alright. But remember what I said. I'll be watching. Are we clear?"

Rita stood, pushing her chair back. "Crystal."

CHAPTER 53

When she got downstairs, the others were waiting in the office. It was almost half six.

"What happened?" Richard asked. Maggie and Rizwan looked up expectantly.

"I got told off," Rita sighed, collapsing on her chair. "We're rattling cages that no one knew existed. And they're making one hell of a sound." She told them the gist of her meeting with Nicola.

"It's time you lot went home," Rita said. "It's late and you've worked hard today." She smiled and waved at them. Reluctantly, one by one, they left. Richard was the last to go. He hung by the door.

"We should get the Post Mortem results on Mark Strong tomorrow. If the same murder weapon was used, there can't be too many of them. An antique axe." He shrugged. "We'll find it."

As he said the words, a memory triggered inside Rita. She frowned, and her eyes flickered down. She had the same feeling the first time Dr Das had told her about the axe. She had seen an axe recently. Where was it?

The memory bothered her. She shook her head, as if jostling the thoughts around her head might help. But she was tired, and a headache was starting in the base of her skull.

"Go home," she smiled wanly at Richard. "Let's get cracking first thing tomorrow. I want the researchers to track down every single child who lived in that care home."

Richard left, and Rita called Angela again. There was no answer. The concern was deeper in her mind now, like a knife pushing deeper into her spine. She rubbed her eyes, and stifled a yawn. A weariness made her limbs ache, and her head felt heavy. But she had to see Angela tonight.

She took her extendable steel baton from the drawer before she left. She turned off the lights, and locked the door.

Her phone pinged as she walked down the corridor. It was Jack. She debated whether to answer. She didn't want to see him tonight, and she wasn't sure if the frequent contact with him was good for her. He seemed interested, but she was here for a short while, and she didn't want to leave this place with any regrets. She had enough of those already. But neither did she want to be rude. Jack had been more than helpful, and she owed him the courtesy of answering his call.

"Hi, how are you?" Jack's warm voice came down the line.

"Not bad. Just leaving work. Everything okay?"

"Yes." He paused. "I was at the station myself actually, dealing with a client. I was wondering if you were here too." It seemed like he wanted to say more, but stopped himself. She felt a little bad. She had already rejected his offer of dinner. It might be harmless, but she didn't know how she felt about it. Not as yet, anyway.

"I've still got work to do," she said. "Guess I'll see you later?"

She had walked to the car park by now, and she came to a stop when she saw him, leaning against the wall with his back to her. For a moment she thought of avoiding him, then scolded herself. She wasn't some confused school girl, she could deal with this.

She walked up to him, and he turned. The lights were on outside, casting a hazy glow over the cars. Jack's handsome, square jawed face split into a smile when he saw her. His brown eyes danced with mirth, then he became serious.

"You alright?"

"Yes," Rita nodded. She realised she needed to ask him something. "Can I speak to Carol, your secretary who told you about the allegations at the care home?"

"Can't see why not. I can ask her to contact you, or you can drop by the office to speak to her."

"Thank you."

"It's odd how none of these rumours hit the newspapers, or leaked out. But the care home was shut down in 2003 so something happened. Did you check with the council?" His eyes were attentive now, resting on her.

"Yes. Got nowhere. And now the CEO has complained about me to my boss."

Jack grimaced. "They're taking this seriously. You need evidence, Rita. A few people talking about what happened won't stand in court."

His head lowered in thought. "We represented a councillor last year in a defamation case. Do you want me to contact him? He might be able to help."

Rita considered for a while. "I don't want to get you into trouble. It might be a better idea to give me the councillor's details and I get in touch with him?"

"Might not have the same impact. You would be going official, whereas I can pick up the phone and have a casual chat with him. Might not get anywhere, but worth a try maybe?"

Rita nodded. That made sense. "Thank you."

"Did you use the power of attorney papers?" He asked.

Rita closed her eyes and mentally slapped her forehead. “No. I forgot completely, thanks for reminding me. I’ve been so busy with the case.”

Concern clouded his features. “If you don’t mind me saying, you look tired. Are you sure you have to work again, now? You should rest this evening.” Then he raised his hands, his face changing. “I’m sorry. Not my place to say anything.”

Rita wasn’t offended. Jack had a habit of speaking his mind, she knew that. He had changed, but not that much.

“It’s ok. Yes, I am knackered, as it happens. But I need to talk to someone. It’s not a big deal.”

“Where are you going?”

She smiled. “Not this again. Are you going to become my cab driver? Do I have to pay you for the lifts?”

“Only if I get to wear a uniform and cap,” he smiled back. “Do a proper job.”

Despite his financial success, he was humble, and could joke about himself. She liked that about him. She glanced at her phone, aware she needed to call a cab.

“Come on,” Jack said. “My car’s right here.”

She looked at him, and at the smile hovering around his eyes. There wasn’t any suggestion there, but she wondered what was really on his mind.

"It's fine. I'll take a cab. They don't take long to arrive."

His face fell, and his smile faded. Her guilt deepened. Jack shrugged. "Just take it easy. I know you get too caught up in things. And for something like this case, I know it's hitting you hard. You can't stop thinking about it, can you?"

"No," she sighed, trying not to show her surprise at how accurate his assessment was. Then again, Jack knew her well, from all those years ago. And he had been around when her world fell apart.

"I'm taking one step at a time. I think I'm close to cracking the case, to be honest," she said.

Jack's eyebrows bunched together. "What about the killer? Any suspects?"

"Yes, I think so. But I'm not sure yet." Rita looked at her phone, and groaned. The cab had cancelled, and now she had to order another one.

"Bad news?" Jack asked.

"You could say that," she sighed. "I might have to get that lift from you, if it's not too much hassle. I'm going to Hedley, just south from here."

"Yes, I know it. Nice village. Your mother's friend lived there, didn't she? I drove you there once."

"Yes," Rita brightened. "Angela. You remember that? You must have a good memory."

"Glad that's still left," he laughed.

They walked to his car and got in. Rita closed her eyes as she sank in the comfortable seat. The headache was pounding in her temples now. She felt uneasy with where the case was, her nerves frayed at what she had unearthed. A susurrus at the back of her mind opened her eyes. She turned to Jack as he drove.

"Did you speak to anyone else about the care home apart from Carol?"

His forefinger tapped on the steering wheel. "Carol said she would ask some of her friends." He glanced at her askance. "What about Angela?"

Rita took a deep breath.

"She's not answering her phone. I've left messages but she's ignoring me. That's why I need to see her." Rita watched the dark shapes of the trees slip past as the car picked up speed. "Given what you said, I am wondering why she kept her silence for so long."

"Or maybe that's why she kept her silence." Rita turned to look at him, and he briefly met her eyes before focusing on the road again.

CHAPTER 54

The narrow streets of Hedley village were submerged in an inky darkness. Lights glowed in some windows, through drawn curtains.

"Cut the lights," Rita whispered. Jack did as told. "Stop and pull over." Jack glanced at her then, but still obeyed.

Rita's adrenaline was spiking, a rush in her ears. "I want you to go home," she said. "I don't want to drag you into this."

"I'm in it already. I'm not letting you do this alone. Besides, if you ask me, we need to find out what happened in the care home."

She could see the outline of his face in the half light from the dashboard. "There's no we, Jack. This is my job, not yours."

He was undaunted. "My town though. If something happened here, people deserve to know. This is not just about your case anymore, Rita."

She stared at him for a while, then relented. In truth, she was grateful for his support, but she didn't want to acknowledge it. She knew she could do this on her own, but Jack being here was helpful.

"I can't ask you to be involved in this. To be honest, I shouldn't have asked you to look up the care home."

"It's alright," he said softly. He started the engine up, but didn't switch on the lights. "Shall we get going? Not far now, is it?"

"No."

Jack drove slowly, using only the starlight to direct him. Rita had driven like this before, and she wished she had the wheels. But for a beginner, Jack wasn't doing badly. They got to Angela's house. It was at the end of a lane, with dense woods opposite. The house stood silent and foreboding, bereft of any lights. Rita watched for a while, then unbuckled her seat belt. Her eyes were used to the dark now. She couldn't see anything moving around the house. She got out of the car, and so did Jack.

"You stay here," she whispered to him.

"No. Two eyes are better than one." He moved before she could stop him. She looked over the house carefully. The front garden was deserted, only the plants moved in a light breeze. The detached house had a large garden, and from her visit last time, Rita remembered the motion detector lights in the front and back.

“Wait,” she whispered to Jack. She picked up a stone from the ground and threw it into the front garden. Nothing happened. The inky darkness remained, and only starlight glowed high above. The motion detector lights were either switched off, or they were not working. Had someone cut the cables?

“I’ll take the front,” Rita suggested.

Jack agreed. “I’ll circle around the back and meet you inside, if you get in. Check your phone, I might call you.”

“OK. Can you stay outside? If I don’t come out in half an hour, then raise the alarm. Okay?”

Jack nodded. He walked off. Rita took out her phone and called Angela one last time. The phone was switched off.

Rita walked in through the front garden. As she got closer to the front door, she felt a chill descending on her. The windows seem to watch her like the eyes of a long dead ghost. Her feet creaked on the porch steps, and then she faced the door, a menacing, silent weight that blocked her way. Heart thumping against her ribs, Rita turned the door handle. To her surprise, the door was open.

If Angela wasn’t in, what about Derek? Or had they both gone out? Rita pushed the door and it opened wider. A clotted darkness lay inside, and her eyes couldn’t see. She pulled out her flashlight, and shone it inside. The beam picked out the wide entrance hall, and the staircase. Nothing stirred inside.

"Angela? Are you there?"

Nothing but her feet creaking on the porch steps answered her question. Rita stepped inside, leaving the door open.

CHAPTER 55

Jack walked slowly down the right side of the house, peering through the dimness. He didn't have a torch on him, so he used the light on his phone. The beam didn't penetrate very far. Dry leaves crunched under his shoes. There was a side fence on his right. Beyond that lay a dense, dark woodland. He heard the buzz of crickets, and the night sounds that emanate from a forest, an assortment of insects, and the occasional hooting of an owl. On his left, the house extended to the rear garden.

He emerged from the side of the house, into a wide garden. He could see the outline of tall conifer trees at the rear, across the grass. The triangular shape of a shed stood on the right. He came upon a patio. The rear doors were concertina, and were locked from the inside. He walked across the patio, and saw two windows. Both the windows were open. He shone his light inside, and a kitchen came into view. After that, he came to the end of the house. A screen of trees lay across a grass verge, and that was the edge of the property boundary, he realised.

He turned back to the kitchen windows. Upstairs, only darkness lingered, the same as the ground floor. Jack felt uneasy. Why would Angela leave the house with the windows open? He guessed Hedley was a safe village…but even then, it was risky. And if Angela was in, then why was this the only house on the street that was sunk in darkness?

He stood there for a while, wondering about what he should do. Rita had asked him to stay outside, presumably to ensure no one else entered the property. He turned back to the garden. Stepping stones were laid out across the back and he walked down the path slowly, listening. His phone light was of no use now. He stopped when he heard a sound. It was the crunch of leaves. In the silent night, the sound came clearly to his ears. Only a foot would make that noise, or perhaps a large animal. Hairs stood up on the back of his neck.

Jack half crouched, eyes scanning the darkness anxiously. Dark shapes seemed to rise out of the darkness, deceiving his mind. He checked out each bush and shadow, but nothing moved.

His eyes fell on the shed to his right. He approached it cautiously. It was big, with two windows on each side of a sturdy door. It had two steps going up to a balcony. The shed door was locked and bolted. He tried to look in through the windows. His phone light wasn't enough to penetrate the darkness properly. But he could still see the shapes of covered objects. Nothing moved inside.

Jack left it alone, and went back to the house. He pulled out his phone and called Rita. She didn't answer. He sent her a message, then put his phone back. His mind was made up now. If Rita was inside, then he should be as well. There was nothing out here for him to do.

He put his hands on the ledge of the kitchen window. That's when he heard the sound again. A crunch, like another footstep. Jack whirled around, sensing something behind him. He gasped when the saw a man's shape. How did he get here? He seemed to have risen out of the earth. The man's shape was thick around the shoulders, arms hanging loose by his sides. His face was hidden in the darkness. He observed Jack quietly

"Who…who are you?" Jack croaked. He tried to pull out the phone from his coat pocket.

The man lunged at him with blinding speed. He tried to move away but it was no use. He saw a flash of movement, and then a searing jolt of red hot pain screamed across his skull. His eyes went black, and he crumpled to the ground.

CHAPTER 56

Rita crept down the hallway, her senses on fire. She could hear her heart cannon balling against her ribs. The lounge door was closed, and she opened it by pressing on the handle gently. The spacious lounge opened into the kitchen and dining area. She had sat here with Angela two nights ago. It was deserted now. Rita's fingers groped on the wall for a light switch. She flicked it, but no light came on. Under the staircase, she found a door. She opened it warily, moving back to make sure there was no one hiding inside. She flicked her torchbeam inside and found the circuit board. The board was working fine, but the lights still didn't come on. Someone had cut the wires, like she suspected.

The beam of her torchlight scythed through the granite blackness. She saw the sofa sets in front of the TV, curtains drawn in the window. An armchair was on the floor, turned over. So was the small coffee table, lying on its side. A wine glass was smashed on the floor. Signs of a struggle.

Rita took out her extendable baton, and flicked it to the full size. Her rubber sole feet were silent on the wooden floor.

Two pots rested on the hob, but there were no plates on the table. The cupboard doors above the hobs on either side were open, and plates had been pulled down, smashed on the floor. Rita's shoes crunched on fragments on glass and ceramic. Her pulse quickened. The beam picked up more open cabinet doors, and destroyed china on the floor.

Breath heaving in her chest, Rita flashed the beam around. She noticed the kitchen windows were open, above the sink. The concertina patio doors were shut. She didn't need any more proof that Angela had been in the house. She had struggled with an intruder. But where was she? There was no blood on the floor, Rita checked carefully.

A wind had picked up outside, and it whistled in through the windows, then died.

She thought about Jack. She pulled out her phone and saw that she had a few missed calls from him. She called him back, but he didn't respond. She needed to check on him.

She went out into the hallway. Before she left, she checked the two other rooms on the ground floor. One was a small bathroom and it was empty. The other room was a study, with a table and chair, laptop, and shelves on the wall. Several of the books were on the floor, and the desk drawers were open. Papers had been removed, and they were also strewn on the floor. Someone had searched this place.

Rita wanted to go upstairs, but first, she had to check on Jack. She went for the main door.

But then she heard the noise.

It was a thud, loud enough to carry to her ears. It came again, from beneath her feet. She went still, and crouched. She could hear sounds again, softer now, like someone was moving on the floor. Did this place have a basement?

She flashed her torch around again. Next to the bathroom, against the far wall, she saw a white door. How had she missed it?

Cursing herself, she tiptoed towards it, and turned the handle. The door opened, and she felt a dank, damp air on her face. Her light picked out a set of stairs going down, swallowed up by the darkness.

From underneath, she heard a scraping sound, like an object being dragged across the floor. Then she heard a moan. It was soft, and from a woman's voice. Her skin broke out in goosepimples, and sudden panic gripped her spine, lashing it straight. She turned the flashlight off.

Then slowly, feeling her way down, she descended the stairs.

CHAPTER 57

Rita's feet touched the ground. It was uneven, parts of it wet. The clotted darkness was like an oppressive weight, blinding her vision, restricting her movements.

She heard the moan again, softer this time, to her far right. She turned on the flashlight. The basement was large. She saw walls on either side, water trickling down one of them, making a wet patch on the floor. To her left she saw an empty space. On her right, the basement extended, and she stepped in that direction.

Fear spasmed in her guts, and her palms were sweaty. The path bent to the right, and she came upon another opening, like a room without doors. In the far corner, her beam rested on a chair, and a woman's figure, tied to it. Her hair fell over her face, and Rita recognised Angela. A duct tape covered her mouth. The ropes held Angela in place, tying her securely. Rita rushed towards her, then stopped abruptly.

A man appeared behind Angela. He was broad around the shoulders, not very tall, but thick set. Her torch beam picked out the flash of metal. The man pulled on Angela's hair, thrusting her head back. She moaned again, against the tape. A weapon rested on

Angela's throat. It was an axe, the metal brownish black, the handle wooden. The sharp edges of the axe were long, and the man pressed it harder on Angela's neck.

The torch shook in Rita's hand. She almost dropped it. Her heart was hollow, and her legs trembled as her knees barely took her weight.

She knew that man. "Rob…McFarlane? It's you?"

"Turn the light down," Robert said. His low, raspy voice echoed around the basement wall. "If you want to see her alive. I suggest you do it now."

Rita thought fast. She hadn't called for help so far because she felt the darkness pulling her in, finally revealing its terrifying secrets. Robert might have escaped if the police arrived, and Angela would be dead by now. But that also meant she was alone now, save Jack. Her radio wouldn't work in the basement. Jack was her only hope.

"I knew you'd come," Robert said softly. His grip on Angela's neck tightened, and the axe blade pressed harder. "Turn the light off. I won't ask again."

"You want me, Robert, don't you? Why don't you let her go and get me?"

"As you wish," He said in a mocking tone. He pulled back on Angela's hair, exposing her neck. He raised the axe high above his head, ready to strike the blow.

"No!" Rita screamed. She dropped the light, and kicked it away. It rolled over and rested against the wall, the beam facing away from them. The light was less now, and in the dimness, Rita saw Robert slowly lower his arm. Angela was still alive. She was moaning louder, wriggling against the chair. Robert struck her on the head with the wooden handle.

"Calm down," he rasped in his guttural tone.

"Leave her alone," Rita said. "She's done nothing to you."

Robert looked up at her. "On the contrary, she can cause the most damage. I listened to the Brotherhood and spared her life. I made a mistake."

"What brotherhood?"

She sensed more than saw the thin smile on his thick jowled face. "That you will never know."

"What damage can Angela cause you?"

Robert paused, watching her carefully. "Put your radio and baton on the floor. Then kick them over to me."

"First answer my question. What can Angela do to you? Or your brotherhood, whatever that means."

Rita knew she had to keep him talking. The longer she got, the more chances she had of planning her escape, with Angela.

Robert gave her another grim smile. The axe remained on Angela's neck. "You're not getting out of here alive, so I guess I can tell you the truth now. Angela worked at the care home. She knew what happened there."

"Tell me what you did." Her voice trembled.

"You must know by now. And if you don't…" He shrugged without speaking.

Rita did know. Ever since she knew of the care home's existence she had suspected. When Jack told her about the abuse, she knew in her heart of hearts that's what her mother had discovered.

"You vile bastard. You and your friends abused children. Poor things who had no voice. Didn't you?"

Her teeth clenched, and she shook in sudden rage like a storm was breaking out inside her. "And my mother found out. Clara Winters. So you killed her. Tell me, you despicable toerag!" She screamed the last words out, hate making her voice shrill.

"Oh, getting emotional, are we?" He laughed. "Just like your mother was. Too hot headed for her own good." He cocked his head to one side, the evil smile lingering on his face. "You know, I told Eddie not to start that property company with her. It was his way of keeping her quiet. And the stupid idiot loved her as well. He was a fool, thinking he could buy her silence."

Rita thought the ground move under her feet. It wasn't a huge surprise, but still unsettling to hear it from Robert.

"Edward Salt? He was with my mother?"

"Yes. She found out, the kids told her things and she believed them. She should've kept it quiet. But instead, the dumb bitch took videos." His lips bent into a vicious snarl. "And guess who had the tapes? This bitch here. Your mother was crafty, I'll give her that. She didn't keep the recorder and the tapes together. We threatened her, told her we would kill you. Duncan Sheldrake saw her with the video recorder one day. She refused to hand it over, until she realised, we might kill you."

Was that the reason why Susan Harrington had seen Clara and Sheldrake arguing?

Rage and regret were mixing into a lethal cocktail in Rita's spine, surging into a tsunami. She gasped.

"And that's why Clara went out to meet you, didn't she? To hand over the video tapes?"

"That's right," Robert said calmly. "Only, she didn't have the tapes with her. After I killed her, I searched the car. That was also empty. We looked inside your house too, but she had hidden the tapes well. Or so we thought. We did ask Angela at the time, but she denied all knowledge."

Rita thought back to her first meeting with Angela. She was uncomfortable, cagey. She had known all this time, but…

"How did you know Angela had the tapes? And why now?"

"Because Mark Strong got in touch with her. When Clara's skeleton was discovered, word leaked out. Both Mark and Angela came to visit the body. I saw them talking. My suspicions were aroused. Then I saw Mark following you. I knew I had to act."

Rita wondered if Angela and Mark had been in contact all these years. She looked at Angela, her face barely visible. Robert had a stranglehold on her hair, but the axe was now removed from her neck. Rita had to keep him talking, play for more time.

"So, you killed Mark."

"He should never have come here, just like you." Robert's face hardened, and the snarl reappeared. "You shouldn't have come back," he repeated, his voice dropping to a whisper. "And now you're going to pay for it."

"The Brotherhood is already exposed," Rita said. "And they blame you for exposing them. If you hadn't killed Mark, no one would've found out." She was guessing, throwing words out, in the hope they would hurt him.

Robert was silent, watching her. She sensed a change in him, a tautness in his posture. His earlier relaxed composure had gone.

"They hate you for the attention you've brought upon them. I went to see Lord Northallerton yesterday. Alfred. You know him, don't you? He's panicking. He knows you've sold out the Brotherhood."

Robert was breathing heavily now, his chest rising and falling. "Shut up," he snarled. "You don't know what you're talking about."

"No?" Rita taunted him now. "Then why is Alfred so spooked? Ed Salt is running scared. Duncan Sheldrake knows his game's up. And they all blame you," She shouted the last word, pointing at him. "You're out of the Brotherhood now. They don't care if you live or die."

Robert let go of Angela's hair. He stepped away from her, and towards Rita. "No!" he bellowed. He pointed the axe at her, then at his chest. "I'm the Guardian. I keep the Brotherhood together."

Rita stepped closer, and Robert didn't seem to notice. She got closer still. The torch beam against the wall was fading. Angela was an outline now, but Rita could tell she was moving, head now aloft. Rita's hands crept towards the radio in her pocket.

"Keep the Brotherhood together?" Rita laughed derisively. "You've done your best to split them apart. You destroyed them."

"Shut up. You bitch!" Robert held his axe up, like he was going to hurl it at Rita.

"They hate you now. They'll hand you over to us, and laugh behind your back. You've become a liability for them. They want you gone."

"No!" Robert howled like a wounded animal and hurled the axe at Rita. She watched hypnotised as the weapon swished through the air, the blade winking in the dying light as it approached her. She kept her eyes on it, and at the last second, she dropped to the floor. She heard the axe zoom over her head, and clatter on the ground behind her. It was a trick that Jack, who played cricket, had taught her.

Keep your eyes on the moving ball if it's a bouncer. If you don't the ball will hit you in the face.

Then she was up, radio in her hand. She hurled it at Robert's figure with all her strength. The radio was heavy, and it made good contact, hitting him squarely in the face. He screamed, and fell backwards. The light vanished, plunging the whole basement into darkness.

CHAPTER 58

Rita ran backwards, to where she'd heard the axe hit the wall. Desperately, she groped along the floor, hoping to find the weapon. Her sweeping hands only came up with dust. The dirt blew into her face, making her eyes sting. She coughed.

Then she heard movement behind her. Shuffling, heavy footsteps. Heavy breathing. Panic bulged in her chest. She coughed again, aware that she was giving her position away by doing so, but she had no choice. The dust blinded her, and she still couldn't find the weapon.

"There you are," Robert growled.

She felt him right behind her now. Like a mad woman, her hands thrashed around, hoping to find the axe. Her hands found nothing but dirt. Robert lurched at her, his meaty hands landing on her back. She fended him off, scurrying away. She was more agile than the older man. That was her only advantage. He was far stronger, and she knew if he got her in his grips, he would break her neck like a piece of cardboard.

Robert cursed as she slipped away and threw himself at her again. This time he landed on her with his body, trying to arch his arms over her. He was too heavy, and although she half escaped, her lower back and legs were trapped under his weight. With another growl, he reached for the back of her neck, slamming her face down on the ground. Rita cried out as pain mushroomed against her skull. Her hands were still out, scrabbling wildly, raising clouds of dust.

She tried to kick, but Robert's heaviness had trapped her legs. He hit her again, and she twisted her neck, trying to get free from his grasp. It was no use, he was too strong. Her vision was fading, nausea bloomed in her stomach, and the waves of pain in her head were too strong.

She wasn't going to last this onslaught for too long.

Her strength was fading. "Got you now," Robert gritted out, trying to heave himself on her back. With one last push, she tried to twist forward, her hands scything on the floor in sheer panic.

Then she felt it. A wooden, long object. It was smooth and hard, and her fingers closed on it. She knew immediately it had to be the axe, or a similar object. The top was heavier than she imagined, and she had to strain to lift it. But lift she did, and once she gripped the weapon firmly, it was easier to manoeuvre. She kicked and buckled, and managed to get Robert slightly off balance. It didn't last, he slapped a palm on her back, sending her down again.

But she had a split second of advantage, and she used it.

She managed to half turn, holding the axe. With a cry of anguish, she hit Robert as hard as she could. He screamed as the sharp blade hit him somewhere just below his face. He fell off her, clutching his neck.

Rita galvanised into action, folding her legs beneath her, and powering herself up with a newfound strength. She held the axe with both hands and swung it at him hard. It hit him in the head and he slumped down on the ground, screaming again.

"You used this to kill my mother, didn't you?" Rita whispered, sweat pouring down her forehead, blinding her eyes. "Didn't you?" She shouted.

Robert croaked, his feet shuffling as he tried to move. Rita stepped over him. Tears now blinded her eyes, mixing with the sweat. Her limbs were on fire, but she was burnt to ashes inside, only the scorched earth of her soul remaining. Robert raised a hand as if asking for mercy. She shook her head. But his hand dipped, and he grabbed her leg, suddenly pulling her toward him. Rita was thrown off balance, and she fell.

Robert rose, and on all fours, bundled into her. She didn't think he had the strength. But the blood loss had made him weaker. Rita landed on her side, and she sliced at his shape with the axe. She made contact again, the axe hitting Robert in the shoulder. She didn't hesitate this time. She raised the weapon above her head and brought it down with savage fury, a scream erupting from her lungs. Robert collapsed, and he stayed there.

Rita wiped her face and moved back, watching him. He didn't move. She heard Angela moving. She stood and heard someone calling her name. It came from behind her. She turned to find Jack, leaning against the wall. She rushed over to him. He was slouching, and when she touched his head, it came away wet.

"You're hurt," she said.

"I'm ok. He didn't take my phone. I called the police, they should be here soon."

Jack pulled out his phone and shone the light. Helping each other, they stumbled over to Angela. Rita removed the gag from her mouth, and hugged her while Jack untied her arms. Rita had to help him, and they managed to free Angela from the tangle of ropes. Angela collapsed into Rita's arm, sobbing.

Jack stumbled over to where Robert lay. Then he came back. "He's out cold. I searched his pockets. I've taken his phone, car keys and wallet. Come on, let's get out of here."

"Wait," Rita said. "Help me tie him first."

They tied Robert's hands and ankles, and left him there. They went back upstairs, and Rita blinked against the harsh over head lights. She slouched against the wall, sliding to the floor, exhausted. She could hear the wail of sirens in the distance, getting louder.

CHAPTER 59

Warm sunlight cascaded in through the windows of Angela's house. Rita stood by the windows, looking at the garden where she had played as a child. At the rear, there was a bird feeding post, and she saw the blue winged jays landing on it and feeding with their tiny beaks. Sun beams skittered from their wings as they flew away into the air.

Angela came back carrying a tray with two cups of tea. They were both dressed in black. Angela also had a hat for the occasion, with a veil, that covered the bruises around her eyes. She had offered one to Rita, but she didn't care. She wasn't going to wear a veil to her mother's funeral. She would stare the past in the eyes, bruises and all. She had waited for this closure for almost three decades. The veil of torture had finally lifted. A new, and more permanent ending was now in sight, and far more peaceful. The circle of life and death, as it should've been for Clara.

Rita had woken up in the morning with tears. Now her eyes were dry. Her heart beat as if it was the only sound in her body. Angela sighed, and looked at her. She motioned at the cup of tea.

"We don't have much time," Angela smiled wanly. That was true. It was half nine, and they had to be at the undertakers to start their journey by half ten. Jack, Richard, Maggie and Rizwan would meet her there. And many of Scarborough's police force would also be at the cemetery. It was as though they were treating Clara as one of their own. Rita was overwhelmed when she heard.

I wish you were here to see how many people came to say goodbye to you.

She thought those words when she got up this morning, and she couldn't stop her emotions running riot. But now she had a job to do.

She sipped at the tea, looking at Angela. She looked alright, despite the ordeal she had been through. Almost relieved, it seemed.

"You lied to protect me," Rita said, in a matter-of-fact voice. "I get that. But did you know who killed Clara?"

Angela put the cup down, her hand wobbling. Rita reached out and touched her arm.

"It's okay," Angela said. She sat back. "No, I didn't know who killed Clara. I could guess it was that group of men, of course. But I didn't know who, specifically."

She sighed. “And yes, I kept it a secret to protect you. I knew how powerful these people are. But I also promised your mother I’d look after you.”

Angela looked at Rita with clear brown eyes. “After all, the reason why Clara went to the cliffs that night was because they threatened you. They said you would end up in a care home like Blue Rise. Or worse.”

Rita had suspected this, of course. Her fingers tightened around the cup.

“When you came back, and started to ask me questions, I didn’t know what to say. I should’ve been honest with you, even if that meant breaking the promise I made to you mother. But I kept my silence, and things got out of control.”

Angela lowered her head. Rita shuffled next to her, and held her hand. Angela’s fingers entwined around hers. The past lay in their hands, interlocked in their lives.

“You did what you thought was right,” Rita said. “I’ll never hold that against you.” She smiled, and Angela nodded, her eyes bright with unshed tears.

Angela had told Rita about the video tapes already. Clara had put them in a bank’s safe deposit box. She had given Angela the details of the that deposit box, without telling her what the contents were. She had made Angela swear she would never look inside the box. Angela had kept her friends secret, all these years.

Until now.

Yesterday, they went to the bank, and discovered the video tapes inside the deposit box. Rita had taken them to the station, and she had watched the first tape with Jack, Richard, Rizwan and Maggie. To say the contents were shocking was putting it mildly. Clara had managed to get videos by filming through an open window. The window allowed her a direct view of another room, across a courtyard. The curtains were not drawn, and what those evil men did with the boys was captured on film.

Ed Salt, Alfred Northallerton and Duncan Sheldrake were all recognizable, albeit thirty years younger. All three were now facing lengthy jail sentences. The trial date had been set in three months time. With the evidence from the videos, Rita knew the men were fighting a lost cause.

"Mum won, didn't she?" Rita said. "She didn't live to see how it worked out, but she got her revenge."

"Yes," Angela agreed. "I don't think she'd ever imagine that you'd help her out though. Her little Rita, all grown up." Angela smiled. Rita felt that flutter of bitter regret in her heart again. She couldn't change the past. But Clara's actions had made sure the future would be different. Those evil men would now face justice.

"Funny how that worked out," Rita said. "I just hope this brings closure now. Mum can rest in peace."

"She will."

CHAPTER 60

The weather had held out, and Rita was more than glad for it. Angela drove her Mini behind the hearse car, and Maggie, Rizwan and Richard followed in a car behind them. The convoy wound slowly around the streets, getting closer to the cemetery. The coffin was a simple affair. Rita had been generous with the flowers, and Clara's name written in marigold, small letters. That was it. She wanted her mother to have a simple burial. Clara deserved an uneventful rest in eternity.

Rita's phone pinged. She stiffened when she saw it was from Jay, her father. She had sent him a text last night. She didn't expect anything back, but it was good of him to reply. He wanted to speak to her. Rita explained to Angela, and she told Rita to go ahead.

Rita called him. He answered on the first ring. "Rita, is that you?"

His voice was warm and bright, but seemed to come from so far away. She didn't know what to say. All of a sudden, on this day, she wished she hadn't got in touch with him. She couldn't deal with more ghosts from the past. And yet, perhaps he deserved to know.

She had given him, in the text, a brief summary of what happened.

"Yes, Dad."

"I got your text last night. I can't believe it. Are you okay?"

She didn't tell him how it ended, or the names of the culprits. That wouldn't be public knowledge till the court case. Salt and Northallerton would plead not guilty, and Rita suspected a trial would drag on. She wasn't looking forward to it.

"Yes, I'm fine." She sighed. "It's the burial today, Dad. I'm on my way to the cemetery."

There was a silence. "I see." He cleared his throat, and another pause. "If you'd told me earlier…Anyway, never mind. Thanks for letting me know. I'm worried about you, that's all."

The incredulity surfaced again. He was worried? What about her childhood? And the rest of her life? He stayed in touch sporadically, but she never really had a father. He read into her quietness, and his next words surprised her.

"I would've come over. I owe Clara that much."

That familiar black weight appeared in her throat again. She opened her mouth to release the regrets. If only they could disperse like a breath, never bother her again.

"I didn't have time to tell you. I'm…" She didn't want to say the word sorry, but it hovered on the tip of her tongue, unable to find utterance.

"No, it's okay. I'm just glad you found her."

Rita clenched her teeth, blinked away tears. "Yes, me too."

"And thanks for letting me know."

"That's okay. Look, I better go. Plenty to sort out today."

"I want to come and see you. Visit the grave, and…you know."

If this conversation went on any longer, she would dissolve into that abyss again. No. She had filled up one void in her life, the other could wait a little longer.

"Thanks, Dad. I'll call you later, okay?"

"Make sure you do. I'd like to come over." He repeated. Was there an entreaty in those words? A desire to bridge the gap? Maybe. Maybe for once, she'd done the right thing.

She hung up, then took a tissue out, and wiped her eyes and nose. Angela gave her space, and she appreciated it.

The cemetery appeared, and the convoy went inside. Jack was waiting for them in the car park. He came forward as Rita got out of the car. After a moment's hesitation, he stretched out his arms, and she leaned into his embrace. He felt warm, and she smelt his nice aftershave.

"Thanks for coming," she whispered.

"I know you've waited for this day all your life." He looked at her. His brown eyes were sombre. "I'm so glad to be here for this."

Emotion choked Rita, but she managed to offer a wan smile, and nod. "I'm glad you're here too," she said.

People from North Yorkshire Police had gathered. Rita walked over and spoke to them, shook their hands. Angela did the same, acting as a family member.

Maggie stood next to her and Angela on the other side, as the service progressed. When it was over, one by one, the mourners left. Richard, Rizwan and Maggie lingered with her and Angela. They sat on the bench, and watched the white marble tombstone as it caught the sunlight. Flowers were heaped over it.

"She would've liked it here," Angela murmured. The cemetery was on a hill, overlooking the North Sea.

"Yes," Rita smiled. Clara and herself used to go for walks on the fields adjacent to the cemetery. There was a path which ended in steps going down to the beach front. Rita watched the sea, green and blue in the sunlight.

Finally, she had laid Clara to rest. It was a day to make peace, and to forgive herself. She looked up, and blinked at the rays of light, filtering in through the trees. It was a time for a new beginning.

They walked back to the car park. Rita was ahead with Maggie, the others were dawdling behind, chatting. As they got closer to Angela's car, Rita saw a white paper on the windscreen, stuck to the wiper. She took it off, frowning. It was a simple envelope, without any names on it. She opened it. Inside, there was a handwritten message.

You took my brothers from me.

Now you will pay.

Get ready for what's coming next.

Rita read it twice, three times. Then she crumpled the piece of paper and stuffed it in her pocket. She looked around, her breathing rapid, heart now restless. She saw no one else in the cemetery. The trees moved in the whisper of a breeze. White clouds tugged along in the sky. The gravel crunched under her feet as she walked around the car, casting her eyes for an intruder. She saw no one.

"All okay, guv?" Maggie asked, concern in her voice.

Rita nodded, still looking around. "Yes, it is."

It would be, she told herself. She would find who wrote that message, even if she had to hound that person to the ends of the earth.

Want to read more? *Book 2 - Dead Cold Hand* is out soon…

THE END

Printed in Great Britain
by Amazon

61512357R00262